PINS & NEEDLES

Twins Tanwen and Donna Evans are as different as chalk and cheese. Tanwen is a bubbly extrovert, slim and sharp as a needle. Donna is plain, placid and shy, as sturdy and useful as a pin. In 1924, when they are both fourteen, they become apprentices at The Cardiff Drapers, where Tanwen eventually becomes the store model. Their mother Gwyneth insists that Donna accompanies her sister on dates, but it isn't until she meets Dylan Wallis that Donna falls in love. Then Tanwen sets her heart on Dylan, with disastrous consequences for them all...

PINS & NEEDLES

PINS & NEEDLES

by

Rosie Harris

Magna Large Print Books
Long Preston, North Yorkshire,
BD23 4ND, England.

British Library Cataloguing in Publication Data.

Harris, Rosie
     Pins & needles.

     A catalogue record of this book is
     available from the British Library

     ISBN   0-7505-2258-5

First published in Great Britain 2004
by Headline Book Publishing

Cover illustration © Richard Jones by arrangement with
Artist Partners Ltd.

The right of Rosie Harris to be identified as the author of this
work has been asserted by her in accordance with the
Copyright, Designs and Patents Act, 1988

Published in Large Print 2004 by arrangement with
Random House UK Ltd.

Magna Large Print is an imprint of Library Magna Books Ltd.

Printed and bound in Great Britain by
T.J. (International) Ltd., Cornwall, PL28 8RW

For Jean with Love and Fondest Memories

Acknowledgements

My grateful thanks to Georgina Hawtrey-Woore, Justine Taylor, Sara Walsh and all the other members of the team at Random House who have been so supportive. Also to Caroline Sheldon and Rosemary Wills of the Caroline Sheldon Literary Agency for all their help.

Chapter One

Tanwen and Donna stood stiffly side by side, staring at their reflection in the big cheval mirror that dominated the front room of their terraced house in Rhymney Street.

Tanwen; tall and slim, breathtakingly lovely with her shoulder-length blonde hair, vivid blue eyes and smooth translucent peaches and cream skin. Donna; shorter, a nondescript shadow with frizzy light brown hair and dark brown eyes.

Tanwen smiled with a mixture of arrogance and disdain as she studied the neat black dress with its white Peter Pan collar and white piping on the cuffs that her mother had made, and which she was wearing for the first time. Although it accentuated her budding figure and made her feel grown up, she hated its uniformity and the fact that Donna was wearing an identical dress.

No one, except their mother, Gwyneth Evans, who was at this moment regarding them proudly, would have thought that the two fourteen-year-old girls were twins.

Not only in looks but also in every other

aspect were they as different as chalk and cheese. Tanwen sparkled, attracted attention, and melted hearts when she smiled. Donna's quiet, sweet nature was easily overlooked. Tanwen had verve and vivacity. Donna was caring and reliable. Tanwen was outgoing and gregarious; Donna was shy and withdrawn. Tanwen bubbled over with confidence; Donna was timid, unsure of herself.

Yet most of the time they appeared to be inseparable. Tanwen was prone to landing herself in scrapes; situations brought about by her sheer vivaciousness. When charm and seduction failed to extricate her then Donna was always there to smooth out any problems. She was even ready to take the blame or responsibility for whatever had gone wrong.

Gwyneth was fully aware of all of this, and ever since they'd been toddlers she had always relied on Donna, because she was so sensible, to take care of her sister. Tanwen not only accepted this as the natural order of things, but took advantage of the situation, knowing she was her mother's favourite.

'There you are then, girls, all dressed and ready for your first day at The Cardiff Drapers,' Gwyneth said proudly as she surveyed her handiwork. 'Off you go, then!'

'Mam, it's only half past seven. It takes fifteen minutes to get to St Mary Street and we don't have to be there until eight o'clock,' Tanwen pouted.

'Better to be fifteen minutes early than one minute late, especially on your first day,' her mother told her firmly. 'Run along now both of you or you'll miss the tram, and if you have to wait for the next one then you really will be late.'

Tanwen pulled a face, but Donna merely smiled and nodded in agreement with her mother's wishes.

'Now remember,' Gwyneth Evans told them as she kissed them both goodbye, 'you are to ask for Miss Price. She knows you are starting work today and she will be expecting you.'

'Will there be any other apprentices starting today as well, Mam?' Donna asked nervously.

'No, not today,' her mother said. 'As a special favour Miss Price is giving you a week's trial first to see if you shape up. If you do then she will keep you on. If you don't...'

She left the sentence unfinished and Donna felt a shiver run through her. She wished her mother was going to be with them when they met Carina Price. They had heard so much about her over the years that she had become something of an icon in Donna's mind. They had only met her a few times, though, and that had been when she had come to the house to see their mother when they were very small. Donna had a hazy memory of a tall woman with a large hat.

Carina Price and her mother had both started as apprentices at James Howell's fashionable emporium, The Cardiff Drapers, over twenty years ago, back in 1904, when they'd both been fourteen years old.

In those days apprentices had to live in, and the two girls had chummed up together. It was a friendship that had remained unbroken even though it was now almost fifteen years since Gwyneth had left the store.

Carina Price had never married, but had made working at The Cardiff Drapers her career. Over the years she had risen to be head of the extensive workrooms and responsible for taking on all the new apprentices each year. From time to time she invited Gwyneth to call in and see her, and Carina would take her into the staff canteen where they would enjoy a meal together and reminisce about the old days.

It had been Carina Price who had suggested, after Silas Evans's boat went down in 1916 and along with everyone else on board he was reported missing, that it would be better for Gwyneth to earn a living at home doing dressmaking and millinery.

'You've got two little girls to bring up, and you don't want them to become latchkey kids, out running around the streets and getting into trouble because you have to leave them on their own,' she'd pointed out.

She had even gone so far as to make it possible for Gwyneth to buy a second-hand treadle sewing machine from the store, and arranged for her to pay for it in weekly instalments.

Gwyneth had found it hard work building up her business. Even when the orders had started coming in, many of her customers were slow in paying, so she had been deeply grateful when in those early days Carina Price had also managed to have some of The Cardiff Drapers' outwork passed on to her as well.

Gradually, though, as Gwyneth became well known for her clever designs and skilled workmanship she built up a faithful following of customers from the streets around where she lived, and outwork from The Cardiff Drapers was no longer necessary.

Shortages dominated in the years immediately following the end of the war. As news of Gwyneth's sewing skills became widely known, more and more women turned to her for help. Desperate for a new dress or coat, but unable to find anything that they could afford to buy, they would ask Gwyneth if she could turn their favourite garment and so give it a new lease of life. Or, they would ask her to cut down one of their dresses to fit a young daughter, or remake their husband's trousers to fit a boy who was about to start work.

They were so grateful when she accomplished this that they remained loyal even when supplies began to come back into the shops. They were happy to purchase a length of new cloth and bring it along to Gwyneth to be made up.

As the girls grew older, Gwyneth dragooned them into helping. Donna was brilliant at unpicking the tiniest of stitches. Tanwen, on the other hand, showed far less aptitude and was inclined to be slapdash. If she was asked to take out tacking stitches the work had to be checked afterwards to make sure it was done properly. Very often she merely pulled at the thread and either left the knot at one end or the double stitch at the other still there.

More often than not it was Donna who checked the work and removed them, knowing how frustrated it made her mother if she found them still there.

While Donna diligently unpicked seams, or helped to brush them and press them flat, Tanwen fooled around. She would drape a length of material over her head or around her shoulders and dance round the room pretending to be Clara Bow the 'It' girl, or some other film star.

However, it was Tanwen, with her long silky gold hair and angelic face, that the customers patted on the head or slipped a penny when they came for a fitting or to collect their finished garment. Donna seemed to fade into the background, even though she was the one who handed them their parcel and opened the door for them.

When people did notice Donna it was to comment on how different she was in every way from her sister. 'You'd hardly think they were sisters, let alone twins!' was the usual comment as they compared the two girls.

Tanwen would giggle and preen at such remarks, but Donna felt hurt no matter how hard she tried not to take any notice.

'Tanwen takes after her dad, and Donna is more like my side of the family,' Gwyneth would say quickly.

When the girls reached their teens, Gwyneth suggested to Carina Price that since Donna enjoyed sewing so much it might be a good idea for her to go and work at The Cardiff Drapers when she left school.

'Could you take Tanwen as well?' she had added quickly. 'I'd like them to be together so that Donna can keep an eye on her. She's not quite as keen as Donna on sewing, mind, but she loves clothes and has a good eye for what's fashionable.'

'If they start as apprentices in the workroom like we did then they will have a thorough grounding in dressmaking and millinery, no matter which department they decide to opt for later on,' Carina said noncommittally.

Now, a year later, they were about to do just that. Gwyneth had gone along to see Carina the day after they had reached their fourteenth birthday on 10 June 1924.

'Tanwen and Donna will be leaving school in the middle of July, so is my idea still feasible, Carina?' she asked hopefully.

'There is a long waiting list of applicants and only eight vacancies,' Carina told her. 'I shall be interviewing them all on Friday the twenty-fifth of July.' She looked thoughtful. 'I don't need to put your two through that ordeal as I know all about them, so send them along the Monday before that and I'll give them a trial. If they are suitable, and I'm sure they will be,' she added hurriedly, 'then of course I'll take them on permanently.'

Gwyneth was so anxious that the girls would be dressed right, even if they were only on trial, that she altered the two black dresses which had been her own uniforms when she'd worked at The Cardiff Drapers. Tears came into her eyes as she adjusted them to fit Tanwen and Donna and renewed the white trims which had yellowed with age, even though she'd kept them carefully wrapped up.

'Have we got to wear these awful old dresses?' Tanwen complained. 'They smell musty!'

'No they don't,' Donna argued. 'Mam's had lavender bags in with them to keep the moths away, that's what you can smell.'

'Can't we have new dresses?' Tanwen persisted. 'These old things look as if they came out of the ark!'

'No, cariad, I can't afford new ones! I'm afraid this is the best I can do,' Gwyneth told her. 'If you get taken on then you'll be issued with a uniform.'

She felt inordinately proud of the two girls as she stood on the doorstep watching them walk down the street towards Crwys Road to catch a tram into the city centre.

She was aware of curtains twitching and neighbours coming to their front doors to watch the girls setting off. She felt her own eyes prickling with tears as Blodwyn Hughes, who lived next door to them and who'd joined her on the doorstep, started wiping her eyes and blowing her nose.

'They do you proud, cariad,' Blodwyn snuffled, her double chins wobbling with suppressed emotion.

It had not been easy earning a living and bringing them up single-handed. In the early days, after she had heard that Silas was missing, there had been times when she wasn't even sure if she was going to be able to keep a roof over their heads and feed them.

Fortunately, both girls, who were six years

old at the time, had already accepted that their dada had gone off to the war, because so had the fathers of most of the other children they knew. When she'd first told them that he was reported missing they'd asked for news daily. Then other things had happened in their lives and with childlike acceptance of the present they'd pushed all thoughts of their father to the back of their minds. When the time came to tell them that he would never be coming home again they were sad but not heartbroken.

The memory of the big tall blond man, whom they only saw every few months when he was home from sea, soon became a misty, faded figure in their minds. They were more concerned with the fact that their mother wasn't able to afford special treats any more, or buy them sweets and biscuits.

'Think yourself lucky that you have food on the table and a fire when it's cold,' she'd told them sharply whenever they'd complained. 'There's plenty of children around here that have no shoes on their feet even to go to school in, and who go to bed hungry.'

Nevertheless, Gwyneth usually followed up her reprimand by making Tanwen a new bow for her hair from some of the offcuts from her sewing, or finding a scrap of lace or ribbon to trim one of her shabby little dresses and give it a different look.

Donna accepted this in silence. She didn't crave something new all the time. She didn't mind that her mother favoured Tanwen over her in such matters because she knew it stopped her sister sulking and that made life easier for all of them.

Gwyneth, too, found that the hardships and traumas of everyday living gradually eroded her husband's memory.

Silas had been an only child. His father, Bryn Evans, a slightly built, dark-haired, dark-eyed Welshman, had fallen in love with Zelda, a statuesque Swedish blonde. Against both their family's wishes he'd married her and brought her back to Cardiff. Her family had refused to even write to her after that.

Bryn Evans's own family had been miners from the Blaenavon region and none of them had been able to accept the foreigner, as they termed her, so Silas had never known any of his grandparents. His own parents had both died shortly before he met Gwyneth.

Gwyneth's father had also been a miner, and had been killed in a pit explosion in Aberfan when she was in her teens. Her mother had died shortly afterwards. By that time she was an apprentice at The Cardiff Drapers, living in the staff hostel along with Carina Price and some forty other apprentices. From then on that had been the only home she'd known until she'd married Silas.

Therefore, with no family at all to turn to for help she was grateful to Carina for her interest after Silas was declared missing, presumed dead.

Neighbours were kindly, especially Blodwyn Hughes, but all of them were struggling to make ends meet and in no way did they feel responsible for the welfare of the young widow and her two children.

Most of them had also suffered losses. Many were nursing injured menfolk of their own and some even thought she was one of the lucky ones. She was fit and healthy and so were her children. Many of them were burdened with a husband who was either crippled in some way or whose lungs were so badly affected by mustard gas that he'd never be able to work again.

Gwyneth knew a few of them envied her, but none of them knew the relief she felt. That was her secret. Silas had been tall, blond and very handsome, but he'd also been arrogant, dominant and cruel.

She'd discovered this last trait of his on her wedding night. All the charm and tenderness that had swept her off her feet had vanished once she'd signed her name and he had their marriage certificate in his pocket.

Silas had lost no time in letting her know that she was now his, body and soul. He had forcibly asserted his marital rights from their very first night together.

In the early days of their marriage Gwyneth had lived in fear and dread of his volatile mood swings. She discovered he was not only a ruthless bully, but selfish and possessive. In the years that followed she'd looked forward to his spells at sea as a well-earned reprieve, and when it appeared he was gone for good she felt sadness but also relief.

Standing there on the doorstep as the two girls disappeared out of sight, Gwyneth's heart filled with pride. Bringing them up single-handed had not been easy, but she was more than content with what she had achieved.

Tanwen was headstrong and frivolous, but she had the sort of looks and personality that made these things attributes rather than disadvantages. She could carry off almost any situation enthusiastically. Gwyneth felt confident that she would, in time, prove herself to be an excellent worker, one who would make her mark at The Cardiff Drapers.

So, too, would Donna, but in a very different way. Donna was so quiet and thoughtful. She worried unnecessarily over what sort of impression she was making. She was always eager to help and Gwyneth knew she could always rely on her to do the right thing.

She sighed as she went back indoors and put the kettle on to make herself a cup of tea. Donna hadn't really wanted to go and work at The Cardiff Drapers. She wanted to be a teacher, or at least work with children in some capacity or other. It had taken a fair bit of cajoling to persuade her to change her mind.

'I need you to be there, cariad, to keep an eye on Tanwen and make sure that her impetuous ways don't land her in trouble,' Gwyneth had insisted.

She wondered what Carina Price would make of them both. It was strange, she reflected, as she poured hot water into the teapot and reached down a cup and saucer from the sideboard, that Carina knew so little about them.

She was so supportive in those long ago days when I was first widowed, Gwyneth thought. Yet, since then, Carina had rarely come to see them. She couldn't even remember the last time she'd paid them a visit.

Perhaps she thinks she's too grand to come here now, Gwyneth thought, looking round her shabby living room at the faded curtains and rag rugs she'd made herself from scraps left over from her sewing.

She'd managed to keep her head above water, though, which was more than many in Rhymney Street had been able to do. She'd never had the means-test man walking in and telling her what she'd have to sell before they'd give her a few shillings to buy food.

Carina had kept in touch, but she never invited Gwyneth to her flat in Pen-y-lan Place, only to meet up in the canteen of The Cardiff Drapers, where Carina always paid for their meal.

As she sipped her tea, Gwyneth found herself wondering about what sort of life Carina Price had been leading all these years. She knew from when they were both apprentices and had shared a dormitory at the hostel that originally she came from Pontypridd.

Even in those days Carina had never talked much about her background. The only thing she'd ever told Gwyneth was that she was the youngest of a large family.

The two of them had lived for their work. Highlights had been the jaunts in spring and summer to Swansea or Barry Island organised by James Howell for all his staff.

They'd worked long hours, from eight in the morning until nine or ten at night. What little spare time they had was spent sleeping because they were so tired, or doing their own personal laundry.

On Sundays, after the compulsory attendance at church or chapel, they would go to Roath Park or Victoria Park and walk round the lake, watching children paddling and enjoying the antics of Sammy the seal as he splashed around and jumped almost out of the water, his silvery pelt glistening in the sunlight.

They'd never bothered with boys. The curfew at the hostel was so strict that it was pointless making arrangements to go out during the week.

Now Gwyneth wondered if there had ever been any romance in Carina's life since those days. She'd never mentioned anyone. She had said very little when Gwyneth had told her she was marrying Silas. Possibly that had been because she didn't like him. She thought him arrogant and had said so. Gwyneth had never confided in her or told her how right she was.

Yet Carina had always been there for her. She had been the only one who had offered any sort of positive help. And now she was doing it once again by giving the girls a good start in life, Gwyneth mused. She was grateful for that and she hoped that they'd both enjoy being at The Cardiff Drapers and make a future there for themselves.

Chapter Two

The minute they turned the corner from Rhymney Street into Crwys Road, Tanwen undid the three small pearl buttons on the bodice of her dress.

'Phew! That's better,' she gasped. 'Having to wear a black dress on a hot summer's day is bad enough, but having it buttoned up to the neck is choking me to death.'

'It's not all that hot, not yet,' Donna demurred.

'I'm roasting,' Tanwen argued, 'and if it is this warm at half past seven in the morning then what is it going to be like by the middle of the day?'

'You'd better fasten your dress up again before we reach James Howell's,' Donna warned.

'Why?' Tanwen's blue eyes gleamed mischievously.

'Mam said it was important that we looked our very best when we presented ourselves to Miss Price,' Donna reminded her primly.

Tanwen flicked her shoulder-length blonde hair free from its black ribbon so that it fell in a glittering cascade around her face.

'Don't worry, Carina Price will give us a job no matter what we look like,' she said confidently.

Donna looked bemused. 'How can you say that, we don't even know her. We were just kids the last time we saw her. I'm surprised she even remembers us at all.'

'That's what I'm trying to tell you. She doesn't know us really, or what to expect.'

'So why is she being so kind, then? Why is she giving us a trial even before she starts to interview any other girls?'

'Because of our mam, stupid,' Tanwen said disparagingly.

'You mean because they were once friends?'

'They still are friends.'

Donna frowned. 'They don't see very much of each other. Miss Price never comes to our house, does she?'

'No, but our mam goes to see her at work now and again, and whenever she does they have a good long chat, don't they!'

'She never takes us with her, though,' Donna argued.

'Of course not! They don't want us to hear what they gabble about, now do they?' Tanwen arched her eyebrows and giggled. 'I bet they talk about all the boys they went out with when they first started work as apprentices.' She sighed. 'Think of the freedom they had living there in the hostel.

28

They were able to go where they pleased and do whatever they liked on their days off.'

'From what Mam says they didn't get very much time off, except on Sundays. Even then they had to go to a church service in the morning.'

The noisy clanking of the approaching tram ended their argument. Even though it was so early in the morning there was a crowd of people waiting for it and they were pushed and jostled as they tried to board.

Tanwen was on first and edged her way towards the front, managing to save a seat for Donna.

'And where are you going so early in the morning, Goldilocks?' the conductor asked, looking directly at Tanwen as he took the two pennies Donna held out and punched their tickets in the machine slung across his chest.

'That would be telling!' she told him with a cheeky grin.

'Do I get three guesses?'

Donna nudged her sharply in the ribs. 'Just ignore him,' she hissed.

Ten minutes later they were scrambling off the tram outside the magnificent five-storey frontage of The Cardiff Drapers.

'I think the staff are supposed to use a side door on Trinity Street,' Donna warned, after Tanwen had walked up to the main entrance on St Mary Street and found the huge glass doors securely locked.

'Shall I show you where the staff entrance is?' a man asked. 'I'm going there myself,' he added, raising his brown trilby politely.

The man was in his early thirties, smartly dressed in a brown three-piece suit, white shirt with a stiff collar, and highly polished brown boots.

He looked very respectable, but Donna felt it was better if they didn't talk to anyone until they had met Miss Price.

'That's very kind of you, but I'm sure we can find it ourselves,' she told him, taking hold of Tanwen's arm and drawing her away.

'School leavers, are you?' he persisted, speaking directly to Tanwen. 'I didn't think the new apprentices started until next week.'

'We're special,' Tanwen told him nervously with a toss of her head.

'Oh, I can see that for myself,' he told her gallantly, his brown eyes appreciative. 'If I can ever be of help, like showing you round or anything, you have only to ask for Evan Jenkins. Do you think you can remember my name?'

'Probably, since my name is Evans,' Tanwen told him coolly.

'It is! Now there's a coincidence. Fated we were, to meet on your first day here, Miss ... Miss Evans. Now are you sure there is no way I can help you?'

'You could tell us where we can find Miss Carina Price,' Tanwen told him.

'I could, but I'm not sure if I should tell you or not since I don't know your full name,' he teased. 'Is Miss Price a friend of yours?'

Donna caught at Tanwen's arm. 'Don't worry, Tanwen, we'll find her once we're inside.'

'Tanwen is it! Tanwen Evans! Now there's a pretty name! Certainly not one I am likely to forget, not when it belongs to such an attractive young lady.'

'Come on, Tanwen!' Donna grabbed hold of her hand and dragged her inside the building, uncomfortably aware that Evan Jenkins was walking alongside them.

Immediately they were through the door they found themselves being elbowed out of the way as more and more workers arrived and hurried towards the bank of machines lined up against one of the walls.

Donna watched in bewilderment as each of them selected a strip of cardboard from amongst rows and rows filed in a series of pockets in front of each machine. They then inserted it into a slot in front of the clock face on the machine and pulled a handle that rang a bell. Then they removed the slip and put it back where they'd taken it from before hurrying away and disappearing into the labyrinth of passages, corridors and stairways that led to the offices and sales floors.

The moment Evan Jenkins went over to clock in, Donna grabbed Tanwen's arm and hurried her down one of the passageways and up the first set of stairs they came to.

'Quick, before he turns round and sees us,' she panted.

'Why are we running away from him?' Tanwen asked. 'He seems nice enough! He would have shown us where to go.'

'You know what Mam said about not talking to strangers.'

'Everyone here is a stranger. We've got to ask someone to show us where Carina Price's office is.'

'It will probably be somewhere at the top of the building.'

'You don't know that for sure, you're just guessing,' Tanwen said sulkily.

'All right, we'll ask one of the girls.' Donna paused and turned to a woman who looked to be in her forties and who was walking just behind them. 'Can you tell us where we will find Miss Price's office, please?' she asked hesitantly.

'Take the stairs at the bottom of this corridor, go up another two floors, turn right at the top and it's the third door on your left.' She smiled apologetically. 'I'd take you there but it would make me late.'

Both girls were breathless by the time they reached the right floor. At the top of the stairs was a wide casement window that let them look down on the tops of the passing trams. They stood there, getting their breath back, intrigued by the spectacular view of the busy street outside.

'Mam never told us about the wonderful view from up here,' Donna said in wonderment.

'Mam never told us very much at all about what working here was like,' Tanwen retorted. 'Or about what she and Carina Price got up to in their younger days.'

'What makes you think they got up to anything that they shouldn't have done?' Donna asked, frowning.

'You mean you believe they were goody-goodies, like you are?' Tanwen scoffed.

Donna went bright red. 'I'm not a goody-goody at all, Tanwen, but I do think you have to be careful about who you talk to, that's all. You speak to absolutely anyone. I haven't forgotten the time when we were walking past Maindy Barracks and you started talking to the soldier who was on sentry duty at the gate. Before we knew what was happening we were surrounded by half a dozen young soldiers all trying to persuade us to go out with them.'

'We didn't, though, did we! You made sure of that! I'll never forget the look on their faces when you threatened to report them.'

'It's always the same, though, Tanwen. Look at the trouble you were always causing in school because you would fool around with the boys.'

'I only did it because lessons were so boring!'

'Wherever we go you always cause some sort of a fracas because you chat up young men, even the tradesmen and delivery boys who come to the door.'

'I'm only being friendly!' Tanwen said defensively.

'Well, don't start being friendly here. You may be boy-mad, but keep it to yourself or we might find we're sacked before we can prove ourselves, and that would break Mam's heart.'

Tanwen shrugged her slim shoulders. 'You sound more like my maiden aunt than my sister,' she muttered. 'Come on, let's get it over with and go and beard the dragon in her den.'

'Tanwen! For heaven's sake, show some respect! This is our big chance to get a job and earn some money.'

'So what do you want me to do? Curtsey when we go through the door?'

Donna sighed. It was useless saying anything at all to Tanwen because it made no difference. She took no notice and always seemed to misbehave. Yet she was the one people liked immediately, the one they remembered and wanted to see again. Her blue eyes and long golden hair and brilliant smile seemed to magnetise people, so that anything she said or did, even though it might be out of order, was accepted.

Could you go through life forever like that, Donna wondered? If so, why was her mam so worried about Tanwen all the time?

'You take after me, see, but our Tanwen is inclined to be a bit flighty,' her mam often commented. 'She'll calm down, given time.'

Whenever her mam said this, Donna wondered if she was implying that Tanwen took after their dad and whether it meant that he had been flighty, but she couldn't bring herself to ask.

Her mam never talked about him.

There was a hand-coloured photograph of her dad hanging on the landing wall and she studied it closely whenever she dusted it. It had been taken in Jerome's Studios, and although he was sitting down he looked to be a very big man. He had a shock of blond hair and eyes as blue as periwinkles, the same as Tanwen's. He had a hard mouth, though, and a jutting chin, and sometimes Donna felt she was glad he wasn't around any more because, secretly, she thought he looked cruel.

It was odd, Donna reflected, how different she and Tanwen were, seeing that they were twins. There was no denying that she had her mam's light brown frizzy hair, brown eyes and her short, plump figure. She had also inherited her mam's introspective manner and inbred concern to always do what was right.

'Come on, Tanwen! No good breaking our necks to get here on time and then being late because we've stood here dawdling,' she told her sister briskly. 'Tie your hair back and do up the neck of your dress, and let's find Miss Price's office.'

It was the third door along, as they'd been directed. They looked at each other, took a deep breath and then Donna knocked on the door.

'Come in!'

Shoulders back, Tanwen confidently opened the door. Donna followed, her knees shaking and her mouth so dry she didn't think she would be able to speak.

Chapter Three

Carina Price studied with interest the two girls who had entered her office, and who were standing like a pair of statues in front of her mahogany desk. She hadn't seen Tanwen and Donna Evans for several years and she had almost forgotten how strikingly different they were.

When Gwyneth had suggested they should come and work at James Howell's, as apprentices in the workrooms, her first reaction had been to refuse. There was too much of an air of *déjà vu* about the idea for her liking. Although she'd kept in touch with Gwyneth all these years she didn't really want to relive the past.

Then, when Gwyneth had persisted, and she had realised how important it was to her that her two girls started their working lives together, she had relented.

Now, seeing them standing there side by side, she wondered what the reason was for Gwyneth's concern.

Tanwen, without a shadow of doubt, took after her father, Silas Evans, who had been arrogant and very full of himself, she thought wryly.

He had been a big, barrel-chested man, who was fully aware of his splendid physique. Tanwen, fortunately, was slim and svelte, though she would possibly run to fat in middle age, Carina thought critically.

In her eyes Donna had far greater appeal. She was a younger version of Gwyneth in every respect. Her shy, deferential manner was identical to the way Gwyneth had behaved when she was that age. Donna also had her mother's dark brown eyes and gentle smile.

It took Carina back to the very first time she and Gwyneth had met. It had been their first day at The Cardiff Drapers. Gwyneth had looked just like Donna did now, with a shock of wispy brown hair that frothed like a tiny cloud around her pretty heart-shaped face, accentuating her big brown eyes and wistful look. She'd been chewing nervously on her lower lip in the same way as Donna was doing now, and looking as though she would burst into tears if anyone spoke to her.

'Would you both like to pull up a chair and sit down?' Carina invited. 'I need to ask you some questions.'

She fiddled with some papers as they each dragged a chair closer to her desk, but her mind went back to when she was their age, and earlier.

She'd been the youngest child with four older brothers. In such a large family it was customary for clothes to be handed down, but her mother had been delighted that she at last had a daughter and wanted to dress her in pretty outfits. However, her father insisted she should wear her brothers' cast-offs.

'It doesn't matter what you look like on the outside, it is what is in your heart and your mind that matters,' her father would tell her when she complained that other children laughed at her because of the way she was dressed.

It had not been a happy childhood. Her father had taken umbrage from the day she'd been born that she was a girl not a boy. Even more, he resented the fact that by the age of twelve she was as tall as he was. None of her brothers had been tall, yet she had gone on and on growing until she reached six foot.

Jacob Price had been a deeply religious man who held prayer sessions every night and always said grace both before meals and afterwards. A church elder, he insisted that all his family attended services three times on a Sunday.

The religious tension in their home was sometimes unbearable. As soon as her brothers were old enough to leave home, two of them opted to go to Africa as missionaries and the other two became sailors. All four had ended up living in foreign countries and for many years she hadn't heard from any of them.

As the youngest, and being a girl, she knew her fate would be to stay at home and look after her parents in their old age. Once her brothers flew the nest, however, it was as if her mother felt she had nothing left to live for and she went into a decline.

Carina's last months at school were cut short so that she could nurse her mother.

Shortly before she died her mother made her father promise that Carina should become an apprentice at The Cardiff Drapers.

'It's the store James Howell has opened in Cardiff,' she told her husband. 'I've already written and asked him to take Carina as an apprentice as soon as she leaves school, and he has agreed. I want her to go there and learn to be a dressmaker. She will live in, as all the apprentices do.'

Jacob Price had been very much against the idea. 'Send her to Cardiff to learn to sew! What nonsense! She'll never be any good at doing anything like that! She's a misfit, always has been. You've only to look at her to see she's more like a lad than a girl.'

Her mother had been shocked by his outburst. It had made her all the more determined that her wishes would be obeyed and she harped on about it non-stop.

'Who is this James Howell? We know nothing about him!' Jacob had ranted and raved.

'James Howell is a good Welshman and The Cardiff Drapers is a fine establishment and has a good reputation.'

'Is he a religious man?'

'Yes, he will make sure that Carina remains a Christian. All his apprentices have to attend church on a Sunday morning.'

After a long drawn-out argument her father finally agreed to the idea and her mother died happy in the knowledge that her daughter's future was assured.

After her mother's funeral, as she was boarding the train for Cardiff, her father told her that he was selling up and leaving Pontypridd.

'I'm going to Africa to join your eldest brother,' he announced.

Carina was already saddened by her mother's death and now she was acutely aware that it was highly unlikely she would ever see any of her family again. She'd arrived at The Cardiff Drapers lonely and disillusioned, knowing that she would never be able to return to her home in Pontypridd.

Her father's outburst had also made her aware that there was something different about her, and she was probably going to have trouble fitting in to her new surroundings. She was far too tall for a girl, flat-chested, and because of the way she had been brought up she was boyish in her behaviour as well as her looks.

Gwyneth had looked even more lost than she was and they had been drawn together as if by an invisible bond. It was only later that she learned that Gwyneth's father had been killed in a pit explosion in Aberfan only a few months earlier, and that her mother was in hospital and not long for this world.

She had felt so protective towards Gwyneth that she had made sure they were sharing the same dormitory. She had even managed to get the bed next to her so that they could talk in whispers to each other after lights-out.

In the three years of their apprenticeship that followed they had retained this closeness. Having no family to go home to at Christmas and Easter or on their days off, they spent their leisure time in each other's company. Secretly Carina had looked forward to the day when they would both be fully waged and be able to afford to move out of the hostel and into a place of their own.

She kept this daydream to herself, and in view of what subsequently happened she was glad she had. If she had divulged her plans then Gwyneth might have felt guilty about marrying Silas Evans because it would mean leaving Carina on her own.

Silas had certainly ruined all her plans. From the moment he met Gwyneth he not only took up all her leisure time, but he dominated her thoughts. Her whole attitude changed. She went round in a dream. Her work suffered and Carina had felt that their friendship was doomed.

When she'd tried to make Gwyneth realise this, Silas had been enraged. He'd called her warped. He'd said that her relationship with Gwyneth was unsavoury. He'd even threatened to kill her if she didn't leave them both alone. Finally, he'd told her to find a man of her own ... if she could.

She looked up from her papers and studied the two girls. It was too late to dwell on the past. Seeing them both sitting there had stirred up memories that were best left buried.

Donna was conscious of an uneasy atmosphere in the room as Carina Price looked up from the papers on her desk and surveyed them with her steely grey eyes. Her look was so stern that for a moment Donna felt frightened of her. It was almost as if she was trying to read their innermost thoughts.

To Donna's surprise she addressed her, not Tanwen, with her questions. In fact, she seemed to almost ignore Tanwen. When she did speak to her it was in clipped, short sentences, her voice brusque.

Donna sensed that for some reason Carina Price didn't seem to like Tanwen and she couldn't understand that. Usually everyone liked Tanwen and she was the one people ignored.

Yet when she speaks to me her voice is quite different. It's softer and far more friendly, Donna thought, bemused.

She sensed that Tanwen had also noticed this because her smile had changed to a scowl. She wasn't used to being ignored or snubbed. She was the one who did all the talking, the one people took to and liked from the moment they met.

Concerned, Donna tried fielding the next question Carina Price asked her by turning to Tanwen for the answer.

Tanwen, now thoroughly disgruntled, merely shrugged her shoulders.

'Right, we'll leave that question for the moment and go on to the next one shall we, Donna?' Carina Price said crisply.

Donna felt mortified. She felt that by being evasive she had annoyed Miss Price and only added to Tanwen's feeling of being rebuffed.

She wished her mother had come with them to meet Miss Price. As it was, she was afraid she was letting her mother down. She was so used to Tanwen taking the lead in everything they said or did that she felt completely out of her depth.

Carina Price closed the folder in front of her, stood up, and walked towards the door of her office, indicating to Tanwen and Donna to follow her.

It was no good, she knew she was behaving in a very unprofessional way, but she couldn't have them sitting there facing her any longer. Donna reminded her so much of Gwyneth that it brought an ache to her heart. Tanwen was so like Silas Evans that it caused such a feeling of rage inside her that she had difficulty being civil to her.

The combination of such contradictory emotions was bringing on a sick headache and making her feel ill. The sooner the two girls were out of her office and out of her sight the better. There were still details about their education and general interests to be noted down, but that could wait. For the moment it might be wiser to take them along to the workroom and hand them over to Aileen Roberts. They would be her responsibility when they officially started work so the sooner she got to know them the better.

From somewhere deep inside her there was a niggling doubt about whether she should be taking them on or not, since they had this disturbing effect on her. She wished she had never promised Gwyneth that she would do so.

It was a dilemma she didn't know how to handle, and one which she was sure was going to cause her many qualms, even heartache, in the future.

She strode down the corridor; a tall, mannish figure in her flat black brogues and severely tailored navy blue pinstriped costume. Even her white blouse was tailored, and looked more like a man's shirt with its button-down white collar and crisp white cuffs fastened by pearl cuff-links that showed at her wrists.

The workroom was a buzz of activity but

there was a momentary hush as Carina Price opened the door and strode in. All eyes were on her as she walked across the room towards where Aileen Roberts was supervising the fitting of an evening dress on one of the papier-mâché dummies.

'Miss Roberts, I would like you to take charge of these two girls. Explain the procedures to them and tell them what will be expected of them if they are taken on as apprentices.'

Aileen Roberts removed the pins she'd been holding between her lips and looked up at her in surprise. 'I didn't realise we had any new girls arriving until next week,' she murmured as she stuck the pins into the pincushion that was fastened to her left wrist.

Carina Price nodded briefly. 'I'll explain the details to you later,' she said curtly. 'Their names are Donna Evans and Tanwen Evans,' she added as she turned to leave. 'I'll come back in an hour or so to see how they are getting on.'

'Well...' Aileen Roberts looked taken aback.

There was a hushed expectancy in the room as everybody waited to see what would happen next. Then, self-consciously, they all began busying themselves. Sewing machines whirred, and there was the rustle of paper as patterns were laid out and the sound of scissors slicing through wads of material. Gradually, the murmur of voices as senior apprentices issued instructions to their juniors filled the silence.

'If you haven't the time to deal with them perhaps you can allow one of your senior girls to do so,' Carina Price called back over her shoulder as she opened the door to leave.

Once out in the corridor, and with the door closed behind her, she took a deep breath. She knew she'd not handled the situation at all well. It was so unlike her to be out of control, but seeing Donna and Tanwen had brought back so many disturbing memories that it had completely unnerved her.

Donna felt relieved that Carina Price had left the room. She wasn't a bit like she remembered and the tension when they had all been in her office had been palpable.

She shot a sideways glance at Tanwen and was relieved to find that the sour discontented look had gone from her face and she was gazing round the workroom with interest.

Donna looked at the busy scene in awe. There were at least fifty girls and women of all ages working there. Some were using sewing machines, feet working like pistons, hands guiding length after length of material beneath the flying needle.

At long tables there were older women carefully pinning paper patterns onto lengths of cloth and then painstakingly cutting round the outlines with scissors that looked more like shears. Other girls were tacking pieces of material together, or removing the long white tacking stitches from parts of a garment after the machinist had finished stitching.

In places the floor seemed to be littered with offcuts of materials and stray ends of cotton, and Donna wondered who had to do all the clearing up at the end of the day. It was probably the apprentices, she thought ruefully.

Miss Roberts was a neat woman with small dark eyes and short dark hair that was marcel waved with a heavy fringe. She seemed to be very preoccupied with what she was doing. It was plain from the look on her face that she was irritated at being expected to deal with the two girls. She seemed to be equally annoyed that they were attracting so many stares and whispers amongst her staff.

'Wait over by the window where you will be out of everyone's way and I'll be with you in a few minutes,' she told them both dismissively.

'This might be better than I expected,' Tanwen breathed excitedly as they moved across the room like they'd been told to do.

'There's a whole crowd of girls not much older than us!'

Donna nodded, but as she looked out of the window into an alleyway at the back of the store she felt apprehensive about having to meet so many new people. She was aware of tears filling her eyes as she looked down at the hive of activity outside; at the vans, horse-drawn carts and lorries pulling up, and the goods being loaded and unloaded into the warehouses by men and boys.

Everyone was so busy and seemed to know exactly what was expected of them. Tanwen would probably fit in all right, but she wasn't so sure that she would. She wished she was back at school where she knew exactly what was expected of her each day.

Chapter Four

It took Donna several weeks to settle in at The Cardiff Drapers. She felt on edge and nervous because she was aware that she and Tanwen were constantly under surveillance from Carina Price.

Not that Miss Price ever gave her any direct cause to feel uncomfortable. On the contrary she was extremely encouraging whenever she spoke to her. It was simply that Miss Price seemed to single her out for praise whereas she completely ignored Tanwen.

This didn't seem to worry Tanwen one iota. By their second week in the workroom she was already happily established and the centre of a group of other apprentices who laughed and chattered and occasionally behaved mischievously as if they were still schoolchildren.

From the very start, Tanwen lorded it over the others, acting as if she knew all there was to know. Donna hated the way she bossed the others, and worried in case they reported her to Miss Roberts.

'Well, I do know more than they do,' Tanwen pouted. 'We started a whole week before any of them.'

'We'll be leaving before any of them as well if you don't shut up. Do you want to be out of work?'

'Not until I've saved enough to buy that blue silk dress that's in the window,' Tanwen giggled.

'Stop being such a bossy-boots, then,' Donna warned her.

For a fair amount of the time Tanwen did try to behave herself, and when their mother asked if they were settling in Donna was able to assure her that they were.

On the odd occasion when a group of

them got together and caused mischief it was Tanwen who was the ringleader. Their pranks were childish. When asked to make the tea, they put sugar into the cups of those who didn't take it and giggled when they saw the look on their faces as they took a sip of their drink. They deliberately mixed up the spools of cotton and silk; they mislaid pieces of the paper patterns, thimbles, tapes and scissors and then caused ructions as they searched for them.

Before the end of her first month Tanwen had been reprimanded several times by Aileen Roberts for causing a disturbance.

In the main, however, the atmosphere in the workroom was extremely congenial. The fully qualified seamstresses had once been apprentices themselves, and although they often treated the new girls as skivvies they were never really harsh or critical as long as they could see that the apprentices were trying to do their best.

Donna certainly did try to do her best. Although she had not wanted to learn dressmaking, now that she was actually doing so she found the work was far more interesting than she had expected it to be.

She was intrigued by the whole process of selecting the right material to suit the chosen pattern, seeing it being cut out and then watching as the miscellany of pieces of cloth were tacked together and gradually took shape and became a fashionable garment.

There was so much to learn that Donna sometimes wondered if she would ever become as expert as some of the older women. She certainly intended to try and she was proud of being able to take her wage packet home each week because she knew how much the extra money was helping her mother.

Aileen Roberts recognised her enthusiasm and encouraged her. She wished Tanwen showed the same industriousness. Tanwen seemed to love fashionable clothes, but she was too eager to get to know all the other apprentices and have fun with them to settle down and work seriously.

Yet she couldn't help liking Tanwen and was well aware that she was being more lenient with her when she made silly mistakes than was fair. She was so pretty, with blonde hair that rested on her shoulders and big innocent blue eyes. She had such a perfect figure that she seemed to stand out from all the other new girls.

Like several of the older women she seemed to accept that if Tanwen did chatter rather more than she should it was quite understandable when she had such a bubbly friendly way with her.

'She has such a sunny nature and she's so well liked by the others that it is hard to believe that she and Donna are sisters, let alone twins,' Aileen Roberts remarked when Carina Price asked for a report on how well the two Evans girls had settled in.

'Are you saying that Donna Evans isn't adjusting?' Carina Price asked, her voice sharp with concern.

'No, no, not at all. She is doing very well indeed. In fact, she is by far the better worker of the two. She is so quiet and withdrawn, though, that if you hadn't asked me to keep a special eye on them I am sure she would be overlooked.'

'Mmm! You could hardly overlook the other one,' Carina Price retorted dryly.

Aileen Roberts looked at her expectantly, waiting for her to expand on her statement, but Miss Price turned away.

Her attitude puzzled Aileen. It was almost as though she didn't like Tanwen Evans, she thought, yet for the life of her she couldn't understand why. The girl was bright and intelligent and full of life.

Perhaps it was Tanwen's tendency to get herself into scrapes, she mused. She had no idea how Carina Price could know about those since such incidents were dealt with within the confines of the workroom. Only very serious breaches of discipline or very bad behaviour were ever reported to Miss Price. Usually these were so bad that they resulted in dismissal.

There had only ever been one such instance in the whole time she had been in charge of the workroom, Aileen Roberts reflected, and it had been so unpleasant that it was engraved on her mind. She hoped that nothing like that would ever happen again. She took great pride in heading a department that was not only happy and industrious, but also incident free.

She knew she expected a lot from her girls, but for the most part they responded well. Teaching the newcomers the basics of their trade was very satisfying. At the end of their first year she liked to guide them towards the area where she felt their skills could be used to their own advantage and that of the company.

For some it was to become machinists, while others showed an aptitude for sewing or hand finishing. Only a few were skilled enough to understand the intricacies of laying out patterns and then cutting out the expensive material. This had to be done with the utmost precision so that when it was made up the finished garment was perfect in every detail.

Aileen Roberts liked to see the girls working in teams so that they could take pride in the finished result. In this way they soon came to realise that it was not simply a question of doing the job they were paid to do, but that a great deal depended on the quality and precision of their work. Whether it was cutting out or finishing, it affected everyone in the team.

Most of them were quick to appreciate this and played their part and gave of their best. There was always the odd girl, however, who was disinclined to make the effort or for some reason failed to keep up, and this could jeopardise the entire programme.

Aileen Roberts hoped that there would be no problems of any kind with the two Evans girls. Indeed, it was in her own interest to make sure that they behaved impeccably since Miss Price seemed to be taking a particular interest in them.

For the first few months everything seemed to be progressing well. Donna was by far the more obedient of the two and learned very quickly. Tanwen tended to play around and was more careless, so on numerous occasions Aileen Roberts found herself having to reprimand her.

'Look, Tanwen, you are part of a team and if you don't fulfil the jobs allocated to you then it holds all the others up,' she told her.

Tanwen pulled a face. 'Picking up cottons from the floor isn't really holding anyone up, is it?' she asked in astonishment.

Aileen Roberts tried to shut her ears to the suppressed laughter coming from some of the other workers.

'That is not the point, Tanwen. It is your

job to keep the floor clear, by picking up pins and threads of cotton.'

'I thought it would save time if I left them until Sylvie had finished and then I could sweep them all up in one go,' Tanwen explained, smiling innocently.

'How will that save any time? You will then have to sort through a jumble of cotton and pins and pick out the pins,' Aileen pointed out.

'They're not worth bothering about, they cost hardly anything,' Tanwen retorted quickly. 'In some shops they even give you a whole packet of pins instead of your change when it's only a farthing.'

'The number of pins we use in this department every day adds up to a fair bit,' Aileen told her, struggling to remain calm. 'If we don't save them and use them over and over again, we will quickly put up the cost of every garment we make.'

'A couple more pennies on the price wouldn't be noticed,' Tanwen argued.

'I'm not prepared to enter into a discussion on that point with you since it is something you do not understand,' Aileen Roberts said frostily, her dark eyes hostile. 'Now, pick up the pins immediately and then you can gather up all the cottons. Make sure there are no pins left in amongst the threads before they go in the rubbish bin,' she added severely.

Although she walked away and busied herself in another part of the workroom, Aileen Roberts watched to see what would happen. To her annoyance she saw that it was Donna, not Tanwen, who carried out her instructions. It was done so quietly and efficiently and with such speed that for a second she wondered if she had imagined it.

She left it for a few minutes and then she went over to where Donna was removing tacking threads from a brown velvet evening skirt.

'Are you enjoying your work here, Donna?' she asked quietly. She noted the speed and accuracy with which the girl snipped one end of the thread and neatly pulled it through the material, then deftly unpicked the few remaining stitches that had been holding the thread in place.

'Yes, thank you, Miss Roberts.' Donna smiled shyly. 'I didn't really want to come here to work. I thought I would like to teach or look after small children, but I can see now that my mam was right, it's a lovely job.'

'Your mother used to work here?'

Donna nodded. 'She started as an apprentice at the same time as Miss Price.' Colour flooded her sallow cheeks. 'Perhaps I shouldn't have mentioned that?' she said uneasily.

Aileen Roberts frowned. So that was why

Donna and Tanwen had started before all the other apprentices and why they had been given preferential treatment.

'Don't worry, Donna, I won't tell anyone that you've told me,' she said with a reassuring smile.

As she walked away her mind was buzzing. She must remember that little bit of news! It might come in handy one day.

Over the next few months she monitored Tanwen and Donna's progress very carefully. Tanwen, or so it seemed to her, was always in trouble of some kind.

She also began to suspect that Tanwen was the ringleader when other junior members of her staff were involved. It happened so often that Aileen Roberts decided to keep a record of these incidents, and if they continued she would have to speak to Miss Price about having Tanwen dismissed.

On every occasion Donna managed to save her sister from trouble before she could intervene or reprimand her. Then came the day when she returned from her lunch break and found Tanwen parading around the workroom wearing a shimmering green satin evening gown and pretending to be a model. The material alone cost more than she earned in a year. To see it being flaunted so recklessly raised Aileen Roberts's blood pressure to boiling point.

'Tanwen Evans! What on earth do you

think you are doing,' she rasped.

Taken by surprise, Tanwen stumbled. Her foot caught in the billowing fabric and there was a sickening tearing sound that brought gasps of dismay from everyone in the workroom.

Shocked at what had happened, Tanwen stared down at the rent in the back of the expensive gown in consternation. Her blue eyes were misting over with tears and she was shaking as she looked up and met Aileen Roberts's angry stare.

Before either of them could move, Donna and another girl were at Tanwen's side. Unfastening the tiny buttons down the back of the gown they eased it off Tanwen's shoulders and Donna helped her to put her uniform back on again.

'I think I can mend it so that no one will be able to see the damage, Miss Roberts,' Donna said timidly, fingering the rent.

'Don't be so stupid! The gown is ruined! It will have to be made again, there is nothing else for it. It's a special order!'

Donna bit her lip. 'In that case then may I try to repair it. Perhaps it can be sold in the shop...' Her voice trailed away as she saw the anger on Aileen Roberts's face.

'Since it is a special order then the customer certainly won't want to see a replica hanging on a rail in our Evening Gowns department, now will she!'

Donna said nothing, realising that the matter was so serious that she and Tanwen could both be dismissed. Even Tanwen was subdued.

Aileen Roberts held her head in her hands. Turning to the youngest of the apprentices she ordered her to make her a cup of tea and to bring her an aspirin.

'My head is spinning. I need time to think, so bring it to the staff restroom,' she muttered.

Taking advantage of this, Donna carried the torn gown over to one of the tables so that she could examine it more carefully.

The skirt was cleverly cut in a series of gored panels so that when the dress was being worn the fullness seemed to skim the ground and float behind the wearer. The part that Tanwen had torn was in one of these panels at the back of the gown. Tanwen's heel had made a vertical rip that was several inches long and parallel with the seam.

Quickly, Donna found matching thread and using the tiniest of stitches reworked the seam making the panel slightly narrower. She was confident that when the torn section was then cut away no one would realise that the gown had ever been damaged.

By the time Aileen Roberts had finished her cup of tea the temporary renovation was complete.

'Miss Roberts, I think the dress will be all right,' Donna said timidly. Hesitantly, she took it across to show her.

'All right! Don't talk such nonsense! How can it be all right when there is a four-inch tear right down the back of it!'

'There isn't any longer. I've mended it. It still needs the damaged material cutting away and the seam neatening, but I thought you would want to see it first before I did that to make sure you think it looks satisfactory.'

Aileen Roberts waved her away. 'Stop trying to cover up for your sister,' she said angrily. 'You do it all the time, I've watched you. Well, this is one occasion where you can't make things right for her!'

Donna chewed uneasily on her lower lip, her brown eyes pleading. 'Please, Miss Roberts. Have a look at what I've done.'

'Oh, very well, then, but I'm quite sure it won't do,' she warned.

Carefully, Donna shook out the dress and held it up in front of Miss Roberts so that she could view the back of it.

'Turn it round then so that I can see where you've repaired it!'

'I'm showing you the part where it's been repaired. It was one of the back panels that was torn.'

Aileen Roberts frowned. The girl was right. The damage didn't show at all. She ran a

61

hand over the back of the dress, pulling the skirt this way and that, to try to see where the tear had been, but she couldn't.

'So what does it look like on the inside?' she snapped.

'Well, I haven't trimmed away the damaged material yet,' Donna told her.

'Why not?'

'As I said, I thought I had better let you see it first, Miss Roberts. Once it has been cut, then...' her voice trailed away uncertainly.

'It's no good showing it to me half done, is it,' Aileen Roberts said sharply.

She bundled the dress up and thrust it back at Donna. 'Finish the job off properly and then I'll decide what I'm going to do about it and about your sister.'

Chapter Five

'Thank you for what you did today, Donna, I really am very grateful,' Tanwen said as they made their way towards the tram stop in St Mary Street after work.

Donna looked at her sister in surprise. It was so unusual for Tanwen to express gratitude that she felt a lovely glow of happiness.

'Do you want to take the tram or shall we

walk home?' she suggested, linking arms with Tanwen. It was a sunny evening, and after a day confined in the workroom it felt so good to be out in the fresh air.

'Lovely idea!'

'Great! We'll cut through Cathays Park. The flowers will all be out and...'

'No,' Tanwen cut her short, 'I'd sooner nip through the Arcade and walk up Queen Street and look in the shop windows.'

'Oh, Tanwen! We've been shut up in a shop all day making clothes. Who wants to look at them again now!'

Tanwen didn't answer but turned right into the Arcade that led through to Queen Street. 'I don't want to look in shop windows, I want to check what's showing at the Capitol and the Empire,' she said when Donna pulled her arm away in protest.

'Miss Roberts can be a right cow,' Tanwen added suddenly. 'Anyone would think that I deliberately put my foot through that skirt. In fact, if she hadn't crept into the room and startled me like she did then it would never have happened.'

'You shouldn't have been wearing it, though, should you.'

'Oh, don't start preaching. It was only a bit of fun!'

'You're not really sorry at all, are you! You did it to make the other girls laugh.'

'So! What if I did?'

'That's the trouble with you, you're always trying to attract attention. Why can't you just get on with your work like everyone else?'

Tanwen pulled a face. 'Are you going to tell me that you really like working there?'

'It's all right,' Donna shrugged. 'In fact, it's better than I thought it would be.'

'It's not like Mam said it would be, though, is it? She made it sound as though we'd have a good time!' Tanwen sighed. 'Perhaps they did in her day when they lived in and there was more socialising with the other apprentices, and they met up with the boys who worked there.'

'Boys! That's all you think about, Tanwen. Showing off and talking to boys. I've seen you making eyes at the delivery lads and trying to chat them up whenever they come to the workroom.'

'Pimply faced youths, most of them!' Tanwen sniffed. 'I wouldn't go out with them even if they asked me,' she added scornfully.

'Which I take it means that none of them have asked you!' Donna retorted.

'Fat chance there is of me being allowed to go out with them anyway, even if they do ask me, unless I agree that you come as well,' Tanwen said sulkily. 'Mam doesn't seem to realise that we're growing up and want lives of our own. We might as well still be kids at school. She even expects us to dress alike!'

'Give her time! She let us go to the firm's Christmas party.'

'That was only because she knew Miss Roberts was in charge and would see that there was no hanky-panky, as she calls it, going on.'

'Well, we both had a good time. In fact it was smashing! Nice things to eat and drink, a band, dancing, and everyone was given a present as they left.'

'It was all right, I suppose, but it's not the same as going out on a real date with just one bloke, is it.'

'She'll let us do that, in time. We are still only fourteen, remember,' Donna said sagely. 'She's probably waiting to hear Miss Price's report on us at the end of our first year.'

'Yours will be all right, but I'm not sure about mine,' Tanwen said gloomily. 'Do you think Miss Roberts will tell her about what happened today?'

'I don't know. Perhaps you should tell Mam yourself so that she hears your side of the story first.'

'Don't be daft!' Tanwen stared belligerently at Donna. 'You're not going to blab to her, are you?'

'Me? I'm not going to say a word. You were the one in trouble, not me!'

'Yes, and you got me out of it, didn't you,'

Tanwen admitted. 'I bet Miss Roberts thinks there's a halo shining round your head. You got her out of a scrape as well, you know. She'd probably have been hauled up in front of Mr Howell himself if that gown had been completely ruined. You want to remember that.'

'What do mean, I should remember it?'

Tanwen looked smug. 'You might find it comes in useful sometime, when you are in a spot of bother with her and want to get out of it.'

'I intend to behave myself and work hard,' Donna told her emphatically.

'I think we had better both keep out of trouble for the next few weeks. We've been there almost a year and that's when they review the apprentices and decide who they are going to keep on and who they'll let go.'

'I hope we don't get the sack,' Donna exclaimed. 'I'm enjoying it there and I've made quite a few friends.'

Tanwen pulled a face. 'I'm fed up most of the time, doing the same thing like pulling out tacking threads and picking up pins over and over again.'

'You'd get other jobs to do if you showed any interest.'

'You mean if I was one of Aileen Roberts's favourites.'

'No! I mean if you stopped fooling around! If we do get the sack then it will be your fault and I shall tell Mam about the silly way you carry on.'

'We'll be kept on, you needn't worry about that,' Tanwen said confidently. 'Miss Price wouldn't dream of getting rid of us unless we'd done something really bad, because Mam's her friend.'

Tanwen was right, of course. Their apprenticeships were confirmed, although Miss Price did hear about Tanwen's escapades, and take it upon herself to warn Tanwen that she needed to improve her behaviour and work harder if she was ever going to get anywhere.

'I know your sister covers up for you and that she gets you out of trouble time and time again, but that isn't good enough,' she said sternly. 'She won't be at your side all your life, remember, so the sooner you accept responsibility for your own actions the better.'

To Carina Price's surprise Tanwen agreed with her wholeheartedly and promised to improve.

'I think it will be better next year when I'm given more responsibility,' she said confidently.

However, she wasn't so enthusiastic in the confines of the workroom. 'I find picking up pins and threads and taking out tacking stitches so utterly boring,' Tanwen sighed when Aileen Roberts also told her that she needed to try harder now that she was starting on the second year of her apprenticeship.

'Everyone in the workroom has to start that way,' Miss Roberts told her primly. 'I haven't seen many signs of you improving, either. The way you take out tacking leaves a lot to be desired. And as for your sewing! When I compare your stitches with those your sister does, well...' She didn't even bother to finish her sentence but walked away shaking her head in despair.

Once the next batch of apprentices were taken on, both Tanwen and Donna found themselves being entrusted with more intricate work.

Donna quickly mastered the skills needed to use a treadle sewing machine and took pride in being able to stitch the pieces that had been cut out into a garment.

Tanwen was inclined to be too slipshod to be trusted to work one of the machines. Although she was shown what to do time and time again she seemed to have difficulty in keeping the stitching straight. Even when she did, she managed to get the cotton caught up underneath the foot of the machine so that everything became a knotted jumble that had to be carefully snipped free so as not to damage the cloth.

When trying to rethread the bobbin Tanwen made such a mess of it that usually someone had to come and help her out.

Often it was Donna whose nimble fingers seemed to be able to untangle the mess Tanwen had made in seconds. She would then complete the complicated rethreading procedure as if there was nothing at all to it, while Tanwen sat there sulking.

When it came to being instructed on how to lay out patterns Donna found it an intriguing challenge that she adapted to with ease. Not only could she lay them out so as to make the best use of the fabric, but she could cut round the flimsy tissue paper with unerring accuracy.

Tanwen, on the other hand, either left a gap of half an inch or more between pattern and cloth or else cut in so close to the paper pattern that there wasn't enough material left to make a seam. Either way, when the pieces were tacked and stitched together the garment was unwearable. It was painstaking work to carefully unpick all the stitching and usually it was Donna who had to try to rectify the faults and put matters right.

Despite all this, Tanwen's confidence that they were as safe as houses remained, and as time flew past and their three-year apprenticeships drew to a close so her escapades became bolder.

At nearly seventeen she was, physically, far more mature than Donna. She was also very conscious of her charms. She spent every moment she could brushing her long golden hair and arranging it in different styles, or experimenting with make-up to make her blue eyes even bigger and brighter, or her cupid-bow mouth fuller and more expressive.

She had made friends with Bron Pritchard, a pretty gamin-faced junior in the cosmetics department that was on the ground floor, and was always popping down to see her. Bron kept Tanwen supplied with damaged tubes of face cream and blocks of face powder, lipsticks and eye make-up, and Tanwen liked nothing better than to experiment with them.

'You'll ruin your lovely skin putting all that muck on your face, Tanwen,' her mother told her. 'You don't need it, anyway. You've got a really lovely complexion, cariad. Now if it was Donna who was trying to do something to improve her looks then I could understand it. A spot of colour in her cheeks or some bright lipstick might do wonders for her.' She sighed. 'She looks just like I did when I was her age, all washed out and pale and wispy.'

Tanwen pulled a face at her reflection in the overmantel that was above the fireplace in their living room, but said nothing as she went on touching up her make-up.

Donna knew why her sister was taking such pains to look her best. A new porter, Phil Paxman, had started work a few weeks ago and Tanwen seemed to have fallen for his rugged good looks and was out to impress him.

Donna thought he was brash and she ignored the trite flattering remarks he made to all the girls whenever he brought boxes up to the workroom. Tanwen delighted in chatting to him, though, and once or twice Aileen Roberts had told her off rather sharply for doing so.

'Paxman has his own work to do, the same as you have, Tanwen, and the pair of you shouldn't be loitering about talking to each other.'

'He's too old for you, Tanwen,' Donna warned her sister the moment she managed to get her on her own. 'He's at least twenty-five. He may even be married.'

'No he's not!'

'You mean you've asked him?' Donna said, shocked.

'Don't be daft, cariad. I don't want him to know that I'm interested in him, now do I!' Tanwen smirked.

'So how do you know that he isn't married, then?'

'I've checked it out with Clive Lewis.'

Donna looked blank.

'Clive's the junior in Accounts. He sees everybody's records. It's easy for him to find out an age, an address, and all the family details.'

71

'I thought that all that information was supposed to be highly confidential!' Donna exclaimed in surprise.

'Well, he told me in confidence, didn't he?' Tanwen giggled.

Donna looked at her speculatively. 'So what did you have to do to get him to do that?'

Tanwen flicked back her long blonde hair and fluttered her eyelashes. 'I don't know what you mean!'

'Oh yes you do! A little kiss when no one was looking, was it?'

Tanwen shrugged. 'So what? There's no harm in that, is there?'

'It depends on how far you let him go.'

Tanwen flushed angrily. 'Trust you to think the worst!' Her voice rose angrily. 'You're only jealous because none of the boys at The Cardiff Drapers ever flirt with you or try to give you a quick kiss.'

'Now then, what are you two quarrelling about,' Gwyneth asked, coming into the room and finding them standing facing each other angrily. 'I could hear you shouting at each other from the kitchen.'

'It's nothing for you to worry about, Mam,' Donna assured her.

'Well, there must be something wrong. You both look as though you're about to tear each other's hair out.'

'Donna's jealous because the boys notice me and not her,' Tanwen said spitefully.

Gwyneth Evans sighed. It worried her when the girls quarrelled and they seemed to have been doing it more and more lately. Tanwen was so very pretty that she supposed she must expect Donna to be jealous when the boys seemed to prefer Tanwen. However, she was proud of the way Donna was getting on at work and she wished Tanwen would show the same zeal.

'You're both too young to be thinking about boys,' she scolded, 'but I'm not surprised that they're showing an interest in Tanwen since she's so friendly towards everybody. Perhaps instead of quarrelling with your sister, Donna, you should get her to help you do something about your hair to make it look prettier. You've got a lovely face, so why don't you ask her to show you how to use powder and lipstick so that you can make the most of yourself.'

'I'm quite happy with my hair and my face as they are, and I've got all the friends I want, thank you,' Donna snapped.

She turned and ran out of the room so that her mother wouldn't see her tears. She felt mortified that even her own mam felt that she needed to ask Tanwen for help if she was ever to be popular and get the boys to notice her.

It seemed that the only person in the world who preferred her to Tanwen was Miss Price.

Chapter Six

Gwyneth hadn't meant to upset Donna or to hurt her feelings. She knew only too well how it felt to discover that other people thought you were drab and that they didn't want anything to do with you. When she had been Donna's age she'd always been the one who faded into the background and was ignored. She could still remember how miserable she had felt.

She had truly only meant to be helpful and give her daughter some good advice. Now she was sorry she hadn't done it more diplomatically.

Donna was so like her in looks and nature that she knew exactly what it was like to be overshadowed, especially by someone as vivacious as Tanwen.

Donna had other talents, of course. Carina Price seemed to be very impressed by her and her standard of work. The last time they'd met she'd even gone as far as to hint that it was only because of Donna's industriousness that she hadn't sacked Tanwen long ago because she caused so much trouble.

Gwyneth sighed. She was sure there was a

lot that Donna could do to improve her appearance and brighten herself up. These days there were so many more ways of doing this than there had been when she was a girl, and who better than Tanwen to tell her sister how to go about it.

There had never been anyone to help her in that way when she'd been growing up. She'd never had anyone to confide in until she'd gone to work at The Cardiff Drapers and Carina Price had become her best friend. She'd understood Gwyneth's problem because she'd been no oil painting either.

They had been two plain, unattractive girls; certainly the most unprepossessing apprentices of their year, so they'd stuck together closely.

Gwyneth had been so timid, afraid to say boo to a goose! The others had only to laugh at her or tell her off and she would dissolve into floods of tears. Carina had always stood up for her. Right from their very first day she'd championed her.

Carina, six foot tall, flat-chested, size eight shoes and with her hair cut in a shingle, had been even more of a misfit than her. If anyone was silly enough to tease her about this fact, though, she soon showed them that she had the strength as well as the physique of a boy. She had only to grab hold of their arm and twist it behind their back to make them yelp with pain and for an apology to come bubbling from their lips.

They both knew that most of the girls they worked with laughed about them behind their backs, and so did the boys when they attended the staff social events. Gwyneth was nervous every time she had to go to these parties, especially the charabanc outings to Barry Island or Swansea that were arranged for the staff's enjoyment every bank holiday.

Looking back, she sometimes wished that Carina hadn't stuck so closely to her. If she'd been on her own then perhaps one of the boys would have sat next to her on the charabanc, or even walked along the shore with her. None of them dared to do that while Carina was at her side or striding along holding her arm.

It had been sheer chance that she'd been on her own when she'd first bumped into Silas Evans. Carina had been laid up with a sore throat and she'd popped out to The Hayes to get her some soothing linctus. Silas had been passing as she was leaving the chemist's and had collided with her, knocking the bottle out of her hand and sending it flying. The bottle had broken, spilling the contents, so he had insisted on buying a new one.

'You'd better let me walk you home and make sure you don't drop it again,' he told her as they came out of the shop.

It was the first time that a stranger had ever taken any notice of her, and she was too overwhelmed to speak. She kept looking up at him as they walked along the street, impressed by how tall he was and what broad shoulders he had. He had thick fair hair and brilliant blue eyes and she thought he was very handsome. He looked like one of the Norse gods they'd been told about in history lessons when she'd been at school.

As they turned into Trinity Street she hurriedly told him that she lived in a hostel that belonged to The Cardiff Drapers where she worked.

'I see.' He frowned. 'I thought you were fetching the linctus for someone in your family!'

'It's for a friend I work with who is not feeling well,' she explained.

'And this must be your day off,' he smiled. 'So why not take the linctus to your friend and then spend the rest of the day with me?'

Gwyneth was taken aback. She looked up at him uncertainly, a feeling of excitement stirring inside her, unable to believe that a man was asking her out!

Then common sense took over. She ought to be careful as she knew nothing at all about him. It would be different if Carina was going with them.

As if reading her mind, he smiled broadly.

'Perhaps I ought to introduce myself.' He held out his hand, 'Silas Evans, and I'm a sailor. I've only just arrived home on shore leave and I was on my way to Cardiff General Station to catch a train to go and visit my family.'

'You've probably missed your train by walking me home,' Gwyneth frowned apologetically.

He shrugged his massive shoulders. 'There are plenty more trains. My family are not expecting me so they won't even notice if it's another day before I get there.'

She'd shaken her head doubtfully, wondering what she should do. She was very tempted, but she was uncertain about what Carina would say when she found out.

She wrestled with her conscience. It didn't seem fair to go out and enjoy herself when Carina was lying there ill. However, Carina was her friend not her keeper, she told herself. Since they had first come to work at James Howell's they'd never spent any time at all apart. Perhaps it was time they did. There were other people in the world.

'Go on, then,' his voice was gently persuasive. 'Take the linctus to your friend, give her a good dose of it, and then tell her you are going for a walk while she has a sleep.'

The enticement was too great. Unable to resist such an opportunity, she succumbed.

The fact that Carina seemed pleased at the thought of being able to sleep undisturbed salved her conscience. Ten minutes later she was hurrying back outside, hoping that Silas Evans was still waiting for her.

He was, and when she shyly suggested that since it was such a lovely sunny day they should go for a walk in Roath Park, he agreed with alacrity.

She felt on cloud nine as they made their way towards the nearest tram stop. She hoped no one from The Cardiff Drapers would see her and report back to Carina. Even if they did, she argued silently with herself, there was nothing Carina could do about it; she was entitled to go out on her own.

She knew, of course, that if Carina heard about her new friendship with Silas Evans then it would be nipped in the bud.

As it was, no one did see her. Carina's chill and sore throat kept her in bed for almost a week. It had meant that Gwyneth had been able to see Silas Evans every day while he was on shore leave, and she had spent every moment she possibly could with him.

In the space of a week she had lost her head, her heart and her virginity, and when Carina had come to hear about it she had almost lost a friend. She'd introduced them to each other on Silas's last night ashore, and they had taken an instant dislike to each other.

He told Gwyneth he would be away for about three months, but he promised that he would write. Carina told her that she should forget about him because she was convinced that Gwyneth would never hear from him again.

The frost between Gwyneth and Carina was on the point of melting when a letter arrived from Silas, telling her how much he missed her and that he was counting the days until he was back in port and could see her again.

1909 had been a momentous year, Gwyneth reflected. It had been the most wonderful twelve months of her entire life. She was nineteen; she'd completed her apprenticeship and had been earning proper wages for over a year, so when Silas proposed she didn't hesitate to say 'Yes!'

They married in the Cardiff Register Office, and, rather reluctantly, Carina had been a witness.

They then rented a three-bedroom terraced house in Rhymney Street and spent the remainder of Silas's shore leave there. They could only afford to furnish it with the barest necessities; a bed, a table and two chairs, and a few pots and pans, but to Gwyneth it was heaven.

They persuaded Carina not to tell anyone at The Cardiff Drapers about their wedding because Gwyneth wanted to go on working while Silas was away at sea, so that she could afford to buy more things for their home.

'Someone is bound to find out, and then you will be sacked,' Carina warned. 'James Howell doesn't approve of married women working.'

'I know. That's why I'm asking you not to tell anyone. You're not likely to give me away, now are you?'

'No, but I don't like being in this sort of situation,' Carina told her angrily. 'If you are found out then they will know that I knew because we are such close friends, and they will say I should have informed them.'

'It's a chance we have to take.'

Even as she said it, Gwyneth marvelled at her own courage. Before she met Silas she would never have dared to contradict Carina.

However, with Silas away their friendship gradually seemed to return to normal. They spent all their leisure time together and Carina even stayed overnight at Rhymney Street and went shopping with her on their days off to help her to find things for her new home.

They spent New Year's Eve together. Gwyneth wasn't feeling too well, so instead of joining in any of the organised festivities at James Howell's, they stayed on their own

81

at Rhymney Street so that Gwyneth could have an early night.

The next morning it was clear there was something radically wrong with her. The moment she tried to get out of bed she was violently sick.

'Probably too much rich food over the Christmas holiday and you're not used to it,' Carina said dismissively. 'Have a lie in, you'll feel better in a while.'

By midday Gwyneth was feeling fine, and although it was a cold, frosty day they went to Roath Park for a walk.

'Well, that's the end of the celebrations. Christmas is over and the New Year has started, so it's back to work again in the morning,' Gwyneth reminded Carina as they returned to Rhymney Street.

'That's not such a bad thing. I shall be glad to get back into a proper routine,' Carina told her.

The next morning Gwyneth was feeling so sick that she was unable to keep any breakfast down.

'You'd better take the day off,' Carina told her grudgingly. 'You can't work in that state. You'd better go and see if the chemist can give you something to settle your stomach. We probably shouldn't have gone out in the cold yesterday when you weren't feeling well.'

By the time she was washed and dressed

and ready to go out it was mid-morning, and by then Gwyneth felt perfectly all right. Like a bolt from the blue, she suddenly realised the reason for her morning sickness.

Stunned, she sat down on her bed and began to work out how long it was since Silas had last been at home. When she calculated that it was slightly over three months she was convinced more than ever that she was pregnant.

She sat there, bemused by it all, knowing it was a doctor not a chemist she needed to see. If she was right then the baby would be due in June.

She couldn't believe that such a thing could be happening to her. She was so plain and mousy, and Silas was so big and handsome! It had astounded her that he had ever asked her to marry him. And now this!

Tears of happiness rolled down her cheeks. She might be plain and insignificant but she was going to be a mother!

Carina was far from pleased by the news. She didn't want to accept that it was happening. She knew that once Gwyneth left The Cardiff Drapers it was bound to be the end of their close friendship.

'What on earth possessed you to let such a thing happen, Gwyneth,' she scolded. 'I warned you that, like all men, he was only after one thing,' she admonished.

'I am married!' Gwyneth protested.

'You wouldn't be if you'd listened to me and used your common sense,' Carina snapped. 'You've ruined everything between us.'

'Why do you say that? We can still be friends. You were one of the witnesses at our wedding, remember.'

'I know, and that is something I'll never forgive myself for. We should have stayed together. Everything was so good as it was. We had each other, so why did you need Silas Evans? He's separated us, torn us apart. Nothing will ever be the same again.'

Gwyneth had been overcome to see Carina so distressed, and she had put her arms around her to try to comfort her.

'Listen to me. You are the dearest, closest friend I have ever had, and I want it to stay that way forever. Do you understand? You are the one person in the world that I can confide in. The one person I know will always be ready to help me.'

Carina hadn't answered, but had pushed her aside.

Even so, Gwyneth reflected, Carina had always been there whenever she needed help. Carina had been at her side when the twins were born, because Silas was at sea. Carina had been the one she'd turned to when he was reported missing in 1916. It had been Carina who had moved heaven and earth to help her set up a dressmaking business in her own home.

And recently Carina had made sure that Tanwen and Donna had been taken on as apprentices, and she was keeping an eye on them. This was why Gwyneth felt she was the right person to turn to now with her latest problem.

She fingered the torn note in her coat pocket. She didn't need to take it out and read it because she had already perused it so many times that the words were engraved on her mind.

Don't worry about anything, my darling. Everything will be all right in the end because I love you and you love me.

If you really are in trouble then we'll run away together. We'll elope and get married before your mother or anyone here at work can stop us.

It was history repeating itself, she thought despondently. It was a repetition of her own story, and now she knew why Carina had been in such despair at the time.

To have to stand by believing that someone you cared so much about was making the biggest mistake of their life, and yet to not be able to do anything about it, was more heartbreaking than she had ever imagined.

There was a difference, though, in this instance. She could do something about it.

She wasn't a mere friend whose advice could be ignored, she was the girl's mother, and the girl in question was not yet seventeen and therefore was under marriageable age.

There was only one problem: she didn't know which of her girls it was who was on the point of taking such a momentous step.

Donna was so quiet, so reserved, that possibly there was quite a lot she didn't know about her.

Recalling the unfeeling way she had spoken to Donna about her appearance she wondered now whether she had pushed her into having a 'secret life' and this was the outcome.

She had to be quite sure, though, before she intervened, and the only person who could help her to find out which of the girls it was, and the name of the man involved, was Carina Price.

Chapter Seven

Gwyneth Evans looked around the foyer of the Capitol cinema complex anxiously, checking the time on the illuminated clock and scanning the faces of the people already waiting there, but she could see no sign of Carina Price.

Knowing what a stickler Carina was for punctuality she'd arrived dead on time, and she wondered whether or not she should be patient a little longer.

Perhaps Carina had already gone on up to the Capitol Restaurant, which was on a higher level. Maybe she wouldn't want to be seen waiting in the foyer in case anyone associated with The Cardiff Drapers came in and saw her, Gwyneth reasoned. Ever since Tanwen and Donna had been working there, Carina had asked her not to visit her at work.

'I don't want people knowing about our friendship,' she'd said brusquely. 'They might think that I will be favouring your girls.'

Gwyneth had understood how she felt about this, but she didn't think that they had to carry matters as far as Carina insisted. They'd seen less and less of each other in the last three years. In fact, most of the news she had had about Carina was what she managed to gather from talking to Tanwen and Donna. From what they told her, apart from the occasional word of praise for Donna, Carina certainly didn't show them any kind of favouritism.

However, she'd accepted Carina's rules, even to the point of writing to her to arrange for them to see each other today.

As she climbed the wide carpeted stairs

she fingered the letter in her pocket that was the reason for their meeting. She hoped that Carina would set her mind at rest, though she didn't see how she could. Carina must have dealt with similar problems, surely, with all the girls that had passed through her hands over the many years that she had been in charge of apprentices.

Carina was indeed waiting for her in the restaurant. She'd chosen a table tucked away in a corner where they could talk without being overheard.

Without very much chance of them being seen, either, Gwyneth thought wryly.

She felt quite nervous as she walked towards the table. It was one of the top restaurants in the centre of Cardiff and not the sort of place she was used to visiting.

Carina was wearing a well-tailored brown costume and a pale blue silk blouse that was fastened to the neck so that it looked like a man's shirt. She wore her hair in a sleek, close-cropped style, and no jewellery, except for a plain gold wristwatch. From the top of her head to her neat brown court shoes, she looked very much the level-headed success-ful businesswoman.

They were such complete opposites, Gwyneth thought ruefully. Her own outfit, a paisley dress that she had made herself, looked fussy and frivolous.

Self-consciously, she raised a hand to her

ear, wondering if she should remove her dangling earrings and the matching pearl necklace that the girls had given her for Christmas. If she did that then she would look even more nondescript, she decided. Her fine hair was already frothing around her face like a halo. She felt feminine but insignificant, and so obtuse that she couldn't even deal with a family problem without asking someone else for advice, she thought disparagingly.

Carina was bound to remind her about what had happened when she'd been of a similar age. Like mother, like daughter: there was no doubt about that.

All Gwyneth wanted to know was the name of the boy or man involved; to know what sort of person he was and which of her girls had been taken in by him.

She shuddered as she recalled the words: *'If you really are in trouble then we'll run away together ... get married...'* She knew only too well what that must mean. She could forgive even that, though, as long as she knew her little girl would be happy with whoever had written the note. She hoped that he was a man who really cared, not some rake out to take advantage of a young girl.

Would Carina know what sort of character he was, and possibly even how long it had been going on? If the gossip had reached her ears then surely she would have taken some action and put a stop to it.

Carina greeted her coolly, checking her wristwatch as she did so. They ordered their meal. Carina refused wine because she would be going back to work, and until their food was served chatted about mundane matters and how the miners' strike, which had taken place the previous year, was affecting all their lives.

'I take it you had a specific reason for wanting to see me?'

'Yes.' Gwyneth sliced the potato on her plate into four small pieces and then pushed them around in the gravy, trying desperately to find the right words.

'Go on, then, what's the matter? Is one of the girls wanting to leave?'

Gwyneth stared at her in astonishment. 'You mean you already know?' she gasped.

Carina took another mouthful of food and shook her head. 'I was merely hazarding a guess. They are almost seventeen and their apprenticeships end in a few weeks, and then, when they are fully qualified seamstresses, it is more than likely that they will want to spread their wings. I can imagine they either want to try for a senior position in another store or consider some other kind of work. Am I right?'

Gwyneth shook her head. 'It's far more worrying than that.'

'Really?'

Gwyneth nodded. Fishing in her pocket she brought out the note and pushed it across the table towards Carina. 'Read that and you'll see for yourself...' She stopped and dabbed at her eyes, too emotional to go on.

Carina picked up the scrap of paper and smoothed it out. Her thin lips curved into a hard, cynical smile as she read it.

'Oh, she's in trouble all right. This time I don't think she'll be able to talk her way out of it, either.'

'You do already know?' Gwyneth was taken aback, the colour draining from her face.

Carina nodded. 'I've been waiting to see what happens next.'

'You never thought to get in touch with me and warn me?'

Carina shot a sharp, disapproving look at Gwyneth, her grey eyes steely. 'It's hardly my responsibility and there's not a lot you can do about it, now is there. Anyway, it's up to her to face up to things and sort this matter out.'

Gwyneth shook her head, her brown eyes sad. She pushed her plate of food aside, only half eaten. 'I know she takes after me and always tries to do what people ask, and that she doesn't stand up for herself,' she said sadly, 'but I never thought it would come to this.'

'Takes after you! What utter rubbish! She takes after Silas Evans if she takes after anyone,' Carina snapped angrily.

Gwyneth looked puzzled. 'I was talking about Donna.'

'Donna!' Carina exploded. 'Donna's no problem. It's Tanwen who's in trouble! She's been a mischief-maker since the day she started. Donna, on the other hand, has been exemplary. Quiet, industrious, and quick to learn. I wish all the apprentices were like her.' Her voice softened. 'She reminds me so much of you when you were that age.'

Gwyneth stared at her in disbelief. Relief mingled with concern. Tanwen was the one in trouble? She found that hard to believe. Tanwen had dreams; her heart was set on becoming a model. She'd never be able to do that if she was pregnant and had to give up working. It would be the end of her career at The Cardiff Drapers and Gwyneth was sure she would never acquiesce to being a wife and mother.

Although she had been saddened when she'd thought that it was Donna in trouble she'd reasoned that at least Donna was quiet and capable like her and would no doubt settle down to domesticity quite happily. Tanwen, though! That was a completely different matter. Tanwen thrived on being the centre of things.

'I take it Tanwen hasn't told you the

details?' Carina asked, cutting across her reverie.

Gwyneth shook her head. 'I only found the note at the weekend.'

'I see, and you immediately thought that it was Donna who was in trouble?'

Gwyneth looked confused. 'You are quite sure that it isn't?'

'Of course I am. I recognise the handwriting. It belongs to Clive Lewis.'

Gwyneth looked bewildered. 'I've never heard either of them mention him!'

'I'm sure you haven't. He's a nondescript little clerk who is the junior in Accounts.'

'Surely Tanwen hasn't taken up with someone like that?'

'Heavens no! He was just a means to an end.' She smiled grimly. 'I'm not sure whether he is serious about his feelings for her or whether he is trying to blackmail her.'

'What exactly has she done that he can do that?' Gwyneth asked in alarm.

Carina pursed her lips thoughtfully. 'I suppose there's no harm in you knowing what I've been told. Promise me you won't take matters into your own hands, though. This will be dealt with through the right channels, I can assure you.'

'Go on!'

'They think I don't hear the workroom gossip but it filters through. Tanwen has been flirting with one of the porters, a chap called Paxman. She wanted to know if he was married or not so she asked Clive Lewis, who as I said is a junior clerk in Accounts, to check his files. As you know, personal files are strictly confidential, but he did it nevertheless and told Tanwen all she wanted to know about Paxman.

'Unfortunately, his boss, Evan Jenkins, caught him in the act. Evan, who's in his mid-thirties, has been infatuated by Tanwen for a long time. He chatted her up on the first day she came to work, it seems, but she refuses to even speak to him if she can help it. Well, he saw this as an opportunity to get his own back. He threatened he would report young Clive Lewis to James Howell himself for divulging confidential information, unless Tanwen went out with him.'

'And she refused?'

'Needless to say, she refused. So then he said he would report Tanwen as being the one who had instigated "the crime", and she would also be called to account and in all likelihood dismissed as well.'

'That's blackmail!'

'Of course it is! Clive offering to elope with Tanwen is his immature way of trying to be gallant and get her out of trouble, I suppose.'

Gwyneth breathed a sigh of relief. 'It's that word "trouble" that put me in such a state. You can imagine what I thought!'

'I can understand that, but I'm astonished that you should think it was Donna. It certainly goes to show how little you understand her,' Carina said irritably. 'I've always suspected you favoured Tanwen from the way you talk about them, though why you do I'll never comprehend. Except, of course, that she is very like Silas in looks.'

'Yes, and headstrong like he was, which is why I've always felt she needed more guidance.'

'I agree she's headstrong and she's also very wilful. She's caused more trouble in the workroom than all the other apprentices put together. She's not nearly as dexterous or industrious as Donna, either. Donna is forever covering up for Tanwen, putting her mistakes right and getting her out of trouble, otherwise Tanwen would have been sacked a long time ago. I've only tolerated her behaviour because I know how much it means to you that she and Donna stay together for as long as possible.'

Gwyneth looked taken aback. 'Why have you never told me any of this before?'

Carina shrugged. 'I didn't want to worry you, and would it really have done any good if I had told you? As far as you are concerned you have never been able to see anything but good in Tanwen.'

'I love them both!'

'Maybe you do, but you've always put the

onus for Tanwen behaving herself onto Donna's shoulders. Over the years on the few occasions that we've met, I've got heartily sick of hearing you sing Tanwen's praises, saying how pretty she is and what winning ways she has.'

'She is pretty! She can charm the birds off the trees! Yet for some reason you've never liked her.'

'Because she's a trouble-maker! She can get herself into more scrapes than anyone I know. When she does, it is always Donna who comes to her rescue. Donna may be quiet and unobtrusive, but she is worth a dozen of her sister. She's nowhere near as plain as you make her out to be, either. Try taking a good long look at her!'

'I know what she looks like,' Gwyneth retaliated. 'She looks exactly like I did when I was her age.'

'Yes, she does,' Carina said quietly. 'And outwardly she's shy and retiring, just like you were. She has an inner strength, though, that will take her far, providing Tanwen doesn't burden her with too many of her scrapes and escapades.'

Gwyneth chewed her lip. 'So what will happen to Tanwen over this matter of the personal files?'

Carina shrugged. 'I'm not sure. It may have to be dealt with at the top level, especially now that I know about this note and realise its implications.'

'Does that mean Tanwen will be sacked?'

Carina's mouth tightened. 'She will be if Mr Howell hears about it.'

'Must you go to him about it?' Gwyneth pleaded. 'I feel it is partly my fault that Tanwen is so thoughtless. I suppose I have been more lenient with her than I should have been.' She dabbed a tear away. 'She reminds me so much of Silas when I first met him.'

'Oh, she's like her father, there's no doubt about that,' Carina agreed. 'Look, don't upset yourself. I know that strictly speaking I shouldn't be doing this but I'll speak to Evan Jenkins. He's sufficiently senior not to want any scandal so the whole incident can perhaps be cleared up discreetly.'

'Thank you!' Gwyneth reached out and placed her hand over Carina's. 'You've always been so ready to help me solve my problems. I really am very grateful to you.'

Carina withdrew her hand as if she had been stung. 'Don't thank me yet, I may not be successful,' she said brusquely. She looked at her watch. 'I must be getting back. Don't, whatever you do, talk to either Tanwen or Donna about this matter. Put it out of your head. Understand?'

Chapter Eight

Carina Price was unable to avoid an internal enquiry being held to find out how it had come about that details from the confidential files about members of staff had been disclosed.

Evan Jenkins, as head of the Accounts department, was given a stiff reprimand for not preventing such a thing from happening. Blame was eventually levelled at the junior in his department, Clive Lewis, and being the youngest and least important member of staff he was dismissed.

Paxman was also sacked because it was felt that he was far too familiar with the girls, and since the management was responsible for their welfare such risks could not be tolerated.

Fortunately, when hc was interviewed, Clive Lewis refused to divulge the name of the girl he had passed the information on to. Carina Price knew who it was, but she, too, kept silent, although she was well aware that Tanwen should also have been dismissed.

Tanwen, who had been in mortal terror that she would lose her job and be dismissed without a reference, treated the matter lightheartedly once it was all over and she knew she was safe.

'I don't know how you can laugh about it when Phil Paxman and young Clive Lewis have both been sacked,' Donna said in disbelief. 'This time you'd better tell Mam before Miss Price does.'

'If I don't then I suppose you will,' Tanwen said sulkily.

'Don't blame me! It was only a bit of a prank,' Tanwen laughed, flicking back her hair as she gave her mother her version of what happened. 'I was only teasing Clive Lewis when I said Phil Paxman had asked me to go out with him. I knew it would make Clive jealous because he was sweet on me. He pinched the records just to prove to me that Phil Paxman was married and had two kids. I wouldn't have gone out with him anyway, he was a right creep.'

Gwyneth was relieved at the outcome, but like Donna it saddened her that two people had lost their jobs. When she tried to remonstrate with Tanwen and pointed out that in Paxman's case his wife and children would probably go hungry if he couldn't get another job, Tanwen had merely shrugged her shoulders.

'You could have lost your job as well over this, you know!'

'It wouldn't have worried me,' Tanwen

said huffily. 'I'm fed up with the workroom and being bossed around by Aileen Roberts and Miss Price. I don't intend to stay there any longer than I have to.'

'So what are you going to do, then?' her mother asked worriedly.

'What I've always wanted to do ... become a model.'

'You aren't old enough,' Donna told her. 'James Howell insists that you have to be eighteen before you can become a model.'

'I'll be eighteen in less than a year, we both will!'

'You won't find it easy to get a job like that, there's very few of them,' Donna argued.

'There's an opening in the Ladies' Costume department, and I've spoken to Miss Owen who is in charge and she's said she's willing to give me a chance. She says I've got the right looks and the perfect figure. So as long as Carina Price doesn't say anything bad about me I've got the job.'

For once Gwyneth looked annoyed at Tanwen's remarks.

'You should both be grateful to Carina Price for taking you on at The Cardiff Drapers in the first place. From what I hear, Tanwen, you have caused a lot of problems for her ever since you started there.'

'Been gossiping to you, has she,' Tanwen said scornfully. 'I bet she only says nice things about Donna and sings her praises.'

'You're lucky she hasn't sacked you long before now,' Gwyneth said sharply. 'Not many bosses would have put up with you, the way you've carried on.'

Tanwen shrugged. 'She's odd! She needs to find herself a life outside James Howell's. Sometimes I've wondered why she lets me stay, and I'm pretty sure she only does so because she likes the idea of having you under her thumb, Mam.'

'Tanwen! I don't know what you mean!'

Donna was shocked by the look of dismay on her mother's face. 'Take no notice of her, Mam,' she said quickly.

Tanwen smirked. 'You shouldn't let Carina Price bully you, Mam. It's time you stood up to her, she's not your boss, you know!'

'I would think Miss Price would be only too pleased to see the back of you after all the trouble you've caused in the workroom,' Donna opined, coming to her mother's rescue.

'Yes, well, I'm not her little pet, am I? You couldn't do any wrong in her eyes if you tried. I'm fed up with always being compared to you and being told how industrious you are.'

'I only do what is expected of me.'

'The difference is that you are good at sewing and I'm not. I know what I want to do, what I've always wanted to do, and now I'm going to do it.'

'It seems a pointless way of living, parading around in new dresses all day showing off!'

'She will probably be very good at it,' Gwyneth intervened. 'As long as you are both happy, that is the main thing.'

'I'll be happy not to have my sister watching every move I make and jumping in to correct my mistakes whenever I get things wrong,' Tanwen pouted.

'I only do it to save you from getting told off!'

'Yes, well, when I become a model it will be something you won't be able to claim you do better than me,' Tanwen told her ungratefully. 'What is more, I'll be earning more than you,' she added triumphantly

To the amazement of both Donna and her mother, Tanwen did get the modelling job in the Ladies' Costume department, even though she wouldn't be eighteen until the following June. Working in separate departments seemed to bring the two girls closer together. At home they were both eager to discuss what had happened to them that day and compare conditions in the two different sections of James Howell's emporium.

Now that she was no longer expected to be responsible for Tanwen's mistakes and find time to rectify them, Donna found that her own life was more fulfilling. Aileen Roberts seemed to look on her as her deputy and give her more and more responsibility in the workroom.

Tanwen was glorying in her new role. She talked incessantly about the lovely dresses and costumes she was called on to model, and about the wealthy women who thought nothing of buying two or even three dresses or costumes at a time.

'It must be wonderful to be able to afford to buy whatever you like,' she said dreamily. 'I'll get there one day,' she vowed.

'So how will you do that? Become a film star or marry a rich man?' Donna laughed.

Tanwen flicked back her long blonde hair and tossed her head. 'I may do both.'

Their choice of boyfriends was now Gwyneth's biggest worry. She knew Tanwen attracted them like bees to a honey pot. She refused to let her go out alone with any of them, insisting that Donna went along as well.

'You're still my responsibility until you are twenty-one. Make up a foursome if you don't like her tagging along,' she told Tanwen when she grumbled about Donna playing gooseberry.

'She doesn't like the sort of boys I go out with,' Tanwen pouted.

'If she doesn't think they are suitable then it is all the more reason that I'm glad she is there to keep an eye on you when you go off to the pictures or out dancing,' her mother insisted.

'I don't mind that so much, it's the fact that they don't ask me out on a date when they know she has to come along as well,' Tanwen argued.

'Then do what I have suggested and make up a foursome, and let me meet them before you go out with them.'

It wasn't what Tanwen wanted to do, or Donna either for that matter. They thought it old-fashioned and outrageous that their mother should dictate such terms.

'They all laugh at me at work when I tell them about it,' Tanwen told Donna. 'Why can't she trust us?'

'I think she does, really, it's simply that she has always worried a great deal because she's had to bring us up single-handed. It was the same when we were at school. Mam always insisted on us coming home together because she was scared about us mixing with the wrong sort of kids,' Donna said thoughtfully.

For the most part they contented themselves with dancing with the boys they met at various local events and then returning home on their own.

Occasionally a boy would insist on coming with them, hoping that Donna would eventually go on home by herself and leave him and Tanwen on their own, but Donna knew this was more than she dared do. If she returned home without her sister then their mother wouldn't have hesitated to put on her own coat and march her back to where she'd left Tanwen and the boy.

Now that they were both nearly eighteen, though, and they both had responsible jobs, Donna felt as Tanwen did. It was time they had their own friends and went their own ways. Tanwen loved dancing, but she didn't. Tanwen floated round the room in the arms of one boy or another the entire evening while she sat on the sidelines watching.

When someone did ask her to dance it was usually a spotty youth who couldn't get any other partner and she always felt conspicuous, aware that others were laughing at her. She was embarrassed at being held so close. She felt clumsy and awkward and she was unable to respond to the music because she couldn't relax and let herself go like Tanwen did. She would far rather have gone for a walk, or even to the pictures. Sitting in the dark, she felt no one was looking at her and comparing her all the time with Tanwen.

For the most part Tanwen was happy to flirt with as many boys as she possibly could. Until, that was, she met Jared Davies, when suddenly she became all dreamy-eyed and serious.

'He's gorgeous,' she told her mother and Donna that evening. 'He's tall, with dark wavy hair, romantic dark eyes, and a smile that sends shivers down your spine.'

'He sounds dangerous to me,' her mother said dubiously. 'The sort of chap who thinks he can have any girl he wants. Where did you meet him anyway?'

'He came into James Howell's today, and he was with his mother.'

'His mother! How old is he, for heaven's sake?'

Tanwen shrugged. 'In his twenties, something like that.'

'So what was he doing out with his mother. Doesn't he go to work?'

'I don't know! He'd brought her there in his motorcar.'

'How do you know that?' Donna asked.

'He asked me to help him carry the boxes down to his car.'

'Why on earth couldn't one of the porters do it? Surely that is what they're there for!'

Tanwen flicked back her hair and giggled. 'He wanted to show me his car. It's a gorgeous red two-seater and he said he'll take me for a ride in it...'

'Oh no he won't,' Gwyneth cut in sharply. 'You can forget all about that, young lady. I can imagine the sort of ride he has in mind.'

'But Mam...'

'No! I've told you before, if you want to go

106

out on a date then you and Donna are to go as a foursome, and I want to meet them first.'

'All right. I'll ask him if he has a friend,' Tanwen snapped. 'Is that all right with you, Donna?'

'Well...' Donna was about to say no but she caught the pleading look in her sister's eyes and nodded in agreement. 'Make sure he's good-looking, then,' she joked weakly.

'And mind you bring them home for me to meet them first,' Gwyneth reminded her.

A week later Tanwen had fixed up an outing for herself and Donna. Gwyneth was suffering from a severe head cold and so she reluctantly agreed that she probably wasn't up to meeting strangers.

'Now make sure you stick together all the time,' she warned Tanwen. 'No splitting up and going off on your own with this Jared Davies. He sounds far too flash to me to be bothering himself with a shop girl. You and Donna keep together, you understand?'

Tanwen promised, although she had no intention of doing so and she made this plain to Donna the moment they were on their own.

'Jared's only got a two-seater so there won't be room for four of us in it. I've said we'll meet at Cathays Park, then you and Harri Jones, that's the friend he's bringing along, can go for a walk or something while

Jared takes me for a spin.'

'Thanks a bundle. You go swanning off for an exciting ride and I'm left to look at the empty flowerbeds in Cathays Park and freeze to death until you get back.'

'Ask him to take you to the pictures and we'll meet up at the Capitol Restaurant afterwards,' Tanwen said airily.

'You mean you are going to be a couple of hours on this ride?'

'I don't know! It's all in the lap of the gods, isn't it!'

'It will be if our mam ever finds out what we've done.'

'Oh, stop being so morbid. You are as bad as she is! For goodness' sake enjoy yourself for once. This Harri Jones may be a real heart-throb!'

'He might. Then again he may be as ugly as sin and twice as boring.'

'Well, you'll be able to judge for yourself quite soon, so get a move on. We don't want to keep them waiting, do we?'

'I'm not particularly worried,' Donna shrugged.

'I think I'll wear something warm if we're going for a spin in Jared's car, because it's an open one,' Tanwen said speculatively. 'Perhaps that new blue costume Mam made me, and then I can wear my new blue and gold paisley scarf over my hair. Or should I wear my little blue cloche hat, would that look more cute?'

'Dressing up a bit, aren't you?'

'I intend to make an impression,' Tanwen said smugly. 'What are you going to wear, then?'

Donna shrugged. 'Well, what do you wear on a blind date?'

'Oh, stop being so goofy! If Harri is a friend of Jared's then he's bound to be pretty nifty, so lighten up and make the best of yourself.'

Chapter Nine

Gwyneth gradually came to accept that her two girls were spending a great deal of their time with Jared and Harri, so she stopped constantly questioning them about who they were going with or where they had been.

Tanwen was obsessed by Jared and talked of nothing else. She claimed she was madly in love with him and she spent hours getting ready. She wasn't content with what she had and was constantly buying new clothes or begging her mother to make her new outfits simply to impress him.

It annoyed Gwyneth to see her frittering her money away so recklessly, when she had to watch every penny to make ends meet because Tanwen was constantly finding excuses for not handing over the money for her keep on a Friday night.

She never had this problem with Donna, and she also knew that Donna had opened a Post Office book and most weeks managed to save a shilling or more in that.

'Do you really need another new dress?' Gwyneth remonstrated. 'This will be the third new one you've had this month! It's costing a fortune to keep you looking fashionable, cariad.'

'I can't wear the same old thing every time I go out, now can I,' Tanwen argued.

'Donna does!'

Tanwen's only answer to this was to pull a face, and curl her lip. 'She doesn't care what she looks like, but I want to look special, see, and make a good impression. Besides,' she added slyly, 'it doesn't make much difference what Donna's wearing, she still looks short and frumpy.'

'Tanwen! That's a dreadful thing to say,' Gwyneth told her crossly.

Her scathing remarks made little impression on Donna. She had already established a pleasant rapport with Jared's friend Harri and knew that, like her, he was shy and reticent and didn't think clothes mattered all that much.

'Those two look as if they were made for each other,' he would laugh as they watched

Tanwen and Jared cavorting together, creating chaos wherever they went. 'They both have to be the centre of attention or else they're not happy.'

Donna agreed. If the four of them went to a dance then Jared and Tanwen frequently caused a scene because of the way they were dancing. Or else they would show off in some other way so that everyone noticed them.

Donna dreaded going for a meal in a restaurant with them. Jared was always so high-handed with the waiters that it embarrassed her. Tanwen would show off, too, by drinking more wine than she should, and then she would start acting silly. She had also started smoking and Jared had bought her a long jade cigarette holder that she used almost as a weapon. She would wave it around as she talked, indiscriminately flicking ash everywhere.

Donna refused to take up smoking. She tried it only once and she'd coughed so much that she'd almost choked. In tears she declared it was a filthy pastime and that she would never smoke again.

She didn't drink very much either. Never more than one glass of wine, and that only when she was having a meal. She preferred orange juice or lemonade to the exotic cocktails which Tanwen insisted were so delicious that she couldn't stop drinking them. Donna was sure that it was drinking so many cocktails one after another that caused Tanwen's silly giggling fits.

'If Mam ever finds out that you're drinking, Tanwen, she'll be ever so upset,' she warned.

'How will she find out unless you tell her? We're hardly likely to bump into her in any of the places we go to, are we?'

Donna was pleased that Harri was so different from Jared. Like her, he preferred going for a walk to dancing. He didn't have a sleek two-seater like Jared, so they sometimes took a tram out to Roath Park or Victoria Park and went for a walk. More often than not, though, they stayed in the centre of Cardiff and explored the streets and parks around the Civic Centre.

'Now that the weather is warmer and the evenings are lighter it would be nice to go to Barry Island or even to Swansea and walk along the seafront together,' Harri suggested. 'We could go by train, you know.'

Donna looked doubtful. 'It would take too long and I've promised to stay with Tanwen and keep an eye on her.'

'But you don't, do you,' he smiled. 'Lately we've gone our own way from almost the moment we all meet.'

'I know, but we always manage to be back with them at the end of the evening so that I can go home with her.'

Harri nodded. 'I understand. We could go

to Penarth, though, and walk along the promenade there. It will only take us about half an hour and we can be back in plenty of time for you to go home with Tanwen as usual.'

Donna grew to love their evenings in Penarth. It was so different from Cardiff, even though it was less than ten miles away. They sat on the sea wall, gazing out over the Bristol Channel towards Flat Holm and Steep Holm, and away in the far distance she could see the Somerset coastline. It was as if they were in another world.

'How long does this business of taking care of Tanwen have to go on for?' Harri asked as they strolled hand in hand along the promenade. 'You're not children any longer, Tanwen certainly isn't!'

'Mam says we can go our own way when we're eighteen.'

'When is that?'

'Soon! In June.'

Harri's face fell. 'Not until then?'

'It's less than a month away!' Donna smiled.

'I know, but I shall be gone by then. My father's taken a government post in India and he wants the whole family to go out there with him.'

'That's pretty sudden, isn't it?'

'Not really. It's been on the cards for months!'

Donna felt stunned. She'd thought he was as serious about her as she was about him. She certainly wouldn't have been so keen to go out with him if she'd known that he was merely amusing himself until it was time for him to move overseas. Thank goodness she'd had the sense not to give in to his demands that they should go all the way when he became passionate.

'Do you have to go with them?' she said weakly.

'I'm afraid so. My dad's arranged for me to start work in one of the government offices as well.'

His news discomfited Donna. She wasn't madly in love with him like Tanwen claimed to be with Jared, but she had started to think of Harri as her boyfriend.

She might have known she couldn't attract a steady boyfriend, she thought bitterly. Who would bother with someone as nondescript as she was. She could imagine how Tanwen would laugh when she told her.

This really was the end of always going everywhere with Tanwen, she vowed. No matter what her mother said she wasn't going to chaperone her any more. She was going to have a life of her own, even if that meant sitting at home every evening. She'd rather be doing that than hanging around dance halls while Tanwen flaunted herself as a flapper or the belle of the ball.

Perhaps, since I love children, I should have become a teacher after all, she thought morosely. The way my life's going I'm hardly likely to get married and have children of my own.

'I'm sorry to hear your friend is going overseas, cariad, but I suppose he has to if his family says so,' her mother said consolingly when Donna told her what was happening. 'He's only twenty, remember. I expect his parents feel responsible for him until he comes of age and that's why his dad has got him a job as well.'

'All I know is that I won't be seeing him any more. He won't even be here for our eighteenth birthday celebrations because he's leaving on the seventh of June.'

'Oh, that is a shame because Tanwen was saying that on the Saturday night you were all planning to go to the Summer Ball at the City Hall as a special celebration.'

'Yes, well she can go on her own with Jared. I'm not tagging along like a spare part, not any more. You said when we were eighteen we could go our own way and go out on our own if we wanted to do so,' Donna added belligerently when she saw her mother was about to protest.

'When you're both eighteen, but that's not until the tenth of June, now is it,' Gwyneth reminded her.

Donna stared at her in disbelief. 'Oh, Mam! You're not going to hold me to that promise, not just for one day, are you?'

Gwyneth nodded, her brown eyes pleading. 'Please, cariad. I will be so worried if Tanwen goes off with Jared to a do like that and you're not there to keep an eye on her. They're bound to have these new-fangled cocktails at such a grand affair, and they make them look enticing but heaven knows what's in them! I've seen how she carries on when she's had a glass of port wine at Christmas so I dread to think what she might get up to after a couple of those sorts of drinks.'

Donna chewed on her lower lip. 'I'm sorry, Mam, I can't do it. I can't go on my own!' she protested.

'Perhaps Jared will bring another friend along?'

'It would be someone I didn't know so I wouldn't feel any happier about things than if I was there on my own, now would I?' Donna explained dubiously.

'Please, Donna!' Gwyneth squeezed her arm coaxingly. 'I've made both of you beautiful new dresses to go in, remember. If you let Tanwen help you with your hair and make-up you'll look so lovely that the boys will be falling over themselves to dance with you.'

'Some hope! No one is interested in me

116

when Tanwen is around.'

'Please, Donna,' Gwyneth begged. 'This is the last time I'll expect you to accompany Tanwen, I promise.'

'All right, just to keep you happy, and as long as you explain it to Tanwen,' Donna agreed reluctantly. 'I'm quite sure she won't want me tagging along with her and Jared when she hears that Harri won't be there.'

Donna was right about that. Tanwen was furious.

'Going to the Summer Ball was supposed to be my birthday treat from Jared. He has known for ages that Harri would be on his way to India by then and he intended taking me to the Ball on my own,' she ranted tearfully.

'You never told me that, or Mam, or she wouldn't have gone to the trouble of making me a new frock for the occasion. Anyway, this is the last time I have to come with you, Mam's agreed to that,' Donna told her.

'Why do you have to come this time, though?' Tanwen pouted. 'The Ball doesn't end until one in the morning so I'll be eighteen while we are there!'

Donna shrugged helplessly. 'It's my birthday, too, don't forget! Mam thought we'd be celebrating together. She was planning a special party here at home like we've always had in the past.'

She knew why her mother wanted her to

be there. If she told her sister that it was to make sure she didn't have too much to drink then there would be an even bigger row, because Tanwen would be livid.

'I don't know what Jared will say when I tell him,' Tanwen grumbled. 'We can't get all three of us into his car, it would mean our dresses would be all squashed to bits.'

'Perhaps we should meet him at the City Hall...'

'And go there by tram?' Tanwen interrupted scathingly.

'If it's a fine evening I suppose we could walk.'

'Are you crazy! Walk through the streets in high heels and wearing an evening gown?'

'I'll talk to Mam about it, she might have some idea about the best way of us getting there.'

'Oh no you don't! Leave her out of it or the next thing she'll say is that she ought to come with us, and that would be the last straw. It's bad enough that she's made us identical dresses so that we both look like kids on a Sunday School outing.'

As it was, Jared dealt with the matter. 'I'll borrow my old man's Austin saloon for the night and come and pick you both up at eight o'clock,' he promised.

Gwyneth fussed and fiddled with their dresses, making eleventh hour alterations until both girls were at screaming pitch. The dresses were pale green organza with a dropped waist, and with the points of the 'handkerchief' style skirt reaching to mid-calf. The low-necked sleeveless style suited Tanwen beautifully. It showed off her slender figure to perfection. Her long fair hair fanned out over her bare shoulders, framing the beaded neckline.

On Donna, because she was not only shorter than her sister, but also plumper, the tight bodice was revealing and the irregular hemline seemed to make her look dumpy. The colour didn't suit her, and because her froth of brown hair was cut level with her ears her bare shoulders were exposed.

While Tanwen preened, adding touches to her make-up and twirling around in front of the cheval mirror admiring herself, Donna wondered if she ought to drape a scarf over her shoulders so that she didn't look half-naked.

Jared arrived ten minutes early. Both girls gasped when they saw the car that drew up outside their door. Jared wasn't driving, and it wasn't his father's Austin saloon but a black taxi-cab complete with a uniformed chauffeur.

'I decided I'd do you both proud since this is a birthday treat,' he pronounced grandly as he helped them into it.

Donna felt embarrassed at such expense,

but Tanwen was impressed. When she saw that most of their neighbours were watching from either their windows or their front doors as the gleaming black car drew away she gave them all a wave.

The City Hall was packed as they alighted outside the main portico. Jared gave the chauffeur instructions to be back to pick them up at one o'clock. Then he escorted both girls up to the ballroom.

By eleven o'clock, Donna was wishing she could go home. For her the evening had been anything but a success. She had spent most of the time sitting on one of the little gilt chairs that were placed at strategic points all along the wall, watching the whirling dancers on the floor in front of her.

From time to time she caught sight of Tanwen and Jared who seemed to be having a wonderful time. They both loved dancing, and Jared was the perfect partner for Tanwen, responding instinctively to her flamboyant style.

As midnight struck, Donna waited for them to come over and invite her to have a drink with them, since it was her birthday as well as Tanwen's.

Instead there was a sudden flurry in the centre of the dance floor as waiters cleared a space. They then brought in a gleaming iced birthday cake, complete with lighted candles, and placed it on a small portable

table. More waiters appeared with champagne and filled two elegant glass flutes, and to the strains of 'Happy Birthday' from the band, and clapping and cheering from many of the onlookers, Jared raised his glass and toasted Tanwen.

Donna couldn't believe what was happening. They were both ignoring her completely! Tanwen didn't even look round to see where she was.

She felt completely stunned, too frozen to move. She couldn't believe that Tanwen could do such a thing. She felt crushed, disillusioned and rejected. All she wanted to do was to get right away from the bright glittering ballroom, with its noisy, overdressed people who were all milling around laughing and dancing, and hide herself away in some dark corner.

As the band struck up a waltz and Tanwen and Jared began to circle the floor in each other's arms, Donna felt she couldn't breathe. Tanwen had gone too far this time, she thought angrily. No matter how much she tried, she couldn't talk her way out this time. She'd never forgive her, never!

Overwhelmed by despair, she headed for the exit, knowing that she had to escape from the confines of the ballroom and all that was going on there, in order to regain her composure.

Chapter Ten

As she emerged out into the cool of the June evening, Donna would have liked nothing better than to go straight home. However, because she was bound by her promise to her mother that she would stay with Tanwen, she knew she couldn't do that.

Miserably, she leaned against the stone-pillared entrance of the City Hall and felt tears trickling down her cheeks. She didn't even notice the black car approaching, not until it drew up in front of her and a voice said, 'Are you looking for me?'

For a moment she felt terrified, thinking she was being accosted. Then she recognised the taxi-cab and the uniformed chauffeur.

'No ... no, I'm just getting some fresh air,' she mumbled.

'So the others are still inside dancing the night away, are they?'

She shivered. 'Something like that.'

'There's no need to stand there and catch cold, you know,' he told her, holding open the car door. 'You can sit in here until they come out.'

'Thank you, but I don't think they are

ready to leave yet... I'd better go back inside and wait for them.'

'Why do that when you can stay out here and talk to me?'

Donna looked taken aback. 'I don't really know you!' she said primly.

He held out a hand. 'I'm Dylan Wallis, and I'm not really a chauffeur,' he grinned. 'Jared wanted to make an impression, see, so I agreed to dress up for the occasion.'

'So what do you really do?' Donna asked, her curiosity piqued.

His dark eyes twinkled. 'I'm still at school!' She studied his lean, handsome features in disbelief. With his short dark hair that was brushed forward, and his fresh complexion, he certainly didn't look much older than her. Yet his firm wide mouth, determined chin and direct gaze seemed to be those of quite a mature young man. 'You look awfully young to be a schoolmaster,' she said dubiously.

'A teacher!' He laughed. 'Oh no, I'm not a teacher, I'm a student.'

Donna frowned. He was certainly too old to still be a pupil so she suspected that he was laughing at her.

'So what are you doing driving a car like this if you are still a schoolboy?'

He shrugged. 'Part-time work. It's my uncle's car, he has a garage. Anything to earn some money.'

'If you are old enough to drive then you could get a proper job,' she persisted.

'I will when I'm qualified.'

She suddenly realised what he meant by student.

'Cardiff Technical College, just across the road there,' he grinned as if reading her mind. 'The same as Jared.'

'And Harri?'

'Yes. We all started there at the same time and became pals. We're not taking the same subjects, mind.'

'So you know that Harri has gone to India?'

'Lucky devil, isn't he! His dad's even fixed up a job for him. Made, he'll be! No daft interviews or special qualifications needed. Wish my old man was around to do the same for me.'

'My dad's dead, too,' Donna said softly. 'He died in the war.'

'Mine's not dead! He buggered off and left my mam to bring my kid sister and me up. That's why we've got no money. Mam was determined I should have a good education, though. She says you need to pass exams and have qualifications if you're going to get anywhere in this wicked old world.' He grinned. 'I've gone along with it because I know it's what she wants, but once I've got that piece of paper saying I'm qualified then I'm off to make my fortune. You need money and plenty of it to get by these days. Look at the way the miners had to strike and hold the whole country to ransom in order to get a living wage. Shameless, I call it.'

'So what are you going to do, become a politician?'

'I might! They're the people who can get things done and change things for the better. Will you vote for me? Since they gave women the vote in March you don't want to waste yours, mind.'

Donna laughed at his enthusiasm. 'I don't get a vote until I'm twenty-one,' she reminded him. 'That's three years away.'

'So you're eighteen?'

She nodded. 'That's right! I turned eighteen at midnight.'

He looked puzzled. 'Jared said it was Tanwen who was eighteen today. That was why he wanted to hire the car, so that he could take her to the Summer Ball in style.'

'Tanwen's my twin sister.'

'You're twins! You don't look a bit alike!'

'I know! She got all the looks.'

'She's flashy and a show-off! I think you're much nicer and far prettier.'

Donna laughed cynically. 'It's all right, you don't have to pretend. I know she's got it all and I'm the frump. I've lived with it for eighteen years, remember.'

'Stop running yourself down. You're different from her, that's all. Anyway, if it's your birthday as well then why aren't you in there celebrating? Jared told me he'd ordered a special birthday cake and champagne to be served on the last stroke of midnight, and arranged for the band to play "Happy Birthday".'

'Yes, it all went to plan,' Donna told him, 'and Tanwen looked very impressed.'

'What about you?'

She shook her head. 'Can we talk about something else,' she said uncomfortably.

'You mean they didn't include you in the celebration?' he asked in amazement.

Donna shrugged. 'It doesn't matter,' she said balefully.

'So that's why you came rushing out as if the old dragon itself had jumped down from the top of the City Hall and was chasing you and breathing fire down on your head,' he said consolingly. He took her hand. 'Would you scream for help if I gave you a birthday kiss? Someone ought to do so; it's bad luck otherwise.'

Very gently he took her face between his hands. His warm lips rested for a fleeting second on hers in a tender kiss that left her longing for more.

'And now that I've done that I'm going to take you back inside and demand a slice of birthday cake for us both, and a glass of champagne if there is any left.'

'Why aren't you in there anyway, didn't Jared invite you?' she asked curiously.

He shrugged. 'I don't like dancing. I'd sooner go for a walk.'

'That's my problem as well,' Donna smiled. 'I've got no ear for music so my feet don't move where they should, and either I fall over them or my partner does.'

'Blame your partner!'

Donna sighed. 'They never ask me a second time so I don't even get a chance to do that!'

'Well, are we going to go in there or not? I think we should,' he added, when he saw Donna start to shake her head.

He took off his peaked cap and tossed it into the car. Then he grabbed her firmly by the elbow and almost frogmarched her back up the steps of the City Hall and through into the foyer.

As they walked up the imposing marble staircase to the ballroom, Donna felt her heart racing. She didn't really want to go back into the ballroom because she was scared Dylan was going to make a scene.

Common sense told her that it was only what Tanwen and Jared deserved. Now that she'd had time to get over the mortification she'd felt at being left out of the birthday celebrations she could see how mean it had been of them to ignore her.

Tanwen had obviously been determined to

hog the limelight. She obviously had no doubt that if I was standing by her side then she wouldn't be able to take all the applause and good wishes herself, Donna thought, nettled.

Still holding her by the arm, Dylan pushed a way through the milling dancers to where Tanwen and Jared were holding court, surrounded by a congratulatory crowd.

Jared spun round when Dylan tapped him on the shoulder, and then frowned in annoyance when he saw Donna was with him.

'We're not ready to leave yet,' he stated. 'If Donna wants to go then drive her home and come back for us.'

'Donna doesn't want to go home. Donna wants her slice of cake and a glass of champagne. Donna is eighteen tonight, the same as Tanwen. You seem to have forgotten that twins have their birthday at the same time as each other,' he added sarcastically.

Jared's face became suffused with colour. His dark eyes narrowed, but he was at a loss for words.

Some of the people standing nearby overheard Dylan's remarks and began to make a fuss of Donna, congratulating her and proffering cake and champagne. Someone went across to the dais where the band were playing and whispered a request in the conductor's ear. The next minute the band was once again playing 'Happy Birthday', only this time changing the relevant words to 'Dear Donna'.

Tanwen's mood was thunderous. She managed to keep a fixed smile on her face, but her blue eyes were glacial as she stared angrily at Donna.

'What do you think you are playing at,' she hissed as she leaned across and kissed Donna's cheek.

'Ignore her,' Dylan whispered, overhearing. 'Drink your champagne and enjoy the limelight while you can.'

Jared looked equally angry, but like Tanwen he was doing his utmost to keep his feelings under control.

'I'll deal with you outside,' he snarled quietly into Dylan's ear.

'Be careful or I might drive home and leave you stranded,' Dylan grinned. 'It's a long walk from here to Gabalfa, and it was starting to rain when we came back inside.'

Jared looked taken aback and quickly changed tactics. 'Why didn't you say you knew Donna? You could have come in with us at the beginning of the evening and made sure she wasn't hanging round our necks like a spare part!'

'I don't know her. Leastwise, I didn't until a short time ago when I found her outside having a weep. Luckily I recognised her as one of the girls we'd picked up earlier in the evening.'

Jared looked mollified. 'Why don't you take her home and then come back for us?' he repeated, slapping Dylan on the back.

'I will if that is what she wants to do, but by the look of things she is having a good time.'

Jared scowled. 'Believe me, she doesn't know how to enjoy herself. She's spent the entire evening looking as miserable as sin. You wouldn't think they were sisters, let alone twins.'

'Since they're both wearing identical dresses it shouldn't be too difficult to work it out!'

'It's ruined Tanwen's evening knowing her sister is wearing a dress that is the same as hers. Not that she needed to worry, since Tanwen looks divine and her sister looks a frump.'

Dylan frowned. 'You're going over the top a bit, aren't you,' he snapped. 'From what I've discovered from talking to Donna she is a very nice girl. She might have different values to her sister, but I would say she is none the worse for that.'

Before Jared could answer, Dylan walked away.

The celebrations for Donna's birthday had ended, and everyone had drifted away. Donna was once again sitting on one of the little gilt chairs at the side of the room.

'Where's Tanwen?' Dylan asked as he

walked across and sat down next to her.

'Gone to the Ladies' Room to comb her hair and to put on some fresh make-up.'

'Do you want to dance?'

She shook her head. 'Not really. I've had my five minutes of glory; I don't want to spoil it by tripping over on the dance floor and making a spectacle of myself, not now, when everyone knows who I am.'

'So would you like me to take you home?'

He felt touched as he saw the look of relief on her face.

'I'm not sure that Tanwen and Jared are ready to leave yet,' she murmured hesitantly.

'I know that, but it doesn't matter. I'll take you home and come back for them.'

She looked at him questioningly, chewing uncertainly on her lower lip.

'It's all right,' Dylan assured her, 'Jared suggested it, as a matter of fact.'

Her face brightened. 'Oh well, in that case, if it's not too much trouble and you are quite sure that you don't want to stay...'

'I only want to stay if you do,' he told her. 'I don't enjoy dancing either, remember.'

'Then let's go. I'd better let Tanwen know that I'm leaving.'

'Why do that? She won't worry, Jared will tell her you've gone home. Come on,' he took her arm. 'Let's be on our way before you change your mind. Your limousine is at the door waiting for you,' he reminded her.

It was a journey that Donna would have liked to last forever. She sat in the front beside Dylan as they drove through the fresh June night. The streets were practically deserted, the moon hung in the velvet sky above them and stars glittered like sparkling diamonds.

'This isn't the way home,' Donna said in alarm as they skirted the River Taff and edged their way over Clarence Road Bridge. 'Where are you taking me?'

'Calm down! We're going to the Pier Head. Once the trams have all stopped it's a magical spot. There's something special about looking out over the Bristol Channel while the rest of the city is sleeping.'

'You always bring girls down here, do you?' she asked nervously, looking sideways at him.

'No, but I do come here on my own sometimes when I want to think. Where do you go?'

She shook her head. 'Nowhere on my own. I usually have to go wherever Tanwen wants to go.'

'Tanwen! Always Tanwen. Why do you let her dominate your life?' he asked, sliding his arm around her shoulders and pulling her closer to him.

Donna shrugged. 'She's my twin, we've always done everything together and gone everywhere together. Mam likes it that way. In fact,' she pulled away from Dylan's encircling arm, 'I think perhaps we should go and collect them from the City Hall, don't you?'

'There's no need. I told you, I've agreed with Jared that I'll go back and pick them up after I've taken you home.'

Donna looked doubtful. She'd been quite prepared to let Dylan take her home when they left the City Hall, but now she was having second thoughts. After the way Tanwen had behaved it would serve her right if I did go home without her, she thought rebelliously. Then her conscience brought her up sharply. 'Mam will be waiting up for us and I promised I would stay with Tanwen and make sure we came home together. It will be the last time I have to do it, though,' she explained. 'Mam said that after tonight we'd both be old enough to live our own lives.'

Chapter Eleven

Donna found Dylan Wallis waiting for her in Trinity Street when she came out of the staff exit on Monday night.

'Whatever are you doing here?' she gasped

in surprise.

'Waiting to see you, of course. I wanted to make sure you were real and not just a figment of my imagination. Come on,' he linked her arm through his, 'I'm taking you for a milkshake before you go home.'

Donna scanned the throng of people still pouring out of the door. 'I have to wait for Tanwen,' she murmured.

'Oh no you don't! Remember what you told me on Saturday night, or,' he grinned broadly, 'should I say Sunday morning? You said that now you were eighteen you could live a separate life from Tanwen, so let's start doing it.'

'Even so, she'll wonder where I am because we always walk home together, so she will probably hang about waiting for me,' Donna protested, gazing up into his dark eyes.

'It won't hurt her. Someone is bound to tell her that they saw us walking off together. Anyway, you've doubtless waited for her often enough, it might do her good to be the one who has to hang around.'

'I had better let her know that I'm going to be late home or Mam will worry,' she protested. 'Look, there she is!'

Dylan held on to her arm as she made to dash away. 'Let her come over here to us.'

Tanwen's eyebrows shot up in aston-ishment when she saw them standing together. She smiled coquettishly at Dylan. 'What are you doing here, shouldn't you still be at school,' she teased, taking his other arm.

'I'm taking Donna to the Kardomah, so will you tell your mother that she'll be home later on,' he said, freeing his arm from Tanwen's grip.

'Aren't you going to take me as well?' she asked with an inviting smile.

'No!'

'Why not?' she challenged.

'I'm trying to make up to Donna for what she missed out on at the Summer Ball,' he told her coldly.

Tanwen pouted prettily. 'Well, it wasn't my fault. We couldn't find her at midnight,' she explained sweetly.

'You didn't look very hard, did you? She was where she'd been all night, sitting on the sidelines while you and Jared enjoyed yourselves and ignored her.'

'I think you've missed your role in life,' she said teasingly. 'You should be riding a white horse, Dylan Wallis, since you seem to think that you're a knight in shining armour.'

'I take it that's what Jared said about me, was it? I don't think you're capable of putting that sort of interpretation on my behaviour,' he told her scathingly.

Tanwen flicked back her long blonde hair disdainfully. 'Well, if you don't want to take me for a milkshake there are plenty of others who do,' she boasted. She turned and gave a dazzling smile at Evan Jenkins who was passing. 'Isn't that right, Evan? You'll take me for a milkshake.'

'Any time!' he agreed, raising his brown trilby with a suggestive leer.

She smiled at him and linked her arm through his. 'How about now, then?'

'If you'll settle for a real drink at the Borough Arms instead of a milkshake?'

Donna bit her lip as Tanwen and Evan Jenkins walked off together, laughing and joking as they headed for the nearby public house. She hadn't liked Evan Jenkins when they'd met him on their first morning at work, and she'd heard so much about his reputation since then that she wondered if it was safe for Tanwen to go for a drink with him, or if she should try to stop her.

'Perhaps we should go to the Borough Arms, the same as them,' she suggested worriedly.

Dylan raised an eyebrow. 'Why? You don't like that sort of drink, now do you. Why do you have to do something you don't want to just because of Tanwen?'

Donna chewed her lower lip uneasily. 'I am just so used to keeping an eye on her,' she said lamely.

'To please your mother?'

'Yes, I suppose it is really. I've always done

so, ever since I can remember. She likes us to stay together, do the same things, and even dress alike.'

'Then it's time you stopped and started living your own life. Simply because Tanwen wants to do something it doesn't follow that you're going to enjoy doing it. When it comes to what you wear then since you don't look a bit alike it stands to reason that the same kind of clothes aren't going to suit you both, now doesn't it?'

'Mam's usually the one who chooses our clothes.'

'In styles and colours to suit Tanwen, I bet,' he said with a derisory laugh.

Donna felt uncomfortable. She wondered if he was trying to say she looked a mess. She probably did, but she didn't want a young man she hardly knew telling her so.

'You are so pretty, so demure,' he told her. 'You should be wearing either strong red or soft blues and pinks.'

'Those sorts of colours wouldn't suit Tanwen. She hates red and pink because they don't go at all well with her hair.'

'You're doing it again,' he scolded. 'You're considering Tanwen's likes and dislikes instead of your own. I tell you what, why don't you let me take you shopping and choose something that I know you would look good in?'

Donna stared at him in disbelief. 'Are you

crazy! What makes you think you could choose the right things for me to wear?'

'Because I have studied clothes! I've always wanted to design costumes for the theatre. Either that or to be a fabric designer.'

'So is that what you are studying at Technical College?'

'Heavens, no! I'm doing a dull but very practical course on Accountancy and Economics. I can dream, though, can't I?'

Donna shook her head. 'Dreaming doesn't do much good, does it? I wanted to become a teacher but it wasn't possible.'

'Why not?'

'Mam wanted me to work at the same place as Tanwen, so that I could keep an eye on her.'

Dylan scowled. 'Tanwen, Tanwen! Why does everything have to be done to suit Tanwen?'

'As a child she used to be a bit headstrong and Mam worried about her,' Donna explained.

'Used to be? She still is! Most people would call it selfish and self-centred, though, not headstrong.'

'Why don't you like her?' Donna asked. She felt puzzled, she couldn't understand Dylan's attitude. Everyone loved Tanwen because she was so beautiful. People were amused by her chatter and only too happy to fall in with her wishes because they wanted

138

to please her. The only other person she'd ever known who hadn't been captivated by Tanwen's charms had been Carina Price.

He shrugged. 'I don't dislike her, but I like you much better and I don't like seeing her take the limelight while you are ignored,' he said, his voice full of concern. 'I don't think you should run your life to fit in with what she wants to do, either. If you'd gone along with your ambition you would have made a wonderful teacher.'

'You would probably have made a wonderful theatre designer, so why didn't you fulfil your dreams?'

His face clouded. 'Money! Isn't that why we all do things we don't want to do?'

Donna looked perplexed. 'If you need money then why are you not working? Surely you could have got a job in a theatre and gone to night school and studied design.' She stopped and gave a little laugh. 'I don't really know what I'm talking about, do I?'

Dylan gave her a warm smile. 'That's exactly what I would have liked to do,' he assured her.

'Then why didn't you?'

'Family reasons. Like you, I wanted to keep my mam happy because she's had such a hard time of it bringing me and my sister up single-handed.'

'So how does going to Technical College help?'

'My uncle who owns the taxi-cab business said he would pay for me to go to college to become a qualified accountant, if I went to work for him afterwards.'

'So that was what your mother wanted you to do?'

'My mam thought it was a wonderful offer, especially since at the time he made it the miners were on strike and practically every man in our village was out of work. The thought of a ready-made job and a good wage packet meant such a lot to her that I went along with it to please her.'

'Both of us seem to have put our dreams on hold, don't we,' Donna smiled.

'Indeed! There is no need for mine to stay locked away, though, is there?'

Donna frowned. 'I don't understand?'

'I told you, I love fabrics and clothes so let me choose some material and design something that I know would suit you.'

'Mam makes all my clothes, she'd be hurt if that happened.'

'Rubbish! You have a job in the workrooms at the famous Cardiff Drapers, so you must know more about cutting out and sewing garments together than your mother does.'

'Yes, I suppose I do, really! Mind, she worked there before she was married so she's a first class dressmaker,' Donna explained.

'I can see it's going to be difficult to

persuade you to change the habit of a lifetime, but at least I'd like to try. As a start let's go and look in the shop windows and I can point out styles that would look wonderful on you.'

In the weeks that followed Donna found that life took on a whole new meaning. Dylan was constantly persuading her to take a leaf out of Tanwen's book and try different things that she'd never dreamed of doing before she met him.

All through the summer they enjoyed long walks, listening to the band playing in Cathays Park or Sophia Gardens, and visiting places which before had merely been names to her.

In the past, apart from her trips with Harri, she had only ever done things that Tanwen or her mother wanted to do, but now she began doing things that took her interest.

When Dylan took her to the museum he pointed out aspects of the exhibits that she would never have noticed. He took her to the Playhouse Theatre, to see live actors performing on stage, and she came away in a daze.

After that she was far more understanding when he talked about his interest in the theatre and his longing to be part of it.

She worried less and less about Tanwen. Even when she heard that she had broken off with Jared Davies and was flirting wildly with every young man she met, she was barely concerned.

Gwyneth was, though. Repeatedly she begged Donna to let Tanwen accompany her and Dylan when they went to the pictures or the theatre.

'Why, Mam? She has her own life and her interests aren't the same as mine. She likes dancing and drinking, but I don't, and nor does Dylan.'

'Perhaps if you took her with you to the theatre, cariad, she'd learn to enjoy going there instead, like you do. I'm sure it would be of help to her if she saw how they behave on stage now that she's modelling clothes full time,' Gwyneth wheedled.

That part of Tanwen's life seemed to be going well. She loved draping herself in beautiful modish outfits and parading around the showroom. She did it so well that very often she was 'borrowed' by the Evening Gowns department and the Fur Room to model their items as well.

When that happened Tanwen radiated excitement and arrived home all smiles as she told them about the gorgeous coats and wraps she'd been wearing.

It was her social life that alarmed and concerned Gwyneth. She seemed to be dating different young men almost every time she went out. It worried her when she came home as late as midnight, smelling of drink, her eyes glazed and her clothes in disarray.

Time and again she begged Donna to take her out. 'One night, that's all. Take Tanwen to the theatre on your birthday, then. I'm sure you can pick the sort of play that will interest her.'

Reluctantly, in order to set her mother's mind at rest, Donna agreed to ask Dylan if he would mind if they did that.

Knowing how much it meant to her, he agreed. 'Only this once, though. It's not to be a regular arrangement, mind,' he warned. 'I like having you all to myself!' he added, pulling her into his arms and kissing her hungrily.

'There's a new musical called *Funny Face* on at the Playhouse Theatre that week, so since your birthday is on the tenth, which is a Monday, we should be able to get tickets for that.'

'This is a bit different from the way we celebrated last year,' Tanwen pouted as they settled into their seats with Dylan sitting between them. 'It's not the sort of way I usually spend an evening. I would have much rather gone to see Al Jolson in *The Jazz Singer*, or even a Greta Garbo film.'

Donna said nothing. She, too, would have preferred to watch a more serious play, but Dylan had thought Tanwen would prefer something more lively.

By the end of the evening Tanwen was bowled over by what she had witnessed. Her enthusiasm was so tremendous that she could talk of nothing else as they walked home. Donna found herself left out as Dylan and Tanwen discussed at great length the clothes worn by the leading members of the cast and commented about their performance on stage.

A week later, Dylan suggested that Tanwen might like to come along with them to the Playhouse again.

'It's amazing how much I've learned in two visits,' she enthused as they left the theatre that night. 'I never knew that there were so many different sorts of plays.'

'Wait until the pantomime season starts,' Dylan laughed, 'then you'll see something different again. You'd probably enjoy a music-hall show. We must keep our eyes open and see if there is one on anywhere. Cardiff is not the only place with a theatre and I can always borrow one of my uncle's cars to get us there.'

'Tanwen has a real feel for the theatre and she's so knowledgeable about the techniques that are being used, as well as the clothes they're wearing, that I think her interest should be encouraged,' he explained to Donna afterwards.

Donna felt piqued. She didn't want Tanwen going to the theatre with them because the way she monopolised Dylan afterwards worried her. It also meant that they had to forgo their own intimate moments together at the end of the evening, when they kissed and cuddled and whispered how much they loved each other. Instead, Dylan gave her a chaste kiss before dashing off to catch the last train home to Tongwynlais.

In the months that followed it became the accepted routine that whenever they were going to the theatre, or even to see a film that Dylan thought Tanwen would enjoy, then she was invited to come along as well.

It worried Donna because Dylan seemed to be a different person when she was with them, so much more alert, witty and entertaining. Tanwen seemed to bring out qualities in him she'd never managed to reach, Donna mused.

When the advertisements for the panto-mime season began to appear he and Tanwen were eager to go to as many as they could. Once again, Donna found their tastes diverged. She preferred serious theatre not burlesque and wasn't anywhere near as enthusiastic as Tanwen.

As his Christmas presents to the two girls, Dylan arranged for them all to go to a dance at the City Hall. Gwyneth was making them both new dresses, using patterns and material chosen by Dylan.

Tanwen's was in flimsy jade green chiffon, cut tubular style with a low-cut back, dropped waistline, and short, undulating skirt. In keeping with the latest vogue she'd had her glorious long blonde hair cut into an Eton crop, and with her slender figure she appeared almost boyish.

Donna's dress was far more demure, although the flame-red taffeta certainly helped to brighten up her image. She refused to have her hair cut into either an Eton crop or a shingle, though.

Gwyneth was not well in the run-up to Christmas so Donna had to finish making the dresses. It was the first time she'd used her mother's treadle sewing machine and she found it slow and heavy to use compared to the ones she used every day at The Cardiff Drapers.

'Well, I've had it for over ten years and it was old then,' her mother admitted. 'Carina Price arranged for me to buy it cheaply when they were replacing them with the new ones you use today.'

By Boxing Day their mother was feeling a lot worse. She looked pale and drawn, complained of pains in her side and seemed to have a temperature.

'I'm not sure that we should go to the theatre tonight and leave Mam on her own, she's looking terribly frail,' Donna said worriedly.

Tanwen looked annoyed. 'Dylan went to a lot of trouble to get us tickets for the first night of the pantomime and he's really looking forward to it.'

'I know that,' Donna told her quickly, 'and I don't want to spoil all his plans.'

Tanwen shrugged. 'Ask Blodwyn from next door to come and sit with her, then.'

'Blodwyn's not there. She's gone to Neath to spend Christmas with her sister. I think one of us ought to stay home with Mam,' she added worriedly.

Tanwen frowned. 'You are better with Mam than I am,' she said speculatively. 'Anyway,' she added quickly, 'pantomime is not really to your taste, is it. You've been saying all along that it's probably going to be vulgar like the music-hall shows and that you prefer something that's a bit more serious.'

Donna looked doubtful. Could she trust Tanwen on her own with Dylan, or would she start flirting with him and leading him on?

She's been to the theatre with him before, she reminded herself sharply, and felt guilty for being so suspicious.

Chapter Twelve

It was well after midnight before Dylan brought Tanwen home after the pantomime on Boxing night. They were both in high spirits, giggling and laughing and exchanging private jokes about their evening out.

Donna kept shushing them to be silent, afraid they would waken her mother who had only just drifted off to sleep. She knew there was a bar at the theatre and she suspected they'd been in there drinking during the interval.

She was annoyed that they were so late back. She knew the pantomime ended at ten-thirty and it would have only taken them half an hour to get home. Going out drinking was something she and Dylan had never done, but judging by the state they were in she wondered if they had stopped off somewhere else for more drinks.

It was still Christmas, she reminded herself, so perhaps a little jollity of that sort was natural, she thought wryly as she held back her criticism. She was probably feeling disgruntled because she'd had such a hard night, she told herself. She felt dog-tired because her mother had needed constant attention all evening. She had been hoping that Tanwen would take over for a while as soon as she came home so that she could snatch some sleep, but the condition Tanwen was in it seemed improbable that she would be able to cope.

A feeble call from upstairs decided her. 'Mam needs me so I'll say goodnight,' she yawned. 'Perhaps you could take a turn with looking after Mam as soon as Dylan leaves, Tanwen,' she murmured. She waited for Dylan to kiss her goodnight and felt hurt when he didn't even move out of his chair.

Tanwen sighed. 'Must I? I feel I could sleep forever,' she proclaimed dramatically.

Donna didn't bother to answer. Wearily she made her way upstairs to attend to her mother's needs. Since it seemed she was going to be the one on call for the rest of the night she wrapped herself in a blanket and made herself as comfortable as possible in the chair by the side of her mam's bed. Then she closed her eyes to try to snatch a few minutes' sleep, but she couldn't stop wondering what was going on between Tanwen and Dylan. They were still downstairs, laughing and talking as if they were thoroughly enjoying each other's company.

It's silly to be jealous, she told herself. Of course I trust them! I was the one who kept saying that Dylan should get to know Tanwen better. Now that he's done just that

I'm getting all worked up about it.

She was so utterly weary that even though she could still hear them chattering and giggling she drifted off to sleep.

The sound of the front door closing roused her. For a moment she thought that someone had broken in. Gathering her scattered wits she threw aside the blanket and rushed to the window. In the early morning greyness she managed to make out the shape of a man disappearing up the road.

Heart in mouth, she wondered if Tanwen had forgotten to lock the front door and they'd had a burglar. She crept downstairs, expecting to find the house in disarray, but everything seemed to be more or less in order. She glanced at the clock on the mantelpiece, noting that it was almost seven o'clock. She must have been asleep for several hours.

As she was making her way back upstairs she noticed a light shining under Tanwen's bedroom door. In a flash she wondered if the man walking down the street was Dylan and the noise she'd heard had been him shutting the outside door as he left!

It took every ounce of her self-control not to push open Tanwen's door, confront her and ask if it had been Dylan leaving. Only the possibility that if she did so a quarrel might ensue, and that might disturb her mother, stopped her.

She didn't want to believe that he would have stayed so late, but she knew Tanwen too well to put it out of her mind. She was aware of how she could monopolise people when she wanted to do so. What good would it do to say anything, she asked herself bitterly. Tanwen would only accuse her of being jealous and deny that there was any harm in her and Dylan talking half the night away.

Men seemed to find Tanwen irresistible, she thought bitterly. Even Dylan, although in the past he had criticised her a great deal, was obviously as fallible as any other man when she set out to hold his attention.

She stood on the landing for a long time, debating what to do. Then she went back into her mam's room and sat down again in the chair at the side of the bed. Wrapping the blanket around her shoulders she eventually drifted back into a fitful sleep.

Tanwen was bright and chirpy the next morning, but Donna felt so utterly weary that she insisted that Tanwen should look after their mother while she had a couple of hours' sleep.

It was early afternoon when she woke up. She felt so refreshed that she wondered if all the things she had thought the night before had simply been figments of her imagination because she had been so tired.

'I'm glad you're awake at last,' Tanwen told her, 'because I'm planning to go out. I met a really fascinating man last night at the pantomime when we went to the bar in the interval, and I'm seeing him again tonight,' she burbled. 'Come and help me choose what I should wear,' she invited.

'I don't think you need any help from me!' Donna snapped.

'Don't be like that,' Tanwen pouted. 'Are you cross because I want to go out again tonight?'

Donna hesitated, wondering whether to voice any of the suspicions raging around in her mind about what she suspected might have gone on between Tanwen and Dylan the previous night. Knowing Tanwen would deny anything of the sort, she decided not to give her the satisfaction of knowing how concerned she'd been.

'Cross? No, but I am fed up that you're not doing your fair share of looking after Mam.'

Tanwen looked contrite. 'I'll stay home tomorrow night, I promise.'

Dylan arrived as Tanwen was on the point of leaving the house, and Donna was acutely aware that his attention was centred on Tanwen and that he didn't even say hello to her.

'You are looking particularly fetching,' he

smiled as he admired Tanwen's outfit. 'That black wool coat with its white fur collar and matching hat makes you look like a movie star!'

Tanwen looked pleased and pirouetted for his benefit.

'Can I give you a lift anywhere, I've got a car outside,' he offered.

Tanwen smiled up at him playfully. 'I don't think my date would like it if I turned up in another man's car!' she told him, fluttering her eyelashes provocatively.

'You could always say I was your chauffeur.'

'Well, you have played that part before, haven't you!' she giggled.

'I certainly have! Now do you want me to give you a lift or not?'

She shook her head, then patted her fur hat back into place. 'I'm only walking as far as the corner of the road. I'm meeting my date there, and he has a car of his own.'

'I don't know where Tanwen gets the energy from,' Dylan laughed after she had pranced out of the door, blowing kisses to them both.

'I don't either,' Donna agreed. 'I was hoping she would sit with Mam for a while this evening so that you and me could spend some time together.'

'Is she no better?'

'A little, but not well enough to be left on

her own.'

'Oh dear!' His face clouded. 'I did wonder if it was any good coming to take you out. Naturally I thought that as Tanwen had a night out last night then she would be taking over in the sickroom. It looks as though I was mistaken,' he said glumly.

'Never mind, I'll make you a pot of tea and we'll sit by the fire.'

Dylan shook his head. 'No, I think I'll head for home. I had a very late night last night and I have a lot of studying I should be doing. My final exams are in less than two months' time.'

'Surely you can stay for ten minutes,' Donna pleaded. 'I didn't see you at all yesterday evening,' she reminded him, 'and you didn't even kiss me goodnight before you left.'

'You went off upstairs when we came home, and when you didn't come down again we thought you must have gone to bed,' he said huffily.

Donna chewed on her lower lip. She wondered if she should face him with her suspicions. Before she could reach a decision he was heading for the door.

'So when will I see you again?' she asked wistfully.

He sighed. 'You'll be back at work tomorrow and I'll be back at college next week, and it's so important that I do some revising. I think we'd better leave it until the following weekend.'

Donna looked taken aback. 'What about next Tuesday, it will be New Year's Eve! Aren't we going to celebrate the New Year together?'

Dylan looked apologetic. 'Didn't I tell you? I promised my mother and young sister that if I spent Christmas with you then I'd go home and spend the New Year with them.'

'Dylan! This is the first time you've mentioned anything of the sort!' Donna said indignantly.

He looked surprised. 'I'm sure I told you. Perhaps you've forgotten as you've been so busy looking after your mother.'

'I wouldn't have forgotten something as important as that,' she argued, frowning.

'Now then, don't get all cross about it.' He took her face between his hands and gently kissed her on the mouth. 'You're overtired, my darling. What you need is a really early night.'

She knew he was right, but she still didn't want him to go.

'A week is not very long, now is it?' he went on persuasively. 'We'll go somewhere really grand and have our own very special celebration for the start of 1930. We'll make Saturday the fourth of January a day we'll remember forever. Now you won't forget that date, will you, cariad?' he added teasingly.

Before she could swallow back the tears of disappointment that were choking her at having to wait until then he had gone. As she heard the front door close behind him its distinctive sound vividly reminded her of the noise she'd heard at five o'clock that morning, and she was more convinced than ever that it had been Dylan she'd heard leaving.

Gwyneth felt so much better on New Year's Eve that she decided to get dressed and come downstairs.

'It will be so nice for the three of us to celebrate the New Year together,' she said happily.

'Sorry, Mam, but I'm going out. I've got a date,' Tanwen told her. 'A new man in my life, see, and he's very special.'

'Then perhaps you'd better bring him home and get him to let the New Year in, seeing as Dylan won't be coming to do it.'

'I'd love to, Mam, but we've planned a special night out so that won't be possible. I'm afraid you and Donna will have to celebrate on your own.'

January the fourth seemed to be an awfully long time to wait before she saw Dylan again, Donna thought unhappily as midnight approached. By then the New Year would have already started and everything would be more or less back to normal.

She wondered what other changes 1930 would bring. Carina Price had told her that she had recommended to Mr Howell that she should be appointed Deputy Manageress of the workroom. If that happened then it would mean a substantial pay rise.

She looked across to where her mother was sitting hunched up in her chair. She was beginning to look so frail that Donna worried about her. Possibly it was time her mother gave up dressmaking altogether, and for her and Tanwen to support her completely now that they were both earning good money.

Dylan would be taking his Accountancy exams in February, and once he had passed those he would leave Cardiff Technical College for good and take up the well-paid job he had waiting for him at his uncle's firm.

Dylan had promised her that they would become engaged at Easter, so then, with his money and her increased wages, they really would be able to start saving up to get married.

The clock chimed midnight and she and her mother both raised a small glass of port to welcome in the New Year. 1930 really was going to be a wonderful time in her life, Donna told herself optimistically.

Chapter Thirteen

Gwyneth Evans wasn't sure whether it was her long, drawn-out illness that had made her more perceptive, or whether it was because she wasn't so involved in her sewing orders, but she sensed that there was an uneasy atmosphere again between Tanwen and Donna.

The two girls seemed to become more estranged by the day. Donna was quiet and introspective, but Tanwen was as bubbly as a cauldron of cinder toffee.

Her blue eyes were shining intensely, though whether with happiness or devilment her mother wasn't too sure. From the look on her face it was almost as though she was laughing at them all. As if she knew something they didn't and yet wasn't prepared to breathe a word about it.

Donna was the opposite. She acted as though she had the cares of the world on her shoulders. She refused to have her hair styled in a shingle or an Eton crop so it was still as it had always been, making her look even more wan and worn out.

Gwyneth knew that while she'd been ill Donna had done the bulk of the work involved in looking after her. She'd nursed her and cared for her all over Christmas, which had probably left her feeling worn out. By now, the middle of January, she should have recovered from that and have been back to normal.

Things were going so well for Donna at work, and she was so delighted by her promotion, that she should be the one whose eyes were shining with happiness. Carina had kept her promise to speak to James Howell about Donna being promoted and she was now deputy to Aileen Roberts in the workroom, and that had meant a very nice pay rise.

Gwyneth was sure that Donna's air of dejection was something to do with Dylan Wallis. He and Donna had only been out together twice since Christmas. When she'd asked why that was, Donna had told her that it was because he was revising hard for his final exams. She'd looked so woebegone as she'd said it, though, that Gwyneth was sure there was more to it than that.

She thought it was strange that he and Donna hadn't spent New Year's Eve together. Since they were talking about getting engaged as soon as he finished at college and started work, she would have thought that they would have wanted to be together at the beginning of the New Year and drink to their future.

Instead, Donna had stayed at home and kept her company. They'd gone to bed the moment they'd toasted 1930 in and all the hooters and klaxons had finished sounding.

Tanwen had been all dressed up and had gone off to a party. Gwyneth had tried to stay awake because it worried her when one of them was out on their own, but she'd drifted off to sleep and she had no idea what time Tanwen had come home. She'd obviously been late because she'd stayed in bed until almost noon on New Year's Day.

The coolness between Tanwen and Donna seemed to have started around then, Gwyneth reflected. She wondered if Donna felt jealous because Tanwen was having such a good time and she wasn't.

Yet she must realise how important these exams are to Dylan if he's going to justify all the extra years he's spent on education, she told herself.

Perhaps, she mused, I'm the one who is to blame. She looked after me so well while I was ill that maybe I've been expecting her to do too much for me ever since. What with caring for me, and her increased responsibilities at work, she's probably feeling worn out.

She'd have a word with both of them, she decided, and try to find out what was really going on.

Donna sensed that Dylan was avoiding her and that somehow things had gone wrong between them. She wasn't sure whether it was something she'd said or something she'd done that had upset him.

She hated the coldness between them. She couldn't stand the way he gave her a quick peck on the cheek when they met instead of taking her into his arms and kissing her properly, since that was still the highlight of their lovemaking.

Another thing that troubled her was the fact that they were meeting less and less. At one time it had been two or three nights a week after he finished classes at the Technical College, and then again at the weekend. Since Christmas she had only seen him a couple of times. It was now the middle of February so she felt justified in asking him what was going on.

Dylan had finished his exams so there was no question that he was studying and couldn't spare the time to take her out. Which meant that the only other reason was that he was tired of her company and didn't want to go out with her any more.

They were supposed to be getting engaged at Easter and then they'd start saving up to get married, yet he hadn't wanted to talk about either of these matters for weeks. She didn't want to go on like this so she resolved she'd have it out with him. It was the only way to set her mind at rest and find out if he still loved her.

'You know I'm leaving college at Easter and starting work full time, so I've got a lot of loose ends to tie up,' he told her evasively.

'Surely you can spare some time for us to be together?'

Dylan shrugged. 'What's the point. You never let me get near you! I'm getting fed up with it!'

She stared at him, wide-eyed. 'What's that supposed to mean?'

'Dammo di! You know quite well what it means. A kiss and a bit of cuddling and that's it with you! The moment I try to go any further you become all agitated and the shutters go up. I'm not allowed to touch!'

Donna felt the heat rushing to her face. 'We agreed when we first started going out seriously that we would both wait until we were married before we did that sort of thing and went the whole way.'

'Did we? I think you mean that you laid down those rules and I agreed. It might suit you to stay a virgin until we tie the knot but it doesn't suit me.'

'I don't want to talk about it,' she said evasively.

'No, you never do! Anyone would think we were still kids of fifteen. Face it, Donna, we're both grown-ups and it's time you accepted that fact.'

'I thought we had, by agreeing to become engaged as soon as you've finished at college and started work.'

'Is that going to make any difference? Are you going to let me sleep with you then?'

'We agreed to wait until we were married,' she repeated stubbornly.

'If you loved me you wouldn't hold out on me like this,' he argued. 'Prove you trust me by changing your mind.'

She shook her head. 'I can't bring myself to do that.'

Dylan turned on her angrily. 'Duw anwyl! You're a sanctimonious little bitch! Well, if you won't come across then there's plenty of other girls who will. There's your sister for a start!'

The colour drained from Donna's face. The shock as his words sank in sent an apprehensive shiver snaking down her back.

'What did you say?' she asked, fighting to keep her voice steady.

'I said your sister doesn't refuse to sleep with me! What's more, she enjoys every minute when she does.'

'You ... you and Tanwen?' Her breath caught in her throat and for one awful moment she thought she was going to choke.

It was like an unfolding nightmare. She wanted to scream at him, to make him take back the words which were searing her brain and making her chest constrict with pain and jealousy.

He was making it all up, she told herself. Tanwen was her twin, she wouldn't do a thing like that ... not with Dylan!

She looked up into his face then recoiled as she saw the contempt in his dark eyes and the sneer on his lips. A nervous tic was playing at the corner of his mouth and she wondered if he was fearful of what her reaction was going to be.

His next words made it clear that not only was it over between them as far as he was concerned, but that he didn't care whether he had hurt her or not.

'Don't start accusing Tanwen of causing the rift between us, you have no one but yourself to blame,' he told her callously. 'If you'd truly loved me then you wouldn't have held me at arm's length like you've always done.'

Donna crossed her arms over her body as if shielding herself from his rejection, clenching her hands into fists to try to stop herself from shaking.

'I think you'd better go, Dylan,' she whispered dully. She rubbed the back of her hand across her eyes. 'You've already said far more than was necessary!'

He shrugged. 'I won't say goodbye because we are bound to see each other from time to time when I call for Tanwen,' he told her jauntily.

'No!' she pleaded. 'You can't do that to me, Dylan! Have you no feelings?' Her voice quavered with the emotion welling up inside her.

'You'll have to make sure you keep out of our way, then, won't you,' he smirked, as he turned on his heel and walked away.

Donna found that Tanwen was as cold and heartless as Dylan when she accused her of stealing Dylan away from her.

'Please, Tanwen, tell me it's not true?' she begged.

Tanwen shrugged. 'It's time you grew up and learned how to please a man,' she jibed smugly. 'You always were prissy, a little goody-goody who constantly behaved as if butter wouldn't melt in her mouth.'

'Now who's being childish?' Donna asked coldly.

Tanwen's blue eyes were icy. She waved a finger menacingly at Donna. 'Don't think you can get him back. Try that and it will be the worse for you,' she warned. 'He's finished with you for good, so make sure you remember that!'

'If he has then I know the reason why,' Donna retorted contemptuously. 'It's because you have no morals at all!'

'Who are you to sit in judgement?' Tanwen defended herself angrily.

'You must be very proud of yourself, but

then I suppose you think it is all right to go around sleeping with anyone who gives you a second glance, don't you?'

'That's better than being a prude and a little cock-tease. I suppose you've forgotten all the promises you made to Dylan; promises that you never intended to fulfil.'

'Yes, I made promises,' Donna told her solemnly, 'and I intended to fulfil them as soon as it was legal for us to do so.'

'And you thought you'd be able to keep a virile man like Dylan faithful to you because you'd made him promises with conditions like that attached to them?' Tanwen exploded into derisory laughter.

'You lost Jared Davies because you were always flirting with his friends,' Donna reminded her. 'You couldn't bear to see me happy so you've stolen Dylan away from me by offering to sleep with him.'

'What's going on between you two?' came a sudden voice.

Tanwen and Donna lapsed into a tense, uncomfortable silence as their mother came into the room. 'I could hear you yelling at each other all over the house,' she told them sharply.

'It's nothing for you to get upset about, Mam,' Donna told her quickly.

'I heard what the row was about so there's no need to gloss things over, or for either of you to repeat the details.'

'Leave it, Mam, we'll sort it out between us,' Donna said sharply.

Gwyneth ignored her. Her eyes were fixed on Tanwen.

'I'm bitterly disappointed. So what have you to say, Tanwen?' she demanded. 'I've known for a long time that you're boy mad and a flirt, but I never thought for one minute that you would stoop so low as this! Dammo di! Stealing your sister's boyfriend from her! What can you be thinking about?'

'I don't want him back, Mam,' Donna snapped. 'Tanwen's welcome to Dylan. I'd never be able to trust him again, not after what Tanwen's told me has been going on between them.'

'All this began when you started going off to the theatre and music halls with him, did it, Tanwen?' Gwyneth said wearily. 'You're a little hussy and I'm ashamed of you, but I suppose I'm responsible for what has happened.'

'Oh, for heaven's sake!' Tanwen exclaimed exasperatedly. 'I'm not listening to any more of this.' Tossing her head defiantly she stormed out of the room.

'How do you make that out, Mam?' Donna asked in astonishment.

'If I hadn't relied so much on you looking after me lately, cariad, then you would have been the one going out with Dylan, not Tanwen. Throwing them together because

I've been ill is what's done this!'

'Not really, Mam. It goes right back to the first time we all went to the theatre together. Tanwen was so enthusiastic that night about everything she'd experienced. Dylan is mad about the theatre, too, so I suppose it was only natural that they ended up spending more time with each other.'

'Rubbish! Anyway, that was my fault as well,' her mother said sadly. 'I was the one who suggested that Tanwen went to the Playhouse with you as a birthday treat, if you remember.'

Donna put her arms round her mother's thin shoulders. 'Don't worry about it, Mam. It's too late to try and turn the clock back and he's not worth it. Tanwen's welcome to him, they're two of a kind,' she said bitterly.

Chapter Fourteen

It was all very well telling her mother that what was done was done and there was nothing that any of them could do about it now, Donna reflected, but deep down she felt quite differently about the situation. For the first time in her life she actually hated her sister.

She'd been going out with Dylan for

almost two years, they were supposed to be getting engaged in a few weeks' time. She'd trusted him implicitly. He'd told her he loved her and she had believed him and had already started collecting things for her bottom drawer. She'd told some of her friends at work that she was in love.

His passionate kisses and caresses aroused her as much as they did him. Her body was ready for him, but he'd agreed with her that the right thing to do was to wait until they were married and so they'd resisted the overwhelming temptation to go further. She desperately wanted to surrender to his exploring hands and for them to make love, but she'd held out because she thought he might think she was flighty like Tanwen.

And because of that she'd lost him! It was so unfair. She was sure she'd never love any other man as she loved Dylan. She would have given in to his desperate needs and her passionate desires once they were officially engaged. Now she would never know the rapture of consummating their love, or a full and joyous climax of passion.

Tanwen could have her pick of dozens yet she'd used her wiles on Dylan and stolen that sensual experience from her. Knowing Tanwen she'd probably dump him in a few months when she was tired of him, throw him over and then laugh about it!

Or did Tanwen truly love Dylan? It was a

disquieting thought; a question Donna asked herself over and over again. It left her feeling uneasy as she and Tanwen walked home from work together each evening.

Tanwen had placidly accepted her mother's ruling that she wasn't to see him again and that he wasn't to come to the house. She hadn't pouted or sulked. She'd stayed in every night, so she definitely wasn't meeting Dylan on the quiet.

It was as if she knew something that they didn't, and she went round humming to herself and with a little half smile on her face, as if she was highly amused by it.

Donna couldn't understand it. It worried her far more than if Tanwen had been stroppy or weepy. She was planning something, Donna was sure of it.

There was only one way to find out, she decided. It would be painful, but she'd go and see Dylan and find out from him what was afoot. He certainly owed her an explanation.

She'd do it on Sunday, she resolved. She'd tell her mam she was going out with one of the girls from the workroom if she asked.

Her mam would be upset when she found out the truth, but it was Tanwen she'd forbidden to ever speak to Dylan again, not her. She wasn't really flouting her mam's authority, she told herself. It would be better for all of them to know what was happening rather than to have to face some more unpleasant surprises.

She had never been to Dylan's home. In fact, all she knew was that he lived in a village called Tongwynlais that was somewhere between Llandaff and Taff's Well.

On Sunday afternoon, when she said she was going out, her mother seemed pleased.

'Wrap up warm then, cariad. It will do you good to go for a walk to get some fresh air.'

Donna's heart was in her mouth when she heard her mam urging Tanwen to go along as well. Then she breathed a sigh of immense relief when Tanwen said, 'Don't be ridiculous, Mam, the weather's too cold. I don't need fresh air that much!'

Donna felt very nervous when she arrived in Tongwynlais. She had never met Dylan's mother and she thought she might have difficulties in explaining who she was. That was if she ever managed to find where he lived.

The only real clue she had was that his uncle owned a garage. Once she found that, she reasoned, then she could get directions to his home.

It was easier than she had hoped. An elderly man, who looked far too old to be Dylan's uncle, was outside a garage in the main street polishing a black taxi-cab. When she asked if he could direct her to where

Dylan Wallis lived, he did so without asking any questions.

She was surprised to find that it was an ordinary little terrace house, not very much different from the house she lived in. Heart in mouth, she knocked on the door.

The woman who answered it was tall and gaunt. She was wearing a plain grey woollen dress covered by a crisp cotton red-and-grey-patterned pinafore. She had dark eyes and brown hair combed back from her face into a bun in the nape of her neck. With her turned-down mouth and forbidding frown she looked as though she had the cares of the world on her shoulders.

'Mrs Wallis? I'd like to speak to Dylan if I may, please.'

The woman regarded her with hostility. 'You're Tanwen Evans, are you?'

'No!' Donna felt taken aback by the rancour in the woman's voice. 'Tanwen is my sister.'

The woman's hard brown eyes scrutinised her from her dark blue woollen hat and dark blue cloth coat right down to her sensible black shoes. 'You'd better come in,' she said shortly.

Donna followed her down a dark little hallway to the living room, which was at the back of the house. The room was plainly furnished with a scrubbed wooden table and wooden chairs, but spotlessly clean.

The cheery fire glowing in the black-leaded grate shone on the highly polished brass fender and fire-irons.

'Sit down, then.' She nodded towards the wooden armchair at one side of the fireplace and sat down herself in the one facing it.

'Dylan's gone,' she said bluntly. 'Packed his bags and cleared off a couple of weeks ago. Left us all in the lurch. His uncle's that mad I think he would kill him if he could find him.'

Donna shook her head. 'I'm sorry, but I don't understand.'

'Neither do I,' his mother said bitterly. 'He's gone off with that Tanwen, I suppose. He's never been the same since he took up with her. And you say you're her sister?'

'He hasn't gone anywhere with Tanwen,' Donna told her quickly. 'Tanwen is still at home.' She smiled. 'I can assure you about that, she was sitting by the fireside with Mam when I came out.'

Mrs Wallis looked bewildered. 'Ach-y-fi! Perhaps we'd better have a cup of tea,' she suggested. 'Sorry if I bit your head off when you arrived, but I'm at my wit's end with worry about him, see. Take your coat off, cariad, and make yourself at home. It will only take a minute to make us a brew and then we'll talk this over.'

'Now then,' Mrs Wallis said as she brought in the tray of tea things and poured them

173

both a cup, 'let's get down to brass tacks, shall we. So you are not Tanwen but her sister?'

'That's right. I'm her twin sister, Donna.'

Mrs Wallis frowned. 'Twin sister? Dylan told me that Tanwen was tall with golden hair and very beautiful!'

'Yes, well, we're not identical twins. I'm the plain one, see,' Donna smiled.

Mrs Wallis looked embarrassed. 'I didn't mean you weren't beautiful, cariad. You are, you know. You've got an angelic look about you. Pretty hair and a lovely face, as well as wonderfully expressive eyes. You've got a caring nature, too, I can tell that. The sort of girl I'd have liked our Dylan to have brought home. You look the sort that would have kept him on the straight and narrow and his nose to the grindstone.'

Donna flushed bright red and sipped her tea, not knowing what to say.

Mrs Wallis stirred her own tea thoughtfully. 'Perhaps I've been a bit hasty, see, judging your sister like I have,' she said grudgingly. 'You say she's safe at home and not gone gallivanting off to London with our Dylan?'

'London! You didn't say that Dylan had gone to London.'

'Well, I don't know if it is London for sure, but I have a hunch that's where he's made for. He's mad about the theatre, see. He probably thinks he can get work in the theatre if he goes there. There's nothing grand enough for the boyo down in Cardiff because he's got such princely ideas,' she added bitterly.

'I thought he was working as an accountant for his uncle?'

'Ha! So you've heard all about that, have you. That's what he should be doing!'

'Look, Mrs Wallis, I think I'd better tell you what I know about Dylan and how well I know him,' Donna told her stiffly.

'Go on, then! Speak out; lay your cards on the table.'

'I've known Dylan for nearly two years. We met on my eighteenth birthday. He was driving a taxi-cab...'

'Him and that Jared Davies?'

'Yes, that's right. Jared was Tanwen's boyfriend at the time and he had arranged to take us to the Summer Ball at Cardiff City Hall as a birthday treat. Harri Jones should have been my partner, but he went off to India with his father the week before...'

'Darro! And our Dylan stepped into his shoes?'

'Well, something like that. Anyway, Dylan was driving the taxi-cab and that's how I met him. He was very kind to me that night. Tanwen was with Jared Davies, and because Harri wasn't there I was all on my own.

After that we started going out together.'

'He told you, then, that his uncle was paying for him to attend Cardiff Technical College?'

Donna nodded.

'Did he also tell you that when he passed his exams and was qualified then he would be going to work for his uncle?'

Donna hesitated, uncertain whether to tell Mrs Wallis about the plans they'd had to be married, then decided she would.

'Yes, he did. We were going to get engaged at Easter and start saving up to get married.'

'You and Dylan?' Mrs Wallis looked puzzled. 'So why did I think it was Tanwen he was going out with all this time?'

Donna looked uncomfortable. 'Quite recently he dropped me and took up with Tanwen. It seems she had more interests in common with him than I did.'

'Like going to the theatre?'

Donna nodded. 'They enjoyed music halls and pantomime more than I did,' she said lamely.

Mrs Wallis reached out and took Donna's cup and refilled it. 'You've been honest and open with me so I'll tell you my side of the story,' she said as she handed it back to her. 'Dylan's dad cleared off when he was a mere nipper...'

'Leaving you on your own to bring up him and his little sister?'

176

Mrs Wallis's frown deepened and she shook her head. 'Rubbish! There was only Dylan.'

'Sorry, I must have got that wrong.'

'He may have told you that because it made it sound more dramatic. He's always been a liar, the same as his dad!' Mrs Wallis said contemptuously. 'I was about your age when I met Dylan's dad. Emlyn was tall, good-looking and charming, just like Dylan. He swept me off my feet. My family was dead set against us marrying, but of course I didn't listen to them,' she said sadly.

'They could see he was wild and my dad was the pillar of respectability. He was an elder at the Ebenezer Chapel,' she went on. 'Emlyn and me ran away together and I never saw my mam or dad again afterwards. She died within the year. Looking back, I suppose it was my wilfulness that led to her heart attack.'

She sighed. 'My dad was devoted to her and he died a couple of years later,' she went on. 'Quite wealthy, he was. We lived in a grand house in those days called Mawr Coch. It's a big place just outside Tongwynlais. He left it to me in his will, and he left his garage business to my brother Twm.'

Mrs Wallis poured herself another cup of tea. 'Emlyn persuaded me that the house was too big and too full of memories. He insisted that the best thing to do was sell it and buy something new. We moved in here as a temporary measure while we looked round.'

'So what happened?'

'Well, Emlyn was all for us building our own place and like the young fool I was I agreed. Our Twm was dead against it, mind. He said I'd come to grief over it. He was right, of course. Once Mawr Coch was sold, Emlyn wheedled the money out of me, and the next thing I knew was that he'd scarpered.'

'Leaving you to bring up Dylan single-handed!'

'Even more to the point, he left me penniless! If my brother Twm hadn't been there to help me out then I'd probably have ended up in the workhouse and Dylan alongside me.'

'You've never told Dylan this?'

'Oh yes, he knows about it all right. That's why I feel so ashamed that he's let our Twm down like he has. My brother not only supported us while Dylan was growing up but he agreed that Dylan could go off to college in Cardiff. Kept him in pocket money into the bargain.'

'In return for Dylan helping out by driving the taxi-cab for him,' Donna defended him.

'Is that what he told you? Load of old rubbish. He never drove the cab in his life.'

'What about when he drove Jared to the

Summer Ball?'

'That Jared egged Dylan on to pinch the damn thing, didn't he! Twm was worried out of his head. He thought the cab had been stolen. He gave our Dylan a right scolding, I can tell you. Not that it did any good, mind. He pinched it again a bit later on.'

'I think he came to take me out that time,' Donna said guiltily.

'To show off, more likely,' Mrs Wallis snorted. 'He took a whole week's takings from the garage safe before he left. He's probably gone to London, he's always hankered after going there. Believe me, he can be trouble. You want to warn that sister of yours to drop him before she gets hurt.

'Twm was all for calling in the police, but it meant dragging our name into the mud because it was bound to be reported in the Cardiff and South Wales newspapers. I didn't want that, so for my sake he let the matter drop.'

'I don't suppose we are likely to see Dylan again, not if he's gone off down to London like you say he's done,' Donna murmured.

'Depends on how well he does when he gets there, doesn't it!'

Donna looked at the clock on the mantelshelf. 'Thank you for the cup of tea and the chat, Mrs Wallis. I'd better be going or Mam will be worried about what's

179

happened to me. I told her I was going for a walk with a friend and she'll be thinking I'm lost I've been gone so long.'

'If you or your sister should happen to hear from Dylan I'd be obliged if you'd let me know, Donna,' Mrs Wallis told her as she showed her to the door. 'I can't help worrying about him and wondering if he is all right. He may be a bad boyo, but when all is said and done he is my son.'

Chapter Fifteen

'Thank God you're home, Donna! I thought you were never coming back, I've been out of my mind with worry.'

'I'm sorry, Mam, but I did tell you I was going for a good long walk.'

'Yes, cariad, I know! It's Tanwen, though, I don't know what to do, she's been taken that bad while you've been out.'

All the way back from Tongwynlais Donna had been going over and over what she would tell her mother about Dylan Wallis and the way he had cleared off to London.

From what his mother had said, Tanwen wasn't entirely to blame. Now she pushed all that to the back of her mind as she tried to make sense of what her mother was trying to tell her.

'What's wrong with Tanwen?' she asked as she slipped off her heavy coat and followed her mother into the living room.

'I don't really know. She's been so sick and bad that I'm worried stiff about her.'

'Where is she now?'

'She's upstairs, lying down. I thought that perhaps if she could sleep for a while she might feel better.'

'Don't worry, Mam. I'll go on up and see how she is.'

Tanwen was curled up on her bed with the eiderdown over her, but she wasn't asleep. Her face was as white as the pillow and streaked with tears.

When Donna placed a hand on her sister's forehead she found it cold and clammy.

Tanwen grabbed her hand as she made to pull it away. 'Don't leave me,' she whispered.

'Of course I won't. Is there anything I can get you?'

'No!' Tanwen snuffled, rubbing her hand across her reddened eyes.

'Is it something you've eaten, do you think?' Donna asked worriedly.

Tanwen struggled up in the bed, bunching the pillow under her shoulders. 'No, it's nothing like that. I've taken some liquid paraffin, slippery elm and two doses of Epsom salts.'

'What on earth for?' Donna frowned. 'Are

you constipated or something?'

Tanwen laughed harshly. 'I wish that was all that was wrong with me. No,' she went on, avoiding Donna's eyes, 'I'm pregnant.'

'Pregnant! You mean you took that stuff to try and get rid of it?' Donna exclaimed in dismay.

'Do you know a better way?'

Donna shook her head. 'Has it worked?'

Tanwen shrugged. 'I don't know. I don't think so.'

'Well, surely you would know if it had.'

'Nothing has happened yet, but I don't know how long it takes.'

'Taking that sort of stuff is a risky thing to do,' Donna said uneasily. 'Supposing it only half works.'

Tanwen frowned. 'What do you mean?'

'Well, I don't know. Supposing it doesn't do what you are hoping it will but harms the baby in some way. That could mean it's born deformed or something.'

'Trust you to think of something like that,' Tanwen scowled.

Donna chewed her lower lip. 'So whose baby is it, Dylan's or Jared's?'

'How could it be Jared's, I haven't seen him since last August!'

'Well, I don't know how far gone you are, do I? I didn't even know you were pregnant.'

'I wasn't completely sure myself until a couple of weeks ago.'

'And did you tell Dylan?'

'Of course I did, seeing it's his.'

Donna's face hardened. 'What did he say when you told him?'

Tanwen didn't answer.

'He cleared off, didn't he! That's why you didn't make any fuss when Mam said you weren't to have anything more to do with him. You agreed because the rotter had already dumped you and gone to London. That was why you didn't make your usual song and dance, but agreed all meek and mild to do what Mam said.'

'How do you know he's gone to London? Have you been meeting up with him behind my back?' Tanwen flared, her blue eyes icy.

'I know because his mother told me so this afternoon.' Donna lowered her voice. 'I didn't go for a walk, I went to Tongwynlais to see Dylan and find out what was going on. His mother said he wasn't there and she seemed pretty certain that he'd cleared off to London. She also told me an awful lot about him. Things I didn't know and I bet you don't know either.'

'What sort of things?'

'About his dad being a rogue! She also told me how his uncle has helped them. She's terribly upset because he has let his uncle down by running away. She said that Dylan stole the takings from the garage before he left!'

Tanwen ran her hand over her ruffled hair. 'It's probably all lies. He doesn't get on with his mam so he's not likely to confide in her, now is he?'

'She knew all about you!'

'That's because he's serious about me. When he gets fixed up in London he's going to send for me.'

'That's what he's told you, is it? Well, I wouldn't bank on it because from what his mam told me he's a liar and a cheat. She's a very nice lady, by the way!'

'She must be if she talks about her son like that,' Tanwen sneered sarcastically.

'You don't believe me, do you?'

Tanwen shrugged. 'Does it matter whether I believe you or not? It's what I think of Dylan and what he thinks of me that counts.'

'If you both think so much of each other then why are you trying to get rid of his baby?'

'Neither of us want a kid, do we. Not yet, anyway. Dylan intends to make a name for himself in the theatre and so do I.'

'You do? What as?'

'An actress, of course! You don't think I want to spend the rest of my life strutting around James Howell's shop, showing off clothes for women who have more money than sense.'

'I thought you loved your job as a model?'

184

'It's all right! It's better than being in the workroom sewing up seams and taking out tackings all day.'

'You were planning to sneak off to London without a word to Mam or to me, weren't you?' Donna exclaimed angrily. 'You've hurt me so much I wish you had, but poor Mam would have been heartbroken.'

'I would have told you when I was ready to leave!' Tanwen muttered sulkily. 'I'm waiting for Dylan to find work and somewhere for us to live before I give up my job. I'm not as stupid as you seem to think!'

'So you are expecting to hear from him again, then, are you?'

'Of course I will! Whatever makes you think I won't.'

'Things his mam said about him.'

'She doesn't know anything. She's never had any time for him or shown any interest in what he really wants to do. He never wanted to go to college to learn to be an accountant. He hates every minute of it.'

Donna sighed. 'So he told me when we first met, but perhaps it's a good thing he can do something sensible like that if he's about to become a father.'

'Oh no he's not,' Tanwen shivered. 'I'm getting rid of this baby one way or the other.'

'How can you? You've taken stuff, which you shouldn't have done, and it's had no effect whatsoever.'

'There are other ways,' Tanwen snapped. 'Can't you find out from some of the girls in the workroom where I can go to get it taken away.'

Donna gasped. 'Are you asking me to find out the name of a back-street abortionist for you?'

'Yes! Unless you know of a proper doctor who will do it,' Tanwen said sarcastically.

'You must be mad. Those sorts of women can kill you!'

'Accidents can happen, I know that, but it's a risk I'll have to take, isn't it!'

Donna shook her head. Furious though she was with her sister, she couldn't let her take those sorts of risks. 'I don't think you should, it's not really safe. How many months pregnant are you, by the way?'

'I don't know! Probably about four and a bit.'

'Over four months! Are you sure? You don't look it! If you're right then it's far too late to do anything like that!' Donna exclaimed.

'Of course it isn't!'

'You'll never find anyone willing to attempt an abortion if you are that far gone,' Donna persisted. 'Anyway, where are you going to get the money from, they're not cheap, you know.'

'I've been saving up, and you've got some

money stashed away, haven't you?'

'You expect me to loan you money to get rid of Dylan's baby after you took him away from me? You've got a cheek, Tanwen!'

'It's better to do that than have Mam find out and get all upset, isn't it?' Tanwen wheedled.

Donna shook her head. 'I don't think there's any way you can keep her from knowing. I'm quite sure you won't find anyone prepared to perform an abortion if you are over four months pregnant. You'd better make up your mind and tell her as soon as possible before she finds out for herself.'

'How can she do that?'

'For heaven's sake, Tanwen, face facts! You can't go on keeping it hidden. If you are over four months pregnant then any day now you'll start to show. After your so-called illness today Mam's bound to guess what is wrong with you. She's not daft, you know!'

'Very well, you tell her, then.'

'Me? I'm not telling her. It's your problem, you tell her yourself.'

'Please, Donna. She'll take it so much better from you. If I tell her she'll start weeping and wailing and lecturing me about how silly I've been.'

'Well, you have. Silly and selfish. How can you expect me to be the one to help you out of this mess? You stole Dylan away from me, remember,' Donna said angrily.

'He wanted me. I didn't take him away from you. He could see you weren't right for him. You didn't care about the theatre and all the things that he was interested in like I did.'

'No, but I loved him. Can you say the same about your feelings for him?'

'Don't start getting all touchy with me, Donna. We've been through all this before,' Tanwen pouted. 'If you care anything at all about Dylan then you'll help me now. I've told you he doesn't want a baby...'

'No, and that's why he's cleared off. He's leaving you to face the music, isn't he! It's just like his mother said, he's feckless and a liar.'

'So does that mean you'll help me?' Tanwen smiled brightly.

'No, it doesn't. I'm sorry if it upsets Mam, but I'm not taking any part in this. You can tell her yourself about the baby.'

Tanwen ran her fingers through her short blonde hair irritably. 'You're not going to even try and help me to get rid of it, then?'

'No, I'm not! For one thing I think it would be dangerous to do so, and for another, why should I help you to commit a crime.'

'Here we go,' Tanwen taunted. Her voice rose shrilly. 'Miss Goody-goody on her high horse. Going all moral and righteous on me.

188

There's times when I wonder how we ever came to be sisters we're so different.'

'Yes, I suppose we are different, and that's something I have to be very thankful for,' Donna retorted.

'Oh, you're different all right. Almost opposite in character as well as looks, I'd say.' The two girls looked round startled as Gwyneth spoke to them from the doorway.

'I was coming up to see how Tanwen was and I heard most of what you've been saying,' she told them grimly. 'If you are over four months pregnant, Tanwen,' she went on, 'then you've left it far too late to get rid of your baby by taking concoctions of that sort.'

'Mam, you don't understand.'

'Oh yes I do, and I want you to promise that you won't even try to get rid of it. For heaven's sake, cariad, don't go taking any more rubbish like you've done today. It's far too dangerous! You could die! Or the baby could be born disabled. It might be crippled, or even worse, its brain might be damaged. What would you do if that happened. Think of the guilt you'd feel knowing that it was because of something you'd done to try and get rid of it!'

'Then what am I going to do?' Tears streamed down Tanwen's cheeks as she stared at her mother in despair.

'You'll have to go through with it, cariad,'

Gwyneth said firmly. 'You'll have to have your baby and bring it up.'

'Mam, you don't understand. Dylan doesn't want a baby. It would get in the way of all his plans to become an actor.'

'You're saying that Dylan isn't prepared to marry you and accept responsibility for this baby?' Gwyneth said angrily.

Tanwen shook her head. 'I don't know,' she said dully.

'Then in that case you will have to bring it up yourself. It can be done,' she affirmed when Tanwen was about to protest. 'I brought you and Donna up single-handed.'

'Yes, I know that, Mam, but I'm not like you. I don't know anything about babies.'

'You'll learn. You'll have to, the same as I did. The same as all women do when they are left to cope on their own,' her mother told her grimly.

Chapter Sixteen

Tanwen didn't react at all well to being pregnant. She hated the way her shape was constantly changing and growing ever larger and rounder. When she looked in the mirror even the outline of her face seemed to be puffy, and her once bright eyes were a muddy blue.

She resented the way her ankles swelled up and her legs ached. She raged when she became clumsy in her movements and started bumping into things, as the child that was growing inside her became ever bigger and bigger.

It infuriated her that none of her pretty clothes fitted her. She'd enjoyed her role as a flapper so much. The outrageously short dresses in filmy frothy materials that ended inches above her knees had looked so stunning on her when her figure had been slim.

She tried in every way possible to hide her changing shape from inquisitive eyes, but friends and neighbours were quick to notice and gossip was rife. Some made snide remarks and were forever questioning her about when the baby was due.

Towards the end of May, Carina Price told her that James Howell had said that it was no longer fitting for her to continue working at The Cardiff Drapers as a model.

'Perhaps I could model clothes for the Maternity department, Miss Price?' Tanwen suggested hopefully when she was told that her services were no longer required.

Carina Price looked shocked. 'I'm afraid not, Tanwen. Ladies who visit that department would be horrified if they found out that an unmarried mother was modelling the maternity clothes they were contemplating for themselves. It would probably deter them from buying!'

'I could always wear a wedding ring. I still have to earn a living,' Tanwen protested sulkily.

'You can return to the workroom, since you trained there and none of our customers are likely to see you, but only for a month or so. No longer, mind,' Carina Price conceded. 'You must make sure that you wear a loose fitting dress, though,' she went on stiffly, 'because it is already quite obvious that you are pregnant. If I have any complaints from any of the other women about allowing you to work there in your condition, then I'm afraid you will have to go. It's not setting a good example for the younger girls, you understand.'

Tanwen felt furious at the criticism, but she knew it would be jeopardising her chances of going on working at all if she argued, or indeed said anything.

'One further point, Tanwen. You will not discuss your condition with any of the others during working hours. Is that also understood?'

'Yes Miss Price, and thank you.'

'Perhaps you should stay at home and help Mam out with her sewing orders,' Donna suggested. 'If you were at home with her then no one would be likely to say anything about you being pregnant.'

'I'd have her moaning on at me all day and every day if I did that,' Tanwen groaned. 'No, I'd sooner stay at work for as long as I'm allowed to do so, even if it has to be in the workroom. By the time Carina Price says I have to leave, Dylan should have got himself fixed up in London and I'll be able to join him.'

'That's if you ever hear from him again!'

'I will, once he gets himself established,' Tanwen replied confidently.

'Yes, but it may take several years for him to get established and make a name for himself in the theatre. What are you going to do if you haven't heard from him by the time the baby is born?'

Tanwen looked smug. 'I've worked that out, I'm going to get it adopted. I'm planning on doing that anyway,' she added bluntly.

'Tanwen! How can you even think of doing such a thing!' Donna gasped. She felt outraged. If Tanwen hadn't stolen Dylan away from her and she'd been the one expecting his baby, she would have been so happy.

'I can't bring it up, can I? It's all very well for Mam to say I'll learn to cope and all that rubbish.'

'I'm sure she's right. It probably comes naturally.'

193

Tanwen shrugged. 'Maybe! I suppose I could learn to care for it if I wanted a kid, but I don't. It's a mistake. One that's getting bigger every day.' She pulled a face. 'Look at me! I'm the size of a house already and I've still months to go! It's growing inside me and I hate it. I resent what it's doing to me and to my life. What's more,' she added angrily, 'I know I'll hate it twice as much when it's born.'

As her pregnancy advanced, Tanwen became ever more determined about what she intended to do once the baby arrived. Her tirades about how she looked and how it was affecting her life became more heated and longer by the day. When Carina Price eventually told her that she must give up work altogether her mood became even blacker. With no work to go to her life seemed utterly pointless and she refused to get out of bed until midday or even later. She sulked or cried at the slightest thing. She refused to listen to her mother's advice about what she should be eating.

'Look at me! What does it matter what I eat since I'm fat all over. Even my face is bloated! If Dylan did come back he wouldn't recognise me, or if he did he wouldn't want to know me,' she wailed.

She still believed implicitly that Dylan was coming back, even though there hadn't been a word from him since he'd left.

Donna began to think that perhaps his own mother's opinion about him being irresponsible was well founded.

'Why don't you help Mam?' Donna said again and again. 'It might help her to get more orders if she could do the work more quickly, and it would give you something to do. Without your money coming in Mam is finding it hard to manage.'

'If you don't want to help me with my sewing then at least start making some things for the baby,' Gwyneth told her. 'Poor little mite, you haven't even got a shawl to wrap him in.'

'Since I'm giving it away from the moment it's born then I don't need to bother with all that, now do I,' Tanwen said airily. 'Whoever adopts it can provide it with clothes or something to wrap it in. I'm not going to do so.'

Between them, Donna and her mother put together a layette as well as cutting up old sheets and blankets to make bedding. As she worked on the little white smocks and a matinée coat Donna felt tears trickling down her cheeks. If only things had been different. If Tanwen hadn't lured Dylan away from her this could have been her baby she was making clothes for, not Tanwen's unwanted child, she thought wistfully.

It was now the height of summer and over four months since Dylan went away, and there hadn't been a single word from him. At the end of July, when Tanwen was eight months pregnant, Donna went to Tongwynlais again to see if Mrs Wallis had received any news of her son.

Mrs Wallis seemed to be even less pleased to see her than she'd been the first time she'd called. She didn't ask her in, but stood on the doorstep, arms folded across her chest in a slightly aggressive manner as they talked.

'Darro! Of course I've not heard from Dylan. Not a word! He might as well be dead for all I know,' Mrs Wallis said, avoiding Donna's eyes.

'His uncle hasn't heard from him either?'

'No! He still rants on about Dylan taking the money from his safe, almost as if it's my fault,' Mrs Wallis said bitterly. 'It's caused a lot of bad feeling between the two of us, I can tell you. The trouble is, there's not much I can say in Dylan's defence.'

'It's not your fault,' Donna sympathised.

'No, but Twm's right, see! Dylan is a liar as well as a thief.'

'I'm afraid I came to ask because Tanwen is expecting Dylan's baby and it is almost due,' Donna told her.

'Duw anwyl!' Mrs Wallis looked shocked. 'Poor dab! How is she doing? I do feel sorry for her, you know, but there's not a lot I can do to help her.'

'She's not taken the pregnancy well at all. She is quite adamant that she doesn't want the baby.'

Mrs Wallis shrugged. 'Not much she can do about that, though, is there,' she sniffed. 'She shouldn't have given in to him! She must have known what she was doing.'

'She's talking about having it adopted the minute it's born. I thought you should know.'

'Darw! There's heartless! Why tell me, though?' Mrs Wallis asked querulously. 'I can't take it!'

'No? Well, I thought you should know what Tanwen is planning to do, seeing that it is your grandchild.'

Mrs Wallis stepped back inside her hallway and began closing the door. 'You lot will have to sort out your own problems,' she said sharply. 'I've got enough on my plate as it is.'

'I'm sure you have, I'm not asking you for help. I only came to let you know what was happening.'

'Yes, well, as I say, there's nothing I can do about it. I don't think you should come here again,' Mrs Wallis added abruptly, slamming the door shut.

Tanwen went into labour early, on the hottest day in August. The weather was swelteringly humid. Everyone had their doors and windows open, trying to get some air into their homes.

At first Gwyneth thought that Tanwen's moans about not feeling very well were caused by the stifling atmosphere. Then, late in the afternoon her waters broke. The backache and niggling pains she'd complained about earlier increased, and her cries of anguish startled people in the street outside.

Tanwen had refused to see a doctor or a nurse all through her pregnancy and now Gwyneth was in a panic about whom she could call on for help.

She hoped she could manage on her own until Donna came home from work. At five o'clock, however, Tanwen seemed to be in such a distressed state that Gwyneth ran next door to ask her neighbour to come and help her.

'Duw anwyl! You need a midwife, cariad, not someone like me at a time like this,' Blodwyn Hughes told her. 'I'll nip along and see if Megan Simmons in Coburn Street can come and give you a hand.'

'She's not a proper midwife, either,' Gwyneth said worriedly.

'No, but she's delivered more babbas than I've had hot dinners, and she'll know what to do.'

By the time Donna reached home after work that evening Megan Simmons and her mother were doing all they could to help Tanwen and quieten down her screams. Blodwyn was in the kitchen making tea for them all.

'I've never heard anyone create such a noise as your sister in my life,' Megan Simmons exclaimed. Wiping the sweat from her forehead she took the cup of tea Donna had brought upstairs for her.

'I'm so glad you're home at last, cariad,' Gwyneth exclaimed as she dabbed at Tanwen's face with a wet flannel. 'Perhaps you can persuade Tanwen to cooperate with us,' she said hopefully.

'If you'd make a bit of an effort, cariad, and push when I tell you to do so instead of simply lying there screaming your lungs out, then it would all soon be over,' Megan Simmons pronounced. She put her empty cup down on the chest of drawers and moved back to the side of the bed. 'Now, come on, girl! Try and help.'

'I'm in such pain,' Tanwen whimpered. 'I feel as if I'm splitting in half.'

'There's foolish you are!' Mrs Simmons guffawed. 'Come on, now, when the next pain starts, you push with all your might and let's get this baby born.'

It took another hour. Donna held her sister's hand, trying to comfort and encourage her. She felt as if it was her as well as Tanwen who was undergoing the ordeal.

As the child was born and she heard its first cry, the sound tugged at Donna's heart-strings. As she studied the perfect features, almost a replica of Dylan's face, and the little head covered in dark down, her eyes filled with tears.

She gathered the tiny child in her arms, cuddling him against her breast. As she moved towards the head of the bed so that Tanwen could see her little son, Tanwen closed her eyes and turned her head away.

'Take it away. I've already told you I don't want to see it or have anything to do with it.'

'A fine mam you're going to make,' Megan Simmons cackled. 'Exhausted you are, my lovely. Come on now, try suckling him, cariad. You'll feel different about him once he's taken a feed from you,' she added, taking the baby from Donna's arms and laying him on Tanwen's chest.

'Don't bring it anywhere near me,' Tanwen screamed. Roughly, she swept the bundle away.

Deftly, Donna grabbed the baby as it was on the point of falling off the edge of the bed.

'Dammo di!' Megan Simmons exclaimed in a horrified voice. 'If that child had fallen onto the floor on its head it might have ended up daft for the rest of its life!' Her small dark eyes were hard, her face stony as she stood looking down at Tanwen.

'You've had a rough time, girl, I'll grant you that, but there's no need to treat an innocent babba in such a way.'

'Oh, go away!' Tanwen turned on her side, burying her face in the pillow. 'I've told you all, time and time again, that I don't want anything to do with the baby. Not now or ever. Take it away! Put it somewhere where I can't hear it or see it and don't mention it to me ever again.'

Megan Simmons peeled off her blood-stained apron and rolled it into a bundle. 'I'm off, Mrs Evans. I've never heard anyone say anything like that in all my days. Your Tanwen is completely heartless.'

'Are you quite sure that she will be all right now? Shouldn't you come back again in a day or two to check her and the baby and make sure?' Gwyneth asked tremulously.

'I should, but I never want to step inside this house again,' Megan Simmons declared. 'The baby seems healthy enough and she'll probably be all right.'

'What if there are any complications?' Gwyneth pressed.

'I shouldn't worry about her too much if I was you,' Megan Simmons said contemptuously. 'She's young and healthy, even if she does have a heart of stone!'

Chapter Seventeen

Tanwen recovered from her pregnancy in an amazingly short time. A couple of weeks later her figure appeared to be back to its normal slim shape. The only difference seemed to be that her breasts were far shapelier than they had been before.

She spent a great deal of her time in front of the cheval mirror, twisting this way and that, so that she could check these facts for herself.

When she wasn't doing that she was trying on all her favourite clothes to see if her slightly changed shape made any difference to the way she looked in them

She resolved to discard her flapper look. Now she aimed to look more elegant in keeping with the changing fashions of the 1930s. Skirts were now being worn to the knee, or even a little below it. Dresses had normal waistlines.

Finally she had two separate piles of clothes; those she intended to go on wearing and those she felt needed some kind of alteration.

She persuaded her mother to update several of her dresses that had short pleated skirts by unpicking the top from the skirt and attaching the skirt to a long bodice so that it would reach to her knees or below. Then she added a trim of different material to the hem of the top so that it became one of the new style jumper-blouses that were worn loose over the top of the skirt.

During the final months of her pregnancy Tanwen had let her Eton crop grow out. Now her silky blonde hair covered her ears and she started wearing it softly waved across her forehead. She also restyled her deep cloche hats to a Greta Garbo coal-scuttle shape that framed her hair and face rather than hid them.

She was impatient for her hair to grow slightly longer so that she could have a row of tight curls at the back. Or to grow even longer still so that it was as blonde and flowing as that of her favourite film star, Jean Harlow, who was the new goddess of the cinema screen.

She adamantly refused to have anything at all to do with the baby, no matter how much her mother nagged and told her how heartless she was being. She left the feeding and care of it entirely to her mother. Donna grumbled at her thoughtlessness, but she helped out when she was at home. She even got up during the night to feed it because she could see the strain the extra work was putting on her mother. During the day it was Gwyneth who changed it and gave it its bottle, even though Tanwen was in the house most of the time.

Donna and her mother decided on the name Barri.

'We have to register his birth. Do you want him to have our surname or do you want him to be called Wallis?' Gwyneth asked.

'Call it whatever you like,' Tanwen shrugged. 'I've already told you that Dylan isn't any more interested in it than I am.'

There was no way of getting in touch with Dylan, and Donna didn't think it was worth making the journey to Tongwynlais to ask his mother, since she didn't seem to be interested, either. They registered the baby as Barri Evans.

Barri was a good baby. He had Dylan's dark eyes and hair and developed an infectious gurgling laugh. He took his feeds without too much fuss. He slept well, except for the occasional night when he was restless, and he seemed to be putting on weight satisfactorily.

Most of the neighbours had heard about Tanwen's tantrums after he'd been born and offered their support. They insisted on lending a pram and a cot and many of them brought along clothes that their own little ones had grown out of but which were still in excellent order.

Even so, it was a tremendous burden on

Gwyneth's shoulders. She found it was hard to manage on Donna's money, and looking after Barri interfered with her sewing schedule so that people who were in a hurry started going elsewhere. In addition, she had already lost many of her regular customers because they were unable to afford new clothes. Many of their menfolk were out of work and on the dole because of the Depression. Any money they had was earmarked for food and heating. Those who did come to her could only afford to spend a meagre amount. This meant they had no alternative but to make do with last year's dresses. Often they would ask to have them turned inside out if the material was good enough. Gwyneth would then trim them with new collars, or some braid or a piece of lace to make them look like new.

Those customers who could afford new clothes gradually stopped asking her to make them because they weren't sure she'd be capable as she looked so distracted. Added to that, there was no guarantee that she would deliver them on time. If the baby took up more of her time than she'd envisaged then it was her sewing time that suffered.

'Tanwen, you could help Mam more, either by looking after the baby or helping Mam with the sewing orders,' Donna told her time and time again.

It was no good. Her words fell on deaf ears. All Tanwen was interested in was dressing up and prettifying herself. She spent hours experimenting with make-up, trying to follow the latest popular trends even though she was going nowhere in particular.

Donna knew that things couldn't go on like this. With all the additional work and loss of earnings her mother was looking more drawn and worried every day. Nothing either of them said to Tanwen seemed to have any impact whatsoever.

Shortly after Christmas, in desperation, Donna plucked up the courage to go and ask Carina Price if there was any chance of Tanwen having her job back.

Carina Price's first reaction was to shake her head emphatically. 'It's out of the question, Donna, you know that. Mr Howell wouldn't stand for it.'

'Does he have to know? It would mean so much to Mam,' she pleaded. 'She probably hasn't let on to you, but she's having such a hard time making ends meet with only my money coming in.'

'She still has her sewing?'

'No, not really. Orders have dropped off. So many of her customers are out of work or have been forced to accept reduced wages, which means they either have to manage on that or be means-tested if they apply for help. Added to that, she hasn't the time, see,' Donna told her sadly. 'The baby takes up so much of her day.'

'Surely Tanwen takes care of the baby?'

Donna hesitated, not sure she should tell her the whole story or not, then decided that if she wanted her full cooperation she'd better do so.

'Mam probably hasn't told you herself, but Tanwen doesn't want anything to do with the baby. It's been on a bottle since the day it was born and Mam looks after it all the time. I help her when I'm at home, but Mam is finding it a struggle. She's not really got any time to do any sewing so there's only my money coming in.'

'Oh, dear me!' Carina Price looked shocked. 'Poor Gwyneth. She's never breathed a word about this to me. Mind,' she added rather guiltily, 'I haven't seen her for ages.'

'So will you consider letting Tanwen come back to work?'

'What you've told me does put a different complexion on things. Leave it with me for a few days, Donna, and I'll see what arrangements I can make.'

It took over a week for a decision to be reached and Donna was on edge the entire time. She was afraid to mention at home that she had spoken to Carina Price in case James Howell refused to have Tanwen back.

She was also concerned about how Tanwen would take the news. If she was told that there was a job for her, would she want to return to work?

Finally, in order to try to put her mother's mind at rest because she was becoming so worried by the mounting bills, she told them what she had done.

'If you think I'm going back to the workroom, picking up pins and taking out tackings and being bossed around by you and Aileen Roberts then you've got another think coming,' Tanwen said angrily. 'It's a pity you can't mind your own business, Donna.'

'I wouldn't have needed to interfere if you'd pulled your weight. If you looked after Barri and Mam was able to get on with her sewing we wouldn't be hard up,' Donna told her tartly.

'She wouldn't need to look after him if he'd been adopted the moment he was born,' Tanwen pouted. 'The place has never been the same since he was born. Look around you! Everywhere there are nappies and baby clothes airing. The smell when you change him is disgusting. And so is all the pap you've started feeding him. Seeing him sitting there in his high chair trying to eat one of those Farley's Rusks you give him turns my stomach over. And what is more, he keeps me awake half the night.'

'May God forgive you for saying things like that about your own child,' Gwyneth exclaimed. 'You are unnatural, Tanwen. How can you not love him? Look at him, cariad, he's the sweetest little babba I've ever set eyes on.'

Tanwen didn't bother to answer but flounced out of the room and up to her bedroom.

The next day, to Donna's relief, Carina Price called her into her office and told her that she had recommended that Tanwen should come back. Donna was almost too scared to ask if it was to be as a model or as a seamstress.

'She was never much good in the workroom,' Carina Price said scornfully. 'No, she's got her modelling job back. I only hope she will behave herself.'

Tanwen accepted the news with a supercilious toss of her head and a shrug of her shoulders.

'I knew they'd never be able to replace me,' she said complacently.

Her more elegant, sophisticated appearance was welcomed. The mood was no longer for frivolous outfits. Customers were taking life and their clothes more seriously. Those who could still afford to buy new clothes were conscious of the economic situation the country was in.

The change in everyone's circumstances

had started with the Wall Street crash in New York, and just as this had spread from America to Britain so had a more sober attitude to life in general.

Frivolous forms of entertainment had given way to more serious music and plays. Apart from the universal enjoyment of Walt Disney's Mickey Mouse cartoon films, which seemed to appeal not only to children but to all age groups, there was a drift towards more serious topics. In the world of fashion it was towards more sophistication and elegance.

The flapper days were over. Women no longer wore tight bodices or bound their breasts to conceal their shape. The waist had returned to its normal place so dropped waist dresses and shapeless tubes were out.

Tanwen's new shape fitted this call for elegance perfectly. She revelled in the new styles and this added an extra element to the way she modelled them.

To try to boost sales, James Howell put on daily fashion shows at The Cardiff Drapers. News of these and their excellence spread. They were regularly reported and photographed by the *South Wales Echo*.

Tanwen thrived on the publicity that resulted. She was rarely at home. Night after night she dressed up in her smartest clothes and went out to dances or to restaurants. She had a constant stream of new men-friends.

'This must stop, Tanwen,' her mother told her. 'You'll be getting yourself a bad name, carrying on like this. It's not seemly when you have a seven-month-old baby. You should be at home caring for him.'

'You know I don't give a damn about the kid,' Tanwen snapped. 'I give you money to do that,' she added blithely.

'That's all very well, but now that he's getting bigger I'm beginning to find him too much for me to lift up and carry around,' her mother pleaded.

Tanwen moved across to the mirror, admiring herself. Turning her head from side to side and lifting her gleaming blonde hair from her slim neck she studied her profile. Her blue eyes had regained their brilliance and her fine pale skin glowed.

'Barri's seven months old now, remember, Tanwen, and he's beginning to take notice of what's going on around him,' her mother persisted. 'He needs someone younger than me, someone who can play with him!'

'Then let Donna do it! She's the one who persuaded you to keep him. If I'd had my way he would be in an orphanage or adopted, and then you wouldn't be saddled with him.'

'Tanwen, don't say things like that. I'm sure you don't mean them. You can't, not when he's your own flesh and blood. Barri is a lovely little boy and no mother can reject her own child permanently.'

'That's where you're wrong, Mam. This mother can. God knows how many times I've told you and Donna that I never wanted a kid. I still don't want him, now or ever.' Her face hardened as she faced her mother. 'If you find him too much for you then stick him in an orphanage. If you do it now, before he gets used to you, he'll soon settle down and never know the difference.'

'Tanwen! How can you talk like that!' Tears streamed down Gwyneth Evans's cheeks.

'For heaven's sake, Mam! I've admitted I made a mistake. I don't intend to go on paying for it for the rest of my life!'

Chapter Eighteen

Donna found she was spending more and more time looking after Barri. On warm, sunny summer evenings, after she came home from work, she loved taking him for walks in the Silver Cross pram one of the neighbours had loaned them. He was sitting up now and taking notice of everything that was going on around him, and in her eyes he grew bonnier every day.

He was so like Dylan that several times she was tempted to take him to Tongwynlais to let Mrs Wallis see him. In some ways she felt it was her duty to do so, seeing that Dylan was her grandchild, but at the back of her mind was the niggling doubt about whether simply seeing Barri would be enough to satisfy Mrs Wallis.

What would she do if Mrs Wallis changed her mind and wanted to take him over? She was his grandmother so she probably had some legal claim on Barri.

Yet, would she? Was Mrs Wallis, or even Dylan any more interested in Barri than Tanwen was?

Even though Barri was too young to know what it was all about, Donna arranged a special birthday tea to mark his first birthday, which fell on a Sunday.

She hoped Tanwen would be there at teatime, but she was afraid to mention it to her, knowing what her reaction would be.

Donna couldn't understand how she could sit in the same room as Barri and completely ignore him. Even when he crawled across the floor to where she was sitting, his big brown eyes shining with delight at his achievement, and pulled himself up by the leg of the chair she was sitting on, Tanwen would simply get up and walk away.

If his pudgy little hand missed the chair and caught her skirt or leg then she would push him aside as if he was a troublesome fly. She wouldn't treat a dog or cat in such an unfeeling way, Donna thought sadly.

She had thought that as Barri became daily more and more like a miniature version of Dylan then Tanwen's heart would soften. And once it did she wouldn't be able to help herself from taking an interest in him, and then she was bound to love him.

Donna knew that whenever she picked him up and felt his little arms grip round her neck, her heart turned over. She was sure that if Tanwen would simply take him in her arms and cuddle him then she'd feel the same way. She wouldn't be able to help herself since she was, after all, his mother.

Tanwen was at home on Barri's birthday. Whether it was because her conscience wouldn't let her go gadding off on that particular evening, or whether it was purely coincidental, Donna didn't know, nor did she ask any questions.

Gwyneth was also pleased to see that she was there, though, like Donna, she didn't voice this aloud. She had made Barri a new romper suit in sunny yellow cotton that was almost the same colour as Tanwen's hair. She had also baked a sponge birthday cake with Barri's name written on top in white icing, and a single red candle in the middle.

Donna had bought him a big cuddly teddy bear. His eyes lit up when she gave it to him. He gurgled with pleasure and cuddled it to him, burying his face in the soft shiny fur.

'So what have you bought your little boy for his birthday, then?' Gwyneth asked, looking across the tea table at Tanwen.

'Why the hell should I buy him anything? He means sod all to me.'

'Tanwen!' The colour drained from Gwyneth's face and for one frightening moment Donna thought she was going to faint.

'Do you know how stupid you both are, putting on a tea-party like this for a baby as young as he is?' Tanwen sneered.

'Barri understands far more than you give him credit for,' Donna told her.

'Then he should know to stay right away from me! I can't stand it when he comes clambering up on the chair I'm sitting on, his sticky little paws all over my clothes.'

'Another few weeks and he'll be toddling round on his own, so how are we going to stop him from coming near you?' Donna laughed.

'Well, you'd better try and find a way,' Tanwen snapped, pushing back her chair and stalking out of the room.

Donna bit down on her lower lip to stop herself from saying anything that might upset her mother.

Blinking back her tears, Gwyneth began to clear away the dishes. As she collected up the plates and stacked them together her face was a frozen mask as she tried to conceal her feelings.

What had she done wrong to make Tanwen so selfish and uncaring and so different from Donna, she wondered. She supposed she'd given in to her more when she'd been small, and now look at the result, she thought bitterly.

Donna reached out and caught her mother's arm. 'Don't let Tanwen spoil our little celebration, Mam! It's not fair on Barri to do that. Look at his little face, he's enjoying every moment of it.'

Gwyneth shook her head wearily. 'It's all getting to be too much for me, Donna. If it wasn't for you, cariad, I'd be thinking of doing what Tanwen wants and getting him adopted.'

'Have another cup of tea, Mam, and pour one for me. We haven't lit the candle on Barri's cake yet and there's nothing I like better than a slice of your sponge cake.'

As they finished their little party they heard the front door slam. They looked at each other, but said nothing. They both knew it was Tanwen going off out for the evening.

'Leave the tea things where they are and go and sit in your armchair, Mam. Take it easy while you've got the chance, you look done in,' Donna told her mother. 'I'll clear away and wash up after I've put Barri to bed.'

Putting Barri to bed was one of Donna's

favourite chores. She loved the little burst of energy he always had the moment she undressed him. Watching him kick his chubby little legs and wave his fat little arms in the air filled her with joy. His gurgling laugh as she put on his clean nappy and his little sleeping suit delighted her. Then came the stranglehold around her neck as he struggled determinedly against being put down in his cot. She was rewarded by his warm, wet little kiss, before his eyes closed and he suddenly relaxed and was fast asleep in moments.

Standing there, looking down at Barri, watching his little chest rise and fall, Donna was acutely aware of how great her feelings were for him. Was it because he was a small helpless baby or was it because he reminded her so much of Dylan, she asked herself?

She couldn't even start to understand why Tanwen didn't love Barri. If she still had any feelings at all for Dylan then surely seeing Barri must stir some sort of tenderness in her heart.

Or was that the reason why she had no time for the baby? Was it because he reminded her so much of Dylan that she ignored him all the time?

The thought that if Dylan came back then he might want to reclaim Barri concerned Donna. If he did take him, and he had every right to do so, it would break her heart. She felt for Barri as if he was her own baby, perhaps even more so because of the way Tanwen ignored him and refused to show him any love or affection. If Dylan did take him away and made a home for the three of them, what sort of a mother would Tanwen be?

Perhaps it was time to confront her. She'd talk to her on their own, not in front of their mother. She hoped she'd be able to find out exactly what her intentions were, if Dylan ever did return.

She looked down at the sleeping child and knew that she had to face her right away, while she felt strong enough to do so.

Her mam was still asleep in the armchair so the dishes could wait. She'd talk to Tanwen now, this very minute. After all, she'd taken Dylan from her so she might do the same with Barri if it suited her purposes?

Full of strong-minded resolve she walked across the landing to Tanwen's bedroom. The door was ajar so she walked in without even knocking first. Taking her by surprise might do the trick and make her speak out and tell the truth. She had to be ruthless, it was no good being soft with Tanwen, she told herself.

The room was empty.

Donna felt cheated. She had hyped herself up to face Tanwen, forgetting that she had heard her go out earlier, and now she felt deflated. She stood in the middle of the room wondering what to do next. If she went downstairs and cleared away the remains of their party Tanwen might be home again by then. No one had called to collect her so she might only have gone out to buy some cigarettes. She seemed to smoke incessantly these days.

Donna walked across to the wardrobe, idly wondering if Tanwen had dressed up to go out. If she had then it would probably be the early hours of the morning before she came home again.

As she opened the wardrobe door, Donna caught her breath. It was practically empty. She pulled open the drawers of the dressing table. They were also almost empty.

Her heart racing, Donna checked on top of the wardrobe and felt numb. Tanwen's suitcases were missing!

Did that mean Tanwen had gone for good, she asked herself.

She stood there, bewildered, wondering what she ought to do next. Should she tell her mother or leave it until the morning in case she had made a mistake?

If she told her now and Tanwen had returned by breakfast-time then she would have distressed her for nothing.

Deep in her heart she knew instinctively that Tanwen had left for good. Where had she gone, though? Had she gone on her own? Was she ever coming back? The questions stung Donna's mind like icy snowballs.

Did it mean Tanwen was relinquishing all hold over Barri, she asked herself, over and over again? She'd always claimed that she didn't want him, nor to have anything to do with him. Could any mother ever really abandon her own child completely?

Bitterness, as acid as bile, filled Donna's throat. She and her mother had done everything in their power to make things easy for Tanwen. All she had to do was earn enough money to help with bringing him up.

A fresh thought wiped everything else from Donna's mind. Without Tanwen's money coming in she wasn't sure how they would be able to manage. Once Barri was toddling it would be impossible for Gwyneth to cope with him and do any sewing at all. Without Tanwen's contribution to the household her own wages would be all they'd have to live on.

The future seemed so uncertain. She was beginning to understand the stress her mother had been under ever since Barri was born. This new development would only make matters worse, Donna thought sadly, as she went downstairs and began to clear up.

It was putting a burden on her as well as

her mother, she reflected uneasily. As her mother grew older, more and more responsibility for Barri would fall on her shoulders. It meant she would always need to work to support him. She could never hope to marry or have a family of her own, not as long as she had to care for Barri.

Perhaps she should have listened to Tanwen and had Barri adopted the moment he'd been born. Before she'd grown to love him so dearly.

Every day Barri grew more like Dylan. Every day the bond between them became closer. She knew she could never give him up, nor could she walk out and leave him like Tanwen seemed to have done. They might be twins, but they were not only so different in looks, but in every other way possible. The way they looked at life, the way they behaved, even the way they handled their problems was in exact opposition to each other. The only thing in which they appeared to be the same was in their love for Dylan Wallis. There were times when she wished so much that Barri really was hers and Dylan's, instead of Tanwen's and Dylan's. Not that she could possibly love Barri any more than she did now, she thought, as she made her mother a cup of tea after she'd finished clearing up.

'I'm so tired I think I'll go on up to bed after I've drunk this,' her mother said when

221

Donna took it in to her. 'Have you made up a bottle ready for Barri's early morning feed?'

Donna shook her head. 'Not yet.'

'It's dreadful that Tanwen won't pull her weight and help more. So unnatural, he's such a little dear.'

'She's selfish, Mam, and she'll never change now!' Donna said brusquely.

'She shouldn't be like that with little Barri, though,' Gwyneth said sadly. 'It's not his fault he's here, poor little dab. You shouldn't be giving up your time to care for him like you do, either.'

'Oh, I don't mind, Mam.'

'These disturbed nights won't be for much longer, cariad. He'll soon be sleeping right through the night,' Gwyneth assured her, patting her arm.

'Yes, I know that, but I'm tired so I think I'll do the same as you and get some sleep before he wakes up.'

'You'll have to leave the door on the latch for Tanwen, then, you never know what time she'll come home,' Gwyneth said as she handed Donna her empty cup.

Chapter Nineteen

Although she felt desperately tired, Donna found she couldn't sleep. Disturbing thoughts raced round her head in a never-ending stream as she stared into the darkness. She closed her eyes, trying to will herself asleep, but it was pointless. No matter what she did she tossed and turned.

She crept downstairs to get a drink of water, drew back the curtains and looked out of the window. It was a warm, humid night, the sky a velvety blue with a sprinkling of sparkling stars.

She went back to bed, willed herself to lie perfectly still, closed her eyes and waited yet again for sleep, but it refused to come. Over and over she thought of all the different scenarios concerning Barri's future. Tanwen's intentions, the mystery about where Dylan had disappeared to, and her mother's increasing frailty went round and round in her head.

She was still grappling with these thoughts when Barri wakened around six. Dawn was already lighting up the sky as she picked him up out of his cot, carried him back to her own bed and gave him his bottle.

He drifted back to sleep before it was completely finished and she was tempted to snuggle down with him. Common sense told her that it would be foolish to accustom him to doing that so she carried him back into his own cot and tucked him in.

Yawning, she crept back to her own bed and once again settled herself under the covers, and this time she was asleep in seconds.

The next thing she knew her mother was shaking her by the shoulder. 'Donna, you've overslept, cariad. Come on, I've only just wakened myself. I'll take Barri downstairs and go and call Tanwen. Don't go back to sleep now, my lovely, or you'll never get to work on time.'

Donna shook herself out of the deep drowsiness that seemed to envelop her.

'I'm getting up now, Mam,' she promised, flinging back the bedcovers and sitting on the side of the bed. She heard her mother walk across to Tanwen's room and from somewhere deep inside her head Donna knew she ought to stop her, but she couldn't think why.

Then, like a tornado, it all came rushing back. She remembered with startling clarity going into Tanwen's room the night before and finding that she had gone. Not out for the evening, as they'd thought when she'd stormed out of the room in high dudgeon. It

224

was more final than that. Clothes were missing from her wardrobe and drawers, and the cases were gone from the top of the wardrobe.

She'd meant to break the news gently to her mother.

Now it was too late. The moment she walked into Tanwen's bedroom she'd see for herself that the bed hadn't been slept in.

Donna dressed as quickly as she could, all the time wondering what she could say to comfort her mother. Should she take the day off work so that she could be with her? She was probably going to be late anyway.

When she rushed into the kitchen she found her mother spooning porridge into Barri's hungry little mouth.

'Come on, Donna, get a move on or you're going to be late. Tanwen's up and gone. Mean of her not to give us a shout, well, to call you, anyway. She knows you have to be at work at the same time as her.'

Donna stared at her mother in bewilderment. It was not going to be necessary to break the news that Tanwen had left, she thought with relief. At least, not at the moment.

If she thinks Tanwen has already gone to work it is better to say nothing, she decided. Tanwen might even turn up at work. She might have taken her clothes because she had decided to move in with one of her friends.

Giving her mother and Barri a quick kiss, she left the house. She felt optimistic. She might have been making a mountain from a molehill after all. Tanwen might be at work and have a plausible explanation.

Her high spirits were dashed by mid-morning when Carina Price came into the workroom to ask her why Tanwen hadn't come to work.

'I ... I don't know,' Donna prevaricated. 'I didn't see her before I left home this morning. I was late getting up... I overslept.'

Carina Price looked concerned. 'Perhaps you should take the day off, you're looking pretty peaky. Is anything the matter?'

Donna hesitated, then feeling the need to confide in someone blurted out her uncertainty about where Tanwen was, and her fear that she might have left home.

'I know she's selfish and irresponsible, but surely even Tanwen wouldn't clear off without a word to either you or your mother?' was all Carina could say.

Donna kept thinking about Tanwen for the rest of the day. She dreaded going home, knowing that she would have to face her mother with the truth. She wondered how her mother would take it when she told her what she had discovered last night.

When she finally summoned up the courage to tell her the news, Gwyneth stared at her in disbelief. 'Duw anwyl! You mean you knew about this last night and yet you didn't say a word?'

Donna looked contrite. 'I didn't know if she'd moved out or simply gone to stay with one of her friends. It seemed pointless worrying you about it, Mam. I thought I would see her in work and find out what was going on.'

'And she wasn't at work,' Gwyneth said heavily. 'So you've no idea at all where she might have gone last night?'

Donna shook her head.

'Haven't any of the girls there any idea about where she might be?'

'Everyone from Carina Price down has been asking me where she is.'

There was no news about Tanwen for over a month. Then, at the beginning of October on her way home from work, Donna spotted a flyer on the stand at the corner of Trinity Street and St Mary Street, where a news-vendor was selling the *South Wales Echo* to passers-by.

It read: *'Cardiff girl to become a Film Star.'*

Even before she bought a copy of the paper, some sixth sense told her that it was Tanwen.

On one of the inside pages there was a glamorous picture that confirmed what she'd thought. Tanwen was smiling and looking even lovelier than Jean Harlow, the film star on whom she had lately tried to model herself.

The caption under the picture gave a fascinating account of how she had been spotted modelling clothes in Cardiff by a talent scout.

Impressed by her photogenic possibilities he had invited her to London for tests. The outcome had been that she was to have a part in a new film that was about to be made.

When Donna showed the newspaper to her mother, Gwyneth read it through several times and still looked bemused.

'She never breathed a word about this to us, yet she must have known for quite some time,' she said at last.

Donna didn't know what to say. She knew her mother was right. She felt sure they wouldn't spring an offer like that on someone, even if they did think they were photogenic, without checking to find out if they could act or not.

'So where is this film being made?' Gwyneth asked worriedly.

'It doesn't say. It must be somewhere in London.'

'So how do we get in touch with her?'

Donna shook her head. 'I don't know. Perhaps if we wrote a letter to her and then sent it to the paper they would forward it on to her,' she suggested.

They debated the matter for several days.

'I suppose if she wanted to get in touch and tell us her news then she would have done so by now,' Gwyneth Evans said resignedly.

'If we simply do nothing then we might lose touch with her altogether,' Donna argued.

'Perhaps it's better that way.'

'She shouldn't just walk away, Barri is her responsibility, even if she does say she doesn't want anything to do with him.'

'Send a letter to the paper, then, if you want to,' her mother said reluctantly. 'As far as I'm concerned she's made her decision. If that's the sort of life she wants to lead then I don't want to hear any more about her. It doesn't matter to me where she is, or even what she's up to if it comes to that.'

'She should help in some way. She could send you money to pay for his food and clothes.'

Gwyneth shook her head. 'We'll manage, somehow. It might be better if she stayed away for good. Barri's thirteen months old; another year or so and he'll understand what she's saying when she rants on about not wanting him. Even at the age he is now they can sense when people don't like them, and I don't want his little life ruined by feeling he's not wanted.'

Although her mother was so adamant and outspoken, Donna suspected that it wasn't really what she felt deep inside. Her face was so drawn that she looked at least ten years older than she should have done. A lot of the time she seemed to be in a complete daze, as if her thoughts were anywhere but in the present.

It worried Donna. Her mother seemed to be so distracted most of the time that she wondered if she was really capable of looking after Barri. He was such a lively little chap. Now that he was toddling around he was into everything and he needed constant supervision.

She wished she could be at home to help look after him, but since her wages were the only money they had coming in she knew that was completely out of the question.

Finally, in desperation, Donna penned a letter to Tanwen to ask if she could help them out financially. She marked it 'Personal', sealed it with sealing wax to make sure no one opened it, took it to the office of the *South Wales Echo*, and asked them if they would forward it to Tanwen.

At first they were reluctant to help her. When she explained that Tanwen was her sister they promised to see what could be done.

'Not sure we have an address for her, see,' the reporter she spoke to explained. 'That piece was sent in by one of our freelancers. He might still be in touch with her, though.

Leave it with me and I'll do the best I can.'

Donna was on tenterhooks waiting for a reply. Then, as the days became weeks and stretched into months, she tried to put it out of her mind.

It was almost Christmas, and there were so many other pressing worries. The weather was damp and cold and her mother was not at all well.

To make matters worse, bills were piling up. Their stock of coal was running low, so as well as worrying about her mother, Donna was at her wits' end trying to make ends meet.

When Carina Price sent for her on Christmas Eve she went along to her office with a heavy heart, knowing that she had been late many times recently, and even taken the odd day off when her mother had been too poorly to look after Barri. When Carina handed her a plain white envelope her hand shook so much she couldn't open it.

As she walked back to the workroom she wondered if it was a reprimand or a letter telling her that her services were no longer needed.

To her relief it was neither. Inside the envelope were two crisp white five-pound notes and a slip of paper informing her that the money was her 'Annual Bonus'.

For a moment she wondered if it was a

mistake. She was sure Aileen Roberts had never mentioned anything about them being paid a bonus. She was on the point of asking her about it, but when she looked at the piece of paper again, and at the envelope, she realised that it wasn't official stationery. The envelope was a plain white one and the writing on the piece of paper was in Carina Price's own hand.

Embarrassment and gratitude swept over her as she realised what Carina Price had done. She didn't know whether to dash back to her office and thank her profusely or whether it would be better to accept the generous help in silence. It was so unexpected that it brought a lump to her throat, that Carina could be so generous and such a wonderful friend.

She slipped the envelope and its precious contents into the pocket of her skirt and tried to control her excitement. She'd put one five-pound note away safely for future emergencies. The other one she'd spend on things for them for Christmas.

Five pounds was enough to buy all the extras that would make Christmas Day special. She'd be able to replenish their stock of coal so that her mother wouldn't need to sit huddled in a blanket throughout the chilly days of January and February.

As a special concession, since it was Christmas Eve, they left work early that night and Donna dashed along to The Hayes to see what bargains she could snap up from the stalls there. She bought a plump chicken, and an assortment of vegetables to go with it for their Christmas dinner. Then she would use the chicken carcass to make soup or broth for the rest of the week. She bought a tin of mixed biscuits, knowing how much Barri loved them, and some oranges and apples.

As she was walking away, a brightly painted wooden train caught her eye. She stopped to examine it, visualising how Barri's face would light up if he was to find that at the bottom of his bed the next morning. Then she saw the price tag and reluctantly put it back down again.

'Not what you're looking for?' the stallholder asked her.

'It's lovely, but I'm afraid it costs more than I can afford.'

'Twelve and sixpence! It's a bargain. Well made, see. Sturdy enough for a small boy to sit on and scuttle himself round the room on.'

'I know, it's a lovely toy.'

'How old is he?'

'Nearly eighteen months.'

'There you are, then, it's the perfect present. It will last him for years. You'll even be able to hand it down to his little brother or sister,' he added with a cheeky grin.

Donna smiled and picked up her shopping bags and made to move on.

'Come on, you can't go home without it. Think of his face in the morning! Tell you what, seeing it's Christmas Eve, what if I drop the price to ten bob. Can you manage that?'

Donna hesitated for a split second as she did some rapid calculations in her head, then she beamed at the stallholder and nodded.

Barri was such a good little boy that she felt he deserved a special present. The stallholder was right about one thing, he'd be able to play with it for the next couple of years. He wasn't right about the second thing he'd said, though, she thought ruefully. It wouldn't be passed down to any little brother or sister.

Chapter Twenty

Barri was playing happily with his new train, and Donna and her mother were enjoying the luxury of sitting down together for a mid-morning cup of tea, when there was a knock on the front door. They looked across at each other, frowning, wondering who it could be calling at eleven o'clock on New

Year's Day.

Donna opened the door and for a moment she didn't recognise either of the people standing there, and wondered if they had come to the wrong house.

The woman was swaddled in a luxurious fur coat with the collar turned up. It covered most of her face, and reached from the brim of her fur-trimmed hat almost to her ankles.

The man standing beside her was wearing an equally long camel coat. When he raised his brown trilby and said, 'Happy New Year, Donna,' her heart pounded in disbelief.

'Dylan?' She stared at his plump face and red cheeks in stunned amazement, shocked by the change in him. He wasn't a bit like the handsome figure she'd held a candle for these last couple of years. She looked speculatively at the woman, unable to see her face in the swathes of fur. 'Tanwen?'

'Aren't you going to ask us in, then, we're freezing to death standing here?' her sister grumbled with an exaggerated shiver.

'Of course!' Donna stood aside to let them enter. As she did so, Barri came shooting out into the hallway on his new train to see who it was.

For a moment there was a shocked silence, then Barri backed away and scooted back to his grandmother where he clutched at her skirt and hid his face.

'Mam, we have visitors. Look who is here.'

'Hello, Mam! Happy New Year! I've brought you all Christmas presents and Dylan has come along to let in 1932 for you.'

Gwyneth regarded the two of them in silence. Mixed emotions flickered over her face as she stared from one to the other. Whether they were of suppressed pleasure or anger Donna wasn't sure.

Tanwen slipped her fur coat from her shoulders and draped it carelessly over a chair. 'I'm dying for a cup of tea,' she told Donna pointedly as she smoothed her clinging black dress down over her slim hips.

Dylan struggled to take off his coat and stood awkwardly holding it, as well as his trilby and the bag of presents, as if he didn't know what to do with any of them.

Wordlessly, Donna took them all from him. She carried them out into the hallway, laid his coat over the banister, with the trilby resting on top and the parcels at the foot of the stairs. As she continued on into the kitchen to make the tea, she wondered what she had ever seen in Dylan and felt a surge of relief that seeing him again left her completely unmoved.

He wasn't at all like the memory that she had carried in her mind all these months. This wasn't the man she had been so desperately in love with, and who had broken her heart and caused her so many secret tears.

She remembered him as lean and handsome with warm brown eyes and a ready smile. This man, in his grey chalk-stripe suit and flashy green satin tie, had a bloated, dissipated face. She noticed, too, that his eyes had a crafty look about them. His gaze seemed to slide away from hers as soon as she looked directly at him.

With a continuing sense of relief, Donna realised that, apart from having the same colour hair and eyes, Barri was nothing at all like him.

When she carried the tray of tea things back into the living room she studied Dylan more closely and experienced a wonderful sense of lightness. He was nothing at all like the man Tanwen had stolen from her.

The feelings she had been harbouring, which had hung like a dark cloud over her head for so long, suddenly dispersed. It was as if one of the many burdens she was carrying had been lifted from her shoulders. What a wonderful start for 1932, she thought happily.

As they drank their tea, Dylan went on and on about their successful careers. He was full of his own self-importance, outlining the part he was playing in furthering Tanwen's career. Donna decided that he was a pompous, over-bearing bore, and as selfish and egotistical as Tanwen. Her sister was more than welcome to him.

Neither of them, Donna reasoned, is in the least bit interested in Barri's welfare or how we are managing. Tanwen didn't even seem to be aware that her own mother was not only in poor health, but growing frailer every day.

All she can do is talk about how she has been discovered, thanks to Dylan, the part she's going to play in the film, the stupendous publicity it's getting and their plans for the future, thought Donna.

'With Dylan working as one of the directors of the company producing the film, this is only my first stepping stone to what I will eventually achieve,' she gushed. She stretched her arms high in the air above her head. 'From now on, the world is my oyster! Isn't that right, darling?'

Dylan agreed enthusiastically. 'Everyone on the set is thrilled with her performance. By this time next year you'll see Tanwen's name in lights outside every cinema in the land.'

When Barri finally got over his shyness and pushed his train across the floor towards where Tanwen was sitting, she drew her silk-clad legs away from it irritably, as if fearful that it might snag her silk stockings.

Sensing her hostility, Barri ambled away. He toddled over to where her fur coat lay across a chair and murmuring, 'Puss, puss,' began stroking it and laying his cheek against it.

'For God's sake, can't you keep that brat under control,' Tanwen screeched. 'I don't want his sticky fingers pawing my fur, it cost a fortune!'

'Take it easy, doll,' Dylan murmured, as Barri started to whimper. 'He won't hurt it, he's only stroking it ever so gently.' Awkwardly he patted Barri on the head.

Tanwen slammed her half-empty cup down on the table. 'I think we'd better be going,' she muttered. Snatching up her fur coat she slung it around her shoulders.

'So soon?' Donna raised her eyebrows challengingly.

Tanwen shrugged her shoulders. 'We've told you all our news.'

'True!' Donna commented caustically, then added, 'You haven't asked us how we are, though.'

A dark red flush crept up from Tanwen's neck to the opalescent skin on her face, making her look hot and uncomfortable. 'I can see how you are, can't I? I don't suppose you've done anything or been anywhere that is worth telling me about.'

'No,' Donna said dryly, 'we can't afford to go anywhere. In fact,' she added, 'Mam seldom goes out of the house at all except to the local shops for food. I only have

239

Sundays off from work so there's not much time for me to go anywhere or to do anything, either. If the weather is good enough I sometimes manage to take Barri out to the park in his pram.'

Tanwen looked uneasy. 'You are managing all right, though?'

'Far from it, since we've only got my wages to keep both of us and your child,' Donna told her bluntly. 'We wouldn't have been able to afford a fire over Christmas if Carina Price hadn't given me what she termed a bonus. I found out that it was money out of her own pocket. I suppose you could call it charity,' Donna said bitterly.

'Still Carina Price's favourite, I see!' Tanwen sniped.

'Donna! You never said that extra money came from Carina,' Gwyneth exclaimed.

'No, I was afraid you might be embarrassed and want me to give it back.'

'That was one of the reasons we called,' Dylan interrupted. 'We wanted to find out if things were all right with you financially.'

'Tanwen knows very well that they're not. I wrote to her asking her for help as soon as we saw the piece in the paper about her getting a film job,' Donna said angrily. 'Didn't you get the letter?' she demanded.

Tanwen shrugged dismissively. 'I've had a stack of begging letters...'

'Princess! Don't be like that,' Dylan

240

pleaded. Tanwen flashed him a smile, fluttering her eyelashes provocatively. 'I'm sorry,' she said with a pert little pout. 'You know how Donna can upset me. Of course I care about how she is managing. That's why we're here. Go on, tell her, explain things to her and then perhaps she'll stop being so cross with me.'

Dylan patted her shoulder, then he reached inside his jacket pocket and brought out an envelope and held it out to Donna. 'We want you to have this and to know that we appreciate the way you are taking care of the child for us.'

'What is it?' she asked, making no attempt to take the package from him.

'Money, to pay you for looking after him,' he replied, putting the packet down on the table.

'Your son's name is Barri.'

He nodded. 'Tanwen did tell me. Please take the money, Donna,' he persisted. When she still made no move to pick it up he retrieved the package and dropped it into Gwyneth's lap.

'So you intend to leave him here with us permanently, do you?' Donna snapped.

He looked startled. 'I thought that was what you had agreed with Tanwen?'

'No! Tanwen walked out without a word to either Mam or me. Until we read that piece in the paper we worried ourselves sick wondering what had happened to her.'

Dylan looked surprised. 'I was under the impression she had already made it clear that she couldn't take the baby to London or look after...' his voice trailed off uncertainly.

'What about you, Dylan? What are your feelings about the baby. After all, you are his father.'

'It's all come as rather a shock to me,' he said apologetically.

'Such a shock that you cleared off to London or somewhere the moment you heard that Tanwen was expecting your baby!'

'That was a coincidence,' he said hastily. 'It had nothing to do with the news about the baby. Anyway,' he added lamely, 'I knew Tanwen was in good hands and that you'd take every care of her.'

'Even so, you're not interested in bringing Barri up any more than Tanwen is,' Donna persisted. 'If you wanted to have him with you, if you loved him and you were concerned about his future then I'm sure you'd find a way to care for him.'

'I am concerned about his future, Donna! That's why I think he is so much better off here with you and his grandmother.'

'You mean that, like Tanwen, you don't really want the trouble and responsibility of bringing him up,' Donna said scornfully.

The smile vanished from Dylan's face, and

with it all his surface charm. He looked shifty and uneasy, his brown eyes hostile.

'I know nothing about kids. Tanwen should have got rid of it the minute she knew she'd been caught. The fact that she didn't isn't my fault, and I don't want to be saddled with it now any more than she does,' Dylan affirmed.

'You're not human,' Donna told him, her voice laden with disgust. 'Your own child and you have no time for him!'

Dylan shrugged. 'That's the way we are. We can't all be flowing with the milk of human kindness.'

'Look at him,' Donna persisted, ignoring his barbed taunt. 'Can't you see how gorgeous he is? Don't you want to pick him up and cuddle him?'

'To me he looks like any other small child, and as for wanting to pick him up, no, I haven't the slightest wish to do so. I've no interest in children at all. I've already tried to make that clear to you.'

'Dylan, for God's sake stop arguing with her, you know how pig-headed she is,' Tanwen snapped. She walked over and kissed her mother on the forehead and then moved towards the door. 'Come on, Dylan, we really must go.'

'Can't you at least say goodbye to Barri?' Donna pleaded.

Dylan patted the child's hair in the same

way as he would have stroked a dog, but Tanwen made no attempt at all to touch Barri. Slipping her arms inside the sleeves of her coat and turning the collar up around her ears, she waited impatiently with one hand on the door for Dylan to join her.

'Goodbye, Donna. I don't know when we are likely to meet again,' Dylan said as he followed Tanwen out of the house. 'There's money in that envelope to cover immediate expenses and I will be sending you more on a regular basis to support the child.'

'Farming him out, you mean!'

Dylan's face darkened. 'Look, Donna, no one asked you to take on this burden. You chose to keep him and to bring him up.'

'So who else was going to do it? Your mother didn't seem very cooperative when I went to see her to tell her that the baby was due almost any day.'

'You went to see my mother?' His face creased and he laughed dryly. 'That must have been a waste of time!'

'Her opinion of you wasn't very high, either,' Donna said disparagingly.

'Look, Donna, let's face facts. We're not a loving close-knit family. We don't like having responsibility thrust upon us. We like to go our own way.'

'And you don't care who you trample underfoot in the process, do you,' she said indignantly.

'Be honest, Tanwen wanted to have the baby adopted as soon as he was born, but you interfered and refused to let her do so. Now if you want to bring the child up instead, then that's entirely up to you, Donna. I'm willing to see that you are recompensed for doing so,' Dylan affirmed stiffly.

'Yes, we'll make sure you are not out of pocket, but we don't want to be constantly reminded of his existence,' Tanwen told her.

'Tanwen is right. It would ruin her career as an up-and-coming star if people knew she had a child. What is more, I have no intention of playing the part of being a father. Is that clearly understood?'

Chapter Twenty-One

Gwyneth Evans refused to even mention Tanwen's visit. She maintained a brooding silence no matter how much Donna tried to draw her out and persuade her to talk about it.

Donna felt sure her mother had heard the heated conversation she'd had with Tanwen and Dylan as they were leaving and that was what she was worrying about.

If that was the case then Donna wished she

245

would speak out so that they could discuss it and make proper plans. It had certainly left her disconcerted about the future, because it now seemed apparent that Tanwen was never going to take her responsibility for Barri seriously.

It wasn't merely a case of helping out and looking after Barri until Tanwen was properly established as an actress, but that he would be remaining with them permanently.

Most of their neighbours in Rhymney Street had read the newspaper headlines and seen Tanwen's picture and the piece about her in the *South Wales Echo*. They'd also spotted her arriving in a posh car, wrapped up in furs and finery, and they were eager for more details.

When they spoke to Gwyneth about it she merely shook her head and looked at them blankly as if she didn't know what they were talking about.

Even Blodwyn Hughes, who had lived next door to them ever since Donna could remember, was unable to get Gwyneth to talk about Tanwen.

'So you've still got little Barri, then,' Blodwyn commented a few days later when she saw Gwyneth setting off to do some shopping. 'Your Tanwen didn't want to take him away with her, then?'

'Tanwen take Barri? What do you mean? Why ever would she want to do that?'

Gwyneth frowned. 'Barri belongs to our Donna.'

'Darw!' Blodwyn's grey eyes rounded. 'I didn't realise that your Donna had adopted him. There's a silly woman I am, putting my big foot in it!'

'Donna doesn't have to adopt him, Barri's her child,' Gwyneth told her brusquely.

'No, he's not, cariad!' Blodwyn corrected her bluntly, her double chins wobbling. 'He's your Tanwen's baby. Dammo di! I should know, I was there with you all the day he was born!'

Gwyneth didn't reply but walked away as quickly as she could.

Blodwyn felt so worried that she made a point of waylaying Donna as she arrived home from work that night.

'Is your mam going a bit scatty, cariad?' she asked anxiously. 'Nearly bit my head off this morning when I mentioned that Tanwen hadn't taken young Barri away with her.' She laughed shrilly. 'Even said he was your babba, not Tanwen's. She seemed to forget that I was the one who fetched that Megan Simmons to help birth the child.'

'Oh, I'm sorry, Blodwyn, don't let it upset you,' Donna said placatingly. 'Mam's a bit off colour at the moment. Had a lot of worry lately, see. I'm sure she didn't mean to offend you.'

'Lot of shocks, too, I shouldn't wonder. I

247

saw the piece in the paper,' Blodwyn sniffed. 'I saw your Tanwen all wrapped up in her furs and finery turn up with that fancy man of hers in their posh car on New Year's Day.'

'Yes,' Donna smiled tolerantly. 'A flying visit, that was all.'

'Well, I knew she'd been, so there was no point at all in your mam clamming up about it, now was there? And as for saying that Barri was yours, well, if she goes round saying things like that those who don't know the truth will be getting the wrong sort of impression about the sort of person you are, cariad.'

Donna looked uneasy, wondering exactly what her mam had been saying. 'I'm sure I can rely on you to put them straight, Blodwyn.'

'I most certainly will! Bloody angel you've been, the way you've taken that baby on and looked after your mam into the bargain,' she said fervently. 'I hope that sister of yours appreciates all that you're doing.'

Donna smiled, but held her tongue. She didn't for one minute think Tanwen was in the least bit grateful and she was pretty sure Blodwyn was waiting for her to say so.

Tanwen was the least of her worries, she discovered in the weeks that followed. What did concern her far more was the fact that her mother's memory seemed to be failing. She was becoming more and more forgetful, and Donna began to worry when she found her doing strange things. At first they had been trivial mistakes like putting salt instead of sugar into the tea, or going out shopping and forgetting the very things she had gone to buy.

The day her mam forgot to give Barri his midday meal, even though it was left all ready for him, Donna felt really alarmed. She didn't know whether to be cross with her or to say nothing in case it upset her even more.

The real crux came when she arrived home from work on a bitterly cold evening in March and found Barri huddled outside on the doorstep, sobbing his heart out. He didn't even have a coat on and his hands were blue with the cold.

The front door was tightly shut. When she finally got into the house Donna found her mother asleep in an armchair, oblivious of what had happened.

Barri was shivering and freezing cold. His teeth were chattering so much he couldn't speak. Even his little legs were blue. Donna wasn't sure what was the best way to get him warm. She knew she had to do it very gradually otherwise he would be in pain as he thawed out. Possibly giving him a bath would be the best way of warming him up, she decided.

Wrapping him in a blanket while she

heated up some water, she sat him in a chair near the fire, but not too close. She didn't want him to finish up with chilblains on his fingers or toes.

As soon as the kettle boiled she half-filled his little tin bath with warm water and sat him in it. For a moment he stiffened and whimpered, then he slowly relaxed as if he found it comforting. She carefully topped it up with more hot water when it began to cool off. In no time he was laughing up at her as he patted on the water sending splashes all over the place.

Donna wondered if he'd had anything to eat since she'd left for work that morning. Leaving him playing in the water she made a bowl of bread and milk, and spoon-fed him while he sat in the bath.

By the time her mother wakened, Donna had taken Barri out of the bath, dried him and dressed him in his pyjamas. She was sitting by the fire cuddling him, ready to pop him into his cot as soon as he became sleepy.

'You've got him ready for bed awfully early, Donna,' her mother told her. 'He hasn't had his dinner yet.'

Donna frowned, wondering whether there was any point in telling her that Barri had been outside when she'd arrived home from work.

'I think you've been asleep, Mam,' she said

gently. 'It is almost Barri's bedtime.'

'Shall I nurse him, then, while you make us both a nice cup of tea.'

Donna looked down at Barri and wondered whether she should pass him over to her mother or take him upstairs and put him down. He certainly looked all right now and none the worse for his adventure. He didn't even look tired, only a little flushed from his bath.

When he looked up at her and gave her one of his heart-wrenching little smiles, Donna felt a surge of love for him.

'Biccy?' he said hopefully.

'All right, then. Sit on Nana's lap and I'll get you one.'

As she made a pot of tea, Donna debated with herself yet again what she ought to do about this sad change in her mother.

She found she was unable to reach a decision. She loved her mother dearly and knew she would never hurt Barri, not as long as she knew what was happening. The problem was that half the time she didn't seem to know what was going on around her or to be aware of what she was doing.

She wasn't like this all the time, Donna reminded herself. She could go for days without a memory lapse. At those times she ran things exactly as she should and had no problems at all looking after Barri. Then, without any kind of warning, she seemed to lose touch with life and withdraw into a world of her own.

Donna felt that these occasions were not only becoming more frequent, but that they lasted longer. Today, she reasoned, her mother must have been either asleep since midday or at least not aware what was going on around her since then. She suspected that poor little Barri hadn't been fed since breakfast-time, and she had no idea how long he'd been outside in the cold.

Fortunately, Barri seemed to be none the worse for his brief interlude of neglect. He slept soundly all night and was his normal happy little self the next morning.

Gwyneth, too, was up bright and early, urging Donna to eat a proper breakfast and hurrying her up to leave on time for work. So although she was still uncertain about leaving Barri alone with her mother, Donna could see no reason for not doing so.

The problem wouldn't go away, though. It was there all the time, niggling away at the back of her mind. She even began to wonder if it was her, not her mam, who was going scatty.

A week later she was feeling so worried that when she spotted Carina Price coming into the staff canteen she decided to confide in her. If she explained the situation then she could ask if it was possible to have some time off work.

'Oh, Donna, I'm so glad you are here. When Aileen Roberts said you'd gone for your break I was afraid you might have left the building. Can you come along to my office, there's a policeman there who wishes to speak to you.'

'A policeman?' Fear gripped Donna like some giant, menacing hand. She felt her chest tighten so much she could hardly breathe.

'Whatever is the matter?' she gasped. 'Is it something to do with Tanwen? Has something happened to her?'

'No, it has nothing to do with Tanwen,' Carina Price said quickly. 'It's about your mother. I think I'd better leave it to the policeman to explain, but if I can help in any way let me know.'

The policeman was a burly middle-aged man. In a bluff, genial way he told Donna that he'd been called to their house by Blodwyn Hughes.

'She lives next door to you?'

Donna nodded.

'Well, she heard your little boy crying. Not his usual sort of crying, but as though he was very, very frightened.'

'Didn't she go to find out why?' Donna asked, perplexed.

'Yes,' he nodded, 'she did. That was why she came to me for help.'

Donna felt her mouth go dry and her

heart start to race alarmingly. She looked at Carina beseechingly. 'I'll have to go and find out what's happened,' she said worriedly.

'We've already done that,' the policeman told her. 'Your neighbour said that she couldn't get a reply when she knocked on the door. She looked in the window and she could see the little boy was in there but she couldn't see anyone else. She said the place looked to be in a bit of a state. There wasn't even a guard round the fire! It's very lucky the child didn't fall in the fire and get burned.'

'Oh heavens! Where on earth was my mam, then?' Donna clapped her hand to her mouth in shock, her eyes wide with distress.

'It's all right, miss. No need to take on so. Your neighbour has taken the boy into her house and she'll look after him until you get home. He's quite safe.'

Donna looked bewildered, aware that he had avoided answering her question. 'My mam must be in the house somewhere.'

'That's what bothers us. She's not in the house, I'm afraid.'

'She must be there! She'd never go out and leave Barri on his own!'

Even as she said it her mind was racing with doubts. Her mother had done so many strange things in recent months.

'There must be some mistake,' she repeated. 'Are you quite sure she wasn't in the house? Did you check upstairs? She might have gone back to bed if she wasn't feeling well.'

'No,' he confirmed, 'she wasn't anywhere in the house, we made sure of that.'

'You'd better run along home, Donna,' Carina Price said, her voice full of concern.

'Thank you.' Donna looked at her gratefully. 'Will it be all right if I take the rest of the day off?'

'Of course you can!'

'I'll see you in the morning, then.'

'Look, Donna,' Carina Price hesitated. 'I think that perhaps you'd better have a few days off. It might be a good idea to take your mother along to see a doctor and get her checked out. It sounds as though she may be ill, or possibly heading for a breakdown with all the worry she has had,' she said anxiously.

Chapter Twenty-Two

Gwyneth Evans was found later in the day. The policeman who had alerted Donna to the fact that she was missing brought her home.

'She was wandering around Tiger Bay and had no idea where she was or what her name was,' he told Donna. 'Fortunately we recognised her from the description you gave me. By rights she should go into hospital, but since she seems to be perfectly all right physically I thought I'd bring her home and set your mind at rest.'

'Thank you!' Donna smiled at him gratefully.

'I think you should get your own doctor to take a look at her and check her over.'

'Yes, of course I will.' Donna took hold of her mother's arm and led her into the living room. The policeman waited while she settled her in her armchair near the fire.

'You will remember to get the doctor to take a look at her?' he repeated.

'Of course I will! I'll take her along to see Dr Morgan in Crwys Road, he has an evening surgery.'

The constable looked dubious. 'I think you should call him out to see her. I think she might collapse if you tried to get her to walk that far. It would be much better if you sent for him. I'll drive round there and leave a message for you if you like,' he offered.

Donna smiled at him. 'That's very kind of you.'

'All in the line of duty! How's the little boyo? None the worse for his adventure, I hope.'

Donna smiled. 'No, he's perfectly all right,' she assured him.

She had only just taken her mother's coat off and made her a cup of tea when the knock sounded on the door.

Dr Morgan was in his late fifties with a short white goatee beard and sharp blue eyes. He examined Gwyneth thoroughly, sounding her chest, testing her reflexes, peering into her eyes and looking at her throat.

'Her lungs are very congested. Keep her indoors in the warm for a few days otherwise she will end up with bronchitis or pneumonia,' he told Donna tersely. 'I understand she has been suffering from memory lapses so she shouldn't be left on her own for any length of time.'

'Can you tell me why this is happening?' Donna asked worriedly.

Dr Morgan stroked his beard thoughtfully. 'Probably something to do with her age,' he pronounced. 'None of us can do anything about that, I'm afraid.'

'She isn't old!' Donna protested. 'She's only forty-two!'

Dr Morgan frowned but made no comment. He took a pad from his black bag and wrote out a prescription. 'Get this medicine from the chemist tomorrow and follow the instructions on the bottle. In the meantime, give her these,' he ordered, handing Donna some tablets. 'Two now, two more when she goes to bed, and two first thing in the morning. Then, tomorrow, start her on the medicine as directed.'

Donna repeated everything he'd said, just to make sure.

'That's right. If she is no better in a week then send for me again.'

Although her mother made no attempt to get up the next morning, Donna was reluctant to leave her in the house alone. Nipping next door she asked Blodwyn Hughes if she would fetch the medicine from the chemist.

'Of course I will, my lovely,' Blodwyn told her. 'I'll get your shopping for you as well for the rest of the week, or until your mam is better.'

Donna felt at a loss being at home all the time. Barri took up a great deal of her time and she enjoyed being with him, but it wasn't enough. She felt that she ought to be doing something other than playing with him all day. Since her mother had rather neglected the house over the last few months she decided she would clean through from top to bottom.

In the kitchen she found half-used packets and bottles of foodstuffs. Those that looked very old, or had fungi on them, she discarded. The others she placed at the front of the shelves so that they would be used up next.

The living room was dusty and untidy. The chairs hadn't been moved for so long that there were spiders' webs behind them and rubbish underneath them.

The weather, though cold, was bright and sunny, so Donna decided on a good spring clean. She took down the curtains, washed them and hung them outside to dry. She took up the rugs, slung them over the clothes-line and gave them a good beating. Before she put them back down she scrubbed the linoleum, making sure that every corner was clean.

Satisfied with how much better the place was looking she decided to turn out all the rest of the rooms.

Half an hour later, after tackling her mother's bedroom, while her mother dozed in the armchair downstairs, Donna was wishing she had left well alone. To her horror she discovered several empty vodka bottles hidden at the bottom of the wardrobe. Then she found a half-full bottle of vodka tucked away in a drawer, and a full one between clothes on one of the shelves of a cupboard.

Sitting back on her heels she stared in alarm at the collection of bottles – some empty, some half-full and others unopened – that she had around her. Vodka seemed to have become her mother's stand-by, and it astounded Donna.

Was this the reason why her mam had become so absent-minded, she wondered?

Was this the underlying cause of their home becoming so neglected? Even more important, was her mother's drinking the reason Barri was not being cared for as well as he should be?

Donna thought back to all the symptoms that had become ever more apparent lately. Was it illness or was her mam drunk much of the time? The more she considered the details of her mother's decline the more the possibility that drink was the cause seemed to be true.

The periods of depression, the absent-mindedness, the drifting off into a world of her own, could so easily be the result of her drinking to excess. The unintentional neglect of Barri also seemed to tell the same story.

Lately, too, there had been her avoidance of Blodwyn Hughes and the other neighbours. At one time there had always been people popping in and out. Many, of course, had come to see her about sewing she was doing for them, but lately there had been fewer and fewer having anything made for them.

Donna wondered if that was why her mother had turned to drink. Was it because the work she had done for so many years had slowly disappeared that she had taken to the bottle?

Yet there had been no need for her mam

to feel lonely, Donna argued with herself. Looking after Barri should have kept her busy. If she had wanted to do so she could have taken him for a walk every day. She could have taken him to the park and met other people that way.

Donna wondered if Blodwyn knew about her mother's drinking. She was pretty observant, so it was more than likely that she did suspect there was something like that wrong with her.

Her mother would die of shame if she thought the neighbours knew about her drinking, Donna thought distractedly. Or would she? Did she care any more about what people thought?

When they had been growing up her mam had always been so proud, so intent on them doing the right thing. She was always warning them to behave themselves so as not to let her down. Worrying about what other people thought was so important in her eyes that it was unbelievable that she should have sunk to seeking consolation in drink.

Donna wondered if it had anything to do with the shame she probably felt over Tanwen having Barri, even though she'd been adamant that they must bring him up.

No wonder they were having such a hard time managing, if her mam was buying vodka, Donna thought exasperatedly. She'd never asked her mother to account for how she spent the money she gave her for house-keeping; that would have been unthinkable. From now on, though, she certainly would have to do so, or take charge of their finances herself.

Her pleasure in restoring the house to order ebbed. There were far more important matters filling her mind. If her mother had a drinking problem then it might take weeks or even months to wean her off it. Barri couldn't be left on his own with her, so what on earth was she going to do? If she stayed home to look after him how would they manage without her wages every week?

The advice Tanwen and Dylan had given her before they went back to London, to 'put him in an orphanage', seared her mind. No! Whatever happened that was something she would not do, she told herself resolutely.

She toyed with the idea of asking Blodwyn Hughes to look after him while she was at work, but she wasn't sure that was a good idea. Blodwyn had a heart of gold, but her ideas and the way she did things were rather different. Donna didn't like the way Blodwyn hugged and kissed Tiggy, her big tabby cat, and she hated it when Blodwyn encouraged Barri to do the same.

Even if she did arrange for someone to take care of Barri, it didn't solve the problem of leaving her mother on her own all day. Once she was prevented from drinking she was bound to be morose and unhappy. For a time she would not only need company but someone who cared enough to respond to her moods.

'If I don't work then what are we going to live on?' Donna asked herself again. Then she remembered the package that Dylan had left on the table when he and Tanwen had called on New Year's Day. He'd said it was money to help recompense them for looking after Barri.

Where was it now? She tried to control her feeling of panic. What a fool she'd been not to pick it up and put it somewhere safe. She had been so annoyed by their attitude that she hadn't even given it a second thought. Which meant that her mother must have put it away somewhere.

The realisation that her mother might have been using the money that was in that package to buy bottles of drink for herself hit Donna like a rock.

She had no idea at all how much had been in the package. As she hunted in vain for it, looking in all the drawers and other likely places, she remembered it had been quite a thick envelope.

Surely her mother couldn't possibly have spent it all, she thought in alarm. They needed that money, every penny of it, to live on if she was to stay at home for the next few weeks.

Donna was in such a state of anxiety that she felt she couldn't stay in the house a moment longer. She needed to get outside in the fresh air. Hopefully it would clear her head. It might help her to think more constructively about where her mother could have hidden whatever was left.

Having checked that her mother was sound asleep she peeled off her apron and dressed Barri and herself in their outdoor clothes. Then she popped him in his pram and set out for the park.

She walked quickly, filling her lungs with the fresh spring air. Almost without realising it she walked down Albany Road and Bangor Street to Roath Park.

Barri gurgled happily, bouncing up and down in his pram. She wheeled him round the lake, pointing out to him the brilliant white snowdrops and early golden daffodils springing up from the hard ground. A number of small children were playing by the lake and she knew he wanted to join them, but she felt it was still too early in the year and that it would be too cold for him.

Instead, she took Barri along to the play area. Lifting him from his pram she sat him on the multi-seater rocking horse, where several other mothers were giving their children rides.

The rhythmical motion seemed to steady

her own nerves. By the time they set off for home again she felt calm, and as she walked she began to think of decisive ways to sort out her problems.

If she couldn't go back to James Howell's to work then she'd have to make a living some other way. Could she do what her mother had done, she wondered. Could she take in sewing? She had the skills, and everyone knew she had been the Deputy Manageress in the workroom of The Cardiff Drapers. That in itself was confirmation of her ability to do top-class work.

In next to no time she would be able to win back those people who had brought their dressmaking to her mother in the past, she told herself.

Would Carina Price see it quite that way, or would she feel let down after doing so much to arrange for her to have time off. When she told her about her mother's drinking and how it was no longer safe to leave Barri alone with her, she was sure she'd understand. She'd see that it all made sense, because if Donna was working at home she would be able to keep an eye on her mother. She would also be able to care for Barri at the same time. Once her mother was fully recovered and back to good health again then she would be able to help. She could do some of the sewing or look after Barri part of the time.

With any luck, Donna thought determinedly, between them they should be able to build up a very worthwhile business. The only problem was how they were going to manage for money while she was starting out. People didn't pay in advance so it could be a month or even longer before she was earning any money at all. Much longer before she was earning enough to cover all their expenses.

If only she knew what her mother had done with the money Dylan had given them, then everything would have been plain sailing, she thought sadly.

However, even the fact that her mother might have spent it all didn't deflate her renewed optimism. She felt so much more positive now that she'd had the chance to think things through that she was sure she could overcome all their problems.

Her mother was still asleep when they arrived home. Donna took Barri out of his pram and left him to play with his train. It was still his favourite toy and she was so glad she had bought it for him.

Still full of restless energy, she decided to give Barri's pram a thorough clear out. They wouldn't be needing it until the next day so she'd give it a good clean and polish and wash all the bedding, even the mattress cover.

As she slipped the cover off, something fell

to the ground by her feet. As she bent to pick it up, Donna's heart did a somersault. It was the brown package that Dylan had left.

It had been opened and it was apparent that quite a lot of the money had gone. Even so, as she counted out what was left, Donna felt elated.

Her immediate problems were over. There was enough left to keep them in food and coal for several months if she was prudent.

She couldn't believe her luck. It meant that she would have ample time to get her sewing business up and running.

Chapter Twenty-Three

When Donna told Blodwyn that she was going to start doing dressmaking from home, the same as her mother had done, Blodwyn applauded her decision.

'There's lovely! I'll let people know what you're planning, cariad, shall I? In a couple of weeks you'll be getting orders, you'll see.'

'Do you really think so?' Donna looked dubious. 'There's not that much money about, you know. This old Depression is still biting into all of us and making most people count their pennies.'

'Precisely! All the more reason that if you want a new dress, or an old one turning, you go to a dressmaker rather than to a shop,' Blodwyn affirmed.

'If you can afford it at all!'

'Remember, Donna, Easter is only a couple of weeks away!' Blodwyn's face creased into a smile. 'It's a time most of us like to make a splash with a new frock or hat,' she added confidently.

Donna sighed. 'That's true enough! I do hope you are right, Blodwyn.'

'Of course I am, cariad! Remember now, if you need any help with the little one you have only to ask, see.'

'That's kind of you, Blodwyn. I'm hoping that now Mam is feeling a bit better she'll be able to keep an eye on Barri some of the time. I'll also be able to work while he is having his nap and when he's in bed at night.'

'Now don't go overdoing things, cariad. We don't want you ill as well! Your first priority is that babba and that mam of yours.'

Carina Price was equally encouraging. 'It's a big step, Donna, but I'm sure it will work out for you, just as it did for your mother.'

'I hope so! I shall miss all the girls here, and being able to come to you with my problems,' Donna said shyly.

'I'll always do anything I can to help, Donna. You have only to ask me.'

'Thank you! Perhaps when you have the time you'll come and see Mam,' Donna said tentatively. 'I know she'd love to see you ... and so would I.'

Donna found everything in her life suddenly changed. From not knowing how to fill in her time she discovered that the days weren't long enough to fit in everything she needed to do.

A great number of her mother's old customers returned. Most of them did so because they genuinely preferred having their clothes made for them by a dressmaker rather than buying ready-made ones. Others came out of curiosity. They had heard that Gwyneth had been very ill and they wanted to see for themselves whether or not she was better.

A few also came because they hoped to hear some gossip about Tanwen. Her name had appeared in the *South Wales Echo* several times since her flying visit on New Year's Day. It had been accompanied by glowing reports about how very successful she was becoming as a film star.

To many people's astonishment, Gwyneth didn't always recognise them at first, even though they had been regular customers for years. When they tried questioning her about Tanwen she often claimed that she didn't know anyone of that name or understand what they were talking about.

Donna found herself spending a great deal of valuable time explaining to people that her mother wasn't fully recovered and that her memory was still causing her problems.

The week before Easter Sunday, which was early and fell on 27 of March, Gwyneth complained about pains in her lower back. They were so bad that she insisted on staying in bed.

A few days earlier she had taken Barri out in his pram for a short walk. He had been well wrapped up and tucked up warmly in his deep pram. He'd been safe from the biting March winds, but Gwyneth had come home shivering with the cold.

'I'm wondering if she's caught a chill,' Donna confided to Blodwyn.

'It's more than likely that she has, cariad. When I saw her she had her coat flapping in the breeze. It wasn't fastened up at all, see! You'd have thought she'd have had the sense to do it up.'

'I'm afraid Mam doesn't notice things like that these days. I usually make sure she has her coat fastened, and that she's wearing a scarf and gloves as well as a warm hat before she goes out. Mad busy I was, though, trying to finish a dress that morning.'

'You've got a lot on your plate, cariad,' Blodwyn sympathised. 'You knock on the wall or give me a shout if you need any help.

I can't sew, mind, to save my life,' she laughed, 'but there's plenty of other things I can do to help you, my lovely.'

Blodwyn's kind offer was uppermost in Donna's mind on Good Friday when her mother woke with a high temperature. Her back was so stiff and painful that she couldn't turn over in bed without help.

'I've put a hot-water bottle where she says her back is hurting. I do hope that's going to ease it,' Donna told Blodwyn when she called in to see if they wanted some hot cross buns.

'I'm going to that baker's in Elm Street, he does lovely ones,' Blodwyn told her. 'It wouldn't take me a minute to pop along Crwys Road and knock on Dr Morgan's door and ask him to come and see your mam.'

'On a Good Friday?' Donna looked doubtful. 'I don't think he'd like that, do you?'

'Well, being a doctor he must be used to being called out at inconvenient times. Better now than in the middle of the night.'

Donna shook her head. 'I don't think she's that bad,' she said hesitantly. 'Perhaps the hot-water bottle will ease her back.'

'Whatever you say, cariad. Leave it until this afternoon, shall we? You let me know if she's no better and I'll pop round for him.'

By the middle of the day it was obvious that Gwyneth was considerably worse, so

Donna asked Blodwyn to fetch the doctor. Since it was Good Friday she expected the surgery to be closed, so she gave Blodwyn a note to push through the letterbox.

The doctor was so long coming that Donna began to wonder if he wasn't doing any house calls because it was a holiday. If that was the case then did it mean he wouldn't come until the following Tuesday, she thought worriedly.

Her mother seemed so much worse that she was on the point of knocking on the wall for Blodwyn when there was a loud rap on the front door. Before she could even answer it the door swung open and a tall, dark-haired man strode into the house.

'Dammo di! Who the devil do you think you are walking into my house without so much as a by-your-leave?' Donna snapped angrily.

Her heart was pounding with fear as she looked at him. She judged him to be in his mid to late twenties. He was so tall and broad-shouldered that she knew she was no match for him if it came to a struggle.

'I'm sorry! I didn't mean to frighten you. I'm Dr Gareth Thomson. You sent for me. Where is the patient?'

Donna gulped, feeling embarrassed by her outburst, colour flooding her face.

'I sent for Dr Morgan,' she said lamely.

'He's retired. I have taken over his practice.

Now, can I see the person who is ill?'

'Yes, of course!'

Donna took him upstairs, and in a slightly tremulous voice explained what was wrong with her mother. She also told him about the treatment she'd received from Dr Morgan and the medicines he'd prescribed.

Dr Thomson's tone was quiet and considerate when he spoke to Gwyneth. Donna studied him a little more carefully, aware how gentle his hands were as he examined her mother. She noted his strong, clean-shaven profile and brushed-back dark hair. One look at his strong face with its firm mouth was immediately reassuring.

In his navy three-piece suit, crisp white shirt and sombre tie, he looked so respectable that she was at a loss to understand why she had mistaken him for an intruder. As she followed him downstairs she wondered if she ought to apologise. When he spoke to her, however, his voice was so impersonal that she felt nettled.

'Has your mother been upset by something that has happened recently?'

'What do you mean?' she prevaricated, her voice trembling.

His wide-set, dark brown eyes were keen and thoughtful. 'Has someone close to her died, anything like that?'

Donna cleared her throat, reluctant to open up about their family problems. Not only was he a stranger but he didn't appear to be very much older than she was.

He tapped impatiently on the prescription pad with his gold fountain pen. 'I am a doctor, you know. Anything you tell me will be in confidence,' he said curtly.

'I do need to know the underlying cause of your mother's condition,' he went on when Donna remained silent. 'Now, can you tell me if she drinks?'

Choking with embarrassment and not looking directly at him, Donna told him about the bottles of vodka she'd found in the house.

Dr Thomson nodded gravely. 'I thought as much! I think her present symptoms are to do with her liver. Probably caused by excessive drinking.'

Donna looked shocked. 'Is it serious? Will she get better?'

Dr Thomson's brown eyes held hers for a moment. 'I'm going to send her into Cardiff Infirmary for observation.'

'Will she have to stay in there?'

'It all depends on the treatment the specialist thinks necessary. Pack a bag for her with anything she is likely to need for the next couple of days.'

For a moment Donna felt as if she couldn't breathe.

Before she could recover from the shock of his words he was looking impatiently at his watch and moving towards the door.

'The ambulance should be here within the hour. Make sure she is ready when it arrives. Good day.'

He let himself out before Donna could reply. In a daze she saw him getting into his car and driving away without even a backward glance.

Donna found it hard to believe what he had said or what was happening. She knew her mother was ill. The fact that she was so desperately ill that she needed to go into Cardiff Infirmary and see a specialist left her dumbfounded.

Blodwyn had seen the doctor arrive and the moment she spotted him leaving she came rushing round to hear what he had said.

When Donna told her that he was sending her mother to the Infirmary, and that an ambulance would be there to collect her in about an hour, she was very shocked and concerned.

'Why is that, cariad. Couldn't he work out what was wrong with your mam, then?'

Donna shook her head. She didn't want to let Blodwyn know about the drinking because she knew it would be all round the street within the hour. Blodwyn was a wonderfully kind and helpful neighbour, but she did love a tidbit of gossip. Donna knew that even if she asked her to keep it to herself,

Blodwyn would find it impossible to do so.

'I've never seen that chap before, mind,' Blodwyn went on garrulously. 'Very young, wasn't he! I wonder if he's standing in for Dr Morgan because it's Easter holiday time?'

'No, it's nothing like that, Blodwyn. His name is Dr Gareth Thomson. It seems that Dr Morgan has retired and he has taken over the practice in Crwys Road.'

'Darw! There's a shock for us all. Lovely man, Dr Morgan. You felt so safe in his hands. Years of experience. Now this chap, he looks so young that I would imagine he has only just finished medical school.'

'You're quite right, Blodwyn, he does seem very young to have his own practice. Bit abrupt, too!'

'Not had time to acquire a bedside manner yet, eh?' Blodwyn chuckled.

'Well,' Donna frowned thoughtfully. 'I wouldn't really say that was the case. He was ever so gentle when he examined my mam and he spoke to her in a lovely caring way.'

'Oh? He said something that upset you, did he, cariad?'

'Not really, but he didn't even wait for me to answer the door, he barged right in. I thought I was being attacked!'

'I wouldn't mind being attacked by someone as young and handsome as that,' Blodwyn chortled. Then her face grew serious. 'What are we standing here gabbing for when you've got to get your mam ready.'

'Yes, you're quite right. He told me to pack a bag with anything I thought she might need for a couple of days' stay. I'd better get on and do it before the ambulance arrives. He said it would be here within the hour.'

'Duw anwyl! He must think it very serious if he's in such a rush to get her into hospital with it being holiday time and all.'

'Don't say that, Blodwyn!' Donna ran her hand over her hair, pushing it back from her face. 'I can't bear the thought of her needing an operation or something serious like that.'

'Come on, my lovely, don't take on so. He's probably being extra cautious because he's so young and new to the place. Doesn't know her history, see, like old Dr Morgan did. You should have told him she's not been well for ages.'

'I answered all his questions and told him all I could,' Donna said tersely.

'I'm sure you did, cariad, so stop worrying. They'll find out what's wrong and have her as right as rain in no time. Now, you run along and get that bag packed and make sure your mam is ready so that you don't keep them waiting.'

Donna sighed. 'I haven't even told her what the doctor said yet, or that she has to go to the Infirmary. It's going to be an awful shock for her to find herself being taken away in the ambulance.'

'Then you'd better go along with her,' Blodwyn said practically.

'To the Infirmary, you mean?' Donna looked doubtful. 'That might be a bit upsetting for little Barri, don't you think?'

'Would you like me to keep an eye on Barri for you for an hour or so?'

A look of relief registered on Donna's face. 'Could you, Blodwyn?' She smiled gratefully. 'That would be such a great help.'

'Of course I can, cariad.' Blodwyn frowned thoughtfully. 'I tell you what, why don't I pop him in his pram and take him out for a little walk. Keep him away from the house.'

'That would be wonderful, Blodwyn.'

'I'll keep him around at my place when we get back until after the ambulance has collected your mam. That will give you a chance to go with her in the ambulance and see her settled in properly. Stay as long as they'll let you, cariad. Barri will be fine with me.'

Chapter Twenty-Four

Gwyneth Evans was kept in the Cardiff Infirmary for over a week, undergoing various tests and examinations. The procedure left her muddled and disorientated. When Donna finally took her home on a bright spring day in early April, she had no idea where she'd been or what had been happening to her.

Blodwyn was a great help in looking after Barri and doing their shopping. Donna felt she was doing more for them than her own sister.

She had telephoned Tanwen to tell her that their mother was in hospital, but Dylan had answered her call. He'd seemed quite unperturbed by her news and for a moment she had the uncomfortable feeling that he was trying to flirt with her. He kept telling her how successful things were with them. He had even asked her if she'd ever thought of becoming an actress, and if so then he could help her.

He had sounded like the old Dylan, the one she had loved so deeply and who'd been so full of charm and hare-brained ideas. Listening to his mellifluous voice took her back to the never-to-be-forgotten time when they had been going out together.

Deep, warm and sensual, his voice washed over her like a comforting wave. It stirred memories of the love she'd had for him, even though she'd thought that she'd managed to consign them to the back of her mind.

The magic of the moment vanished in a flash when Dylan refused to let her speak to Tanwen.

'She's far too busy rehearsing! Her part is so critical to the success of the film that I couldn't possibly disturb her!' he declared pompously.

When she tried to persuade him because she felt that it was only right that she should be the one to tell Tanwen about their mother's illness, he refused point-blank.

'Bad news at this stage might have a disastrous effect on her performance, Donna,' he said gravely. 'Like all dedicated artists she is extremely sensitive and very easily upset.'

She could picture him standing there in his flash suit, looking pompous and self-satisfied. He was probably rubbing his hands together at the thought of the success they were achieving, she thought balefully.

'Look, Donna, you can always phone again if Gwyneth gets any worse,' he told her in a patronising voice.

She didn't answer. Taking a deep breath to restrain herself from slamming down the phone, she replaced the receiver.

Outside, the sun was shining with all the brilliance of a fresh, clean spring morning. Knowing that her mother was in bed in a deep sleep and unlikely to be awake before midday, Donna felt the need to get out of the house. She dressed Barri in his outdoor clothes and popped him in his pram, and set out for a brisk walk as far as Cathays Park.

It was a spot she loved visiting. Framed by the beautiful City Hall that was built of sparkling Portland stone, and the imposing Law Courts and Technical College, she always felt that it was the true heart of Cardiff.

The green lawns and colourful flowerbeds in Alexandra Gardens always brightened her mood. The National War Memorial in the centre, with its bronze figures of a soldier, sailor and airman, enclosed by a double circular colonnade of gleaming white stone, never failed to impress her.

She would have been happy to walk round the park all day, but because she had left her mother on her own she contented herself with only a brief visit.

She walked home past The National Museum of Wales. The impressive group of monoliths that stood outside always made her think of a group of workmen waiting to go inside the gleaming Portland stone edifice.

Minutes later she had cut through St Andrew's Place, across the top of Senghennydd Road into Salisbury Road, and was back in Rhymney Street.

She was surprised to see a car outside her front door and Blodwyn standing there talking to a man who was wearing a navy blue suit and a dark trilby.

For a fleeting moment she thought it was Dylan bringing Tanwen to see her mother. Then her heart pounded as she recognised the broad shoulders and stern profile of Dr Gareth Thomson.

He raised his hat as she approached, but there was anger in his dark brown eyes and in the steely tone of his voice.

'Have you left your mother locked in the house on her own,' he asked accusingly.

'She was asleep. I took Barri for a walk. I needed some fresh air,' she defended herself, colour flooding her face.

'Oh, I see!'

The sarcasm in his voice cut through her and she found it difficult to stop herself from saying something she might later regret. Her mother was seriously ill, she reminded herself. She must try to cooperate with him, not antagonise him.

'Donna has a hard time of it looking after her mam and the babba night and day all on

282

her own,' Blodwyn put in quickly.

'Really! Doesn't your husband help you with the child at all?' His dark eyes searched Donna's face enquiringly.

'Darro! Donna's not married!' Blodwyn exclaimed, her double chins shaking with laughter.

Dr Gareth Thomson's eyebrows went up even further. 'Perhaps we should go inside and see if your mother is all right or not,' he said abruptly.

'Yes, of course!' Trembling with confusion, Donna fumbled to unlock the front door.

Impatiently he took the key from her and opened the door. He then went straight upstairs leaving her to follow.

Donna felt incensed. Who did he think he was to act in such a cavalier fashion?

Parking the pram in the hallway, with Barri still strapped inside it, she followed hot on his heels. She was still boiling with anger as she went into the bedroom, but the sight of her mother looking so pale and fragile brought a lump to her throat. Momentarily she forgot how outraged she was feeling about Gareth Thomson's attitude.

Although her mother had appeared to be sleeping she opened her eyes and smiled up at the doctor when he lifted one of her hands so that he could check her pulse.

'She's very weak,' he said, turning to Donna after he had listened to Gwyneth's chest with his stethoscope. 'Is she taking any food?'

'Only soups and milky drinks.'

He frowned. 'Does she get up at all?'

'Oh yes, but not until mid-morning. She sometimes dozes off in her armchair during the afternoon. She's usually back in bed again by about eight o'clock because she says she feels so weak and tired.'

'Yes, I'm afraid that's not going to get any better. It's a lot on your shoulders,' he commented thoughtfully.

'I manage all right,' Donna said quickly. 'If you are thinking that she should be in hospital or somewhere like that then it's out of the question. She would hate that. She likes her home and she loves having Barri around.'

'I see.' He snapped his teeth together sharply as if biting back something he had been about to say. Returning the stethoscope to his bag he shut that with an equally sharp snap.

'I'll look in again in a couple of days' time. If you are worried or her condition deteriorates then call me. Understand?'

Before she could answer he had gone.

Donna stood looking down at her mother with tears in her eyes. She wished Tanwen were there to share some of the responsibility. She kept remembering what a strong, bustling woman her mother had always been, and now she looked so frail that it was heartbreaking. If Dylan had kept the news from Tanwen then she probably didn't even know how ill Mam was, Donna thought sadly.

The sound of Barri crying and the realisation that it was well past his usual mealtime brought Donna out of her reverie. As she prepared food for him she tried to think of ways of stimulating her mother's interest about what was going on. She wondered whether, if she told her about the picture Tanwen was starring in, it might cheer her up. Perhaps they could make plans to go and see it when it came to one of the Cardiff cinemas and that would give her something to look forward to.

Whether it was this or whether it was the medicine that Dr Thomson had given her, Donna wasn't sure, but her mother did seem to improve over the next couple of weeks.

By the middle of May, Gwyneth was not only up and about but feeling well enough to manage a short slow walk as far as the corner shop. On the way home, though, she would lean heavily on Barri's pram for support. It was almost as if her legs were too weak to carry her.

Donna tried to persuade her to sit in a chair in the open doorway so that she could look out and see people passing by, but she frowned on the idea. The only time she would agree to do that was when Barri was playing nearby on his little train.

'You get on with your sewing, then, while I'm keeping an eye on him,' she'd tell Donna.

Donna knew her mother was trying to help, but she found it more and more difficult to put her mind to what she was doing. She still had to keep a close watch on Barri while he was playing. She knew her mother couldn't do anything if he fell over or hurt himself in any way.

Dr Thomson called in once or twice to check on Gwyneth's progress, and on each occasion he managed to say something that made Donna feel he was criticising her.

'I know he's a good doctor, probably better than Dr Morgan, and he's done wonders for my mam, but sometimes he gets right under my skin,' she confided to Blodwyn.

'Duw! I thought you said he had a good bedside manner?'

'It's not his bedside manner I'm talking about! It's the way he speaks to me as if he thinks I'm stupid or something.'

'I don't think that's the case at all, cariad,' Blodwyn said thoughtfully. 'In fact, I think he admires you and the way you are managing to deal with all your problems.'

'I doubt it!' Donna laughed bitterly. 'He's

forever telling me what I should and should not do. He's very good at offering advice that I don't want, or need, on how I should be bringing up Barri.'

'Rubbish, girl! You're imagining it. Think yourself lucky that he does show an interest in the young boyo.'

'Yes, I suppose you're right,' Donna agreed reluctantly. 'Perhaps I'm starting to get jaded in my old age,' she added with a laugh.

'What you need, my lovely,' Blodwyn told her, 'is a break from all this. A bit of a holiday, like. It's time that sister of yours took her turn at looking after your mam. Even if it was only for a few days so that you could get away from it all.'

'I'm not even sure that Tanwen realises how ill Mam is.'

'Dammo di!' Blodwyn's eyes widened. 'Surely you've been in touch with her, cariad, and let her know how poorly her mam is?'

'I tried to. I spoke to Dylan on the phone, but he said he didn't want to tell her at the moment.'

'Why ever not?'

'He said it would distract her while she's working on this new film.'

Blodwyn stared at Donna in disbelief. 'I never heard such nonsense in all my life. It's her mam! She has a right to be told how

287

poorly she is. If he won't tell her then you write a letter to her, cariad. It's your duty to let her know.'

As the days became warmer and were filled with sunshine, Gwyneth seemed to improve so much that Donna put off writing to Tanwen.

Barri was now almost two years old and quite a chatterbox. He was a bundle of joy with his glossy curls and ready smile. She couldn't understand how Tanwen could completely ignore him as if he didn't exist.

It amused her to see that Barri actually managed to win over the stony heart of Dr Gareth Thomson. Whenever he called at the house, Barri would rush to meet him. He would fling his arms round the doctor's legs and then run away squealing with laughter and looking back over his shoulder to see if he was following him.

At first, Donna had tried to restrain Barri's exuberance, but Gareth Thomson had waved her away and joined in Barri's little game. More often than not it would end in a rough and tumble with Barri shrieking with excitement and the doctor looking more than a little dishevelled.

Donna often found herself thinking about Gareth Thomson when she was on her own. His handsome face, dark eyes and strong brow seemed to be engraved on her mind.

Although he was a regular visitor to see her mother she knew absolutely nothing about his background except that he had taken over Dr Morgan's practice.

She'd discreetly questioned Blodwyn, knowing she garnered every scrap of gossip imaginable, but even Blodwyn didn't know if he had a family or not.

Donna considered him to be a good doctor and knew her mother trusted him implicitly, even though he was young enough to be her son.

It was his manner towards her that Donna still found disturbing. When he spoke to her he avoided her eyes and his tone always seemed to be so curt. It was as if for some reason he didn't like her.

In the early days, because he was a doctor, she'd treated him with deference. Now she was far more spirited in her replies and she no longer brooded over any criticism he levied.

Secretly, though, she did glow with pleasure whenever he managed a word of praise, and lately this had become more frequent.

He was very pleased with the way her mother had progressed. He even went as far as to say that it had a lot to do with the care and encouragement that Donna had given her.

When she'd expressed her relief and commented that perhaps the time had come to dispense with his services, he looked taken aback.

Before she could add that she would send for him immediately if she thought her mother needed him, he'd picked up his bag and walked out of the house.

Chapter Twenty-Five

Donna found she was not the only one who missed Dr Gareth Thomson's regular visits. Almost every day her mother asked plaintively why the nice young doctor hadn't been to see her.

Whenever there was a knock on the front door Barri would rush towards it squealing, 'Doco, doco,' at the top of his voice. When he found it was someone else he would retreat, thumb in mouth and a woebegone look in his dark brown eyes.

Donna grew tired of trying to placate them both. She missed Gareth Thomson every bit as much as they did, although she refused to admit it even to herself. Every day she hoped he might stop by to see how her mother was getting on.

The knowledge that he was looking after her mother so well had been a tremendous comfort. The fact that he had become so fond of Barri, and brought some fun into his little life, had filled her with pleasure.

This was what she missed most of all, she told herself; his sessions with Barri. It had been wonderful to see them playing together. Their rough and tumble games were always sufficiently restrained to ensure that Barri was never hurt. He might end up completely breathless and exhausted, but always laughing and without any bruises or tears.

Gareth Thomson was, after all, the only man Barri ever saw, Donna reminded herself. All the other people who came to their house were women. Usually customers who wanted some sort of sewing done for them or who were calling to collect finished work.

The moment Dr Gareth Thomson came into the house, Donna reflected, the entire atmosphere seemed to change for the better. He was always so smartly dressed, self-assured and knowledgeable, that he inspired trust and confidence in all of them.

Although initially he had often been critical, or had spoken to her sharply, recently he seemed to have become more tolerant and had praised her far more than he criticised.

Donna found herself fantasising about him more and more. When she was depressed or worried about something, she tried to imagine what he would say if she asked him for advice. As the weeks passed, these fantasies became part of her life.

Her mother kept remarkably well all through July and the beginning of August. She was still weak and disinclined to do very much, but she was surprisingly cheerful.

It sometimes worried Donna that her mother never mentioned Tanwen or asked about her. Then common sense took over and she realised that to some degree it was better that way. At least she wasn't fretting because she never saw Tanwen.

The much-promoted film that Tanwen was starring in still hadn't reached Cardiff. Anyway, she doubted if her mother was well enough to go to the cinema to see it even if it did.

Donna had to admit that Dylan had kept to his word about supporting Barri. On the first of every month a substantial money order arrived. More and more, though, Donna found that she was using it to meet their bills instead of saving it for when Barri was older as she had planned to do.

There was never even a brief note in the envelope from them, though, or even an address. She did have a telephone number, which she assumed would still reach them if ever there was an emergency. She hadn't used it since she had phoned to tell Tanwen that their mam was ill and Dylan had refused to let her speak to Tanwen.

It seemed incredible to her that neither of them wanted to see Barri. He was now such a sturdy little boy with a winning smile and enchanting chatter. He would soon be two, and Donna was planning a little party for him. She had already invited Blodwyn.

She bought Barri a big cuddly rabbit with long floppy ears for his birthday She left it at the bottom of his cot, knowing he would spot it as soon as he wakened.

She could hear him crowing with delight even before she went into the room that had once been Tanwen's. His face was radiant as he hugged it to him, burying his face in the golden furry pile.

Blodwyn also brought him a present when she came to his little party. Donna helped him to unwrap the bright paper and then showed him how to use the rubber hammer to knock the wooden pegs into the holes of the little wooden stand.

At first his aim was so wild that each blow went wide of the mark, but he soon got the hang of it. He banged it down on them as hard as he could, chortling with glee when he hit one of the pegs and managed to knock it in level with the surface of the stand.

He refused to let go of the hammer when it was time to eat his tea so Donna let him hold on to it rather than have him tearful. She ignored his antics completely until he banged it down hard on his china dish.

The accident happened in seconds. One minute they were enjoying their little party, and the next fragments of china were flying everywhere. There was a penetrating scream from Barri and to her horror, Donna saw that his face was covered in blood. There was blood spattered all over his new red shorts and little white shirt that Donna had made him for his birthday.

Thinking a piece of the broken dish must have flown up and cut him she wiped it away quickly, worried in case it had done any damage to his eyes. To Donna's amazement there was no sign of any cut or gash anywhere on his little face.

As he rubbed his hand across his eyes to brush away his tears, however, a heavy smear of blood appeared all over his face again.

'Darro! It must be his little arm that's cut and bleeding, not his face at all,' Blodwyn exclaimed agitatedly.

Between them they managed to calm Barri's screams and hold him still while they tried to find out where he had hurt himself.

The cut, they discovered, was across his wrist. It seemed to be quite deep and the blood was pumping out steadily.

'What do we do now? He'll bleed to death if we aren't careful,' Blodwyn gasped.

'It needs pressure on it,' Donna said. 'Put

your thumb hard down on his arm just above the cut while I find a bandage.'

Barri's piercing screams and the sight of so much blood distressed Gwyneth. She began to shake and the colour drained from her face as if she was about to faint.

'Try putting your head down onto your lap, Mam, or take some deep breaths, while I see to Barri,' Donna told her anxiously.

'What's happened to him, though?' Gwyneth gasped. 'He's got blood all over him. It's coming right through that piece of bandage.'

'Your mam's right,' Blodwyn said worriedly. 'Do you think he may have cut an artery? All this blood, see! It must be something serious, you know. Look, I'd better go and fetch the doctor.'

Donna nodded rather cautiously. She knew Blodwyn was right. The cut must be very deep from the rate that Barri was losing blood. Putting a bandage on it probably wasn't enough, she thought worriedly.

'Go on, then, Blodwyn. I'll try and staunch it until you get back. If Dr Thomson's not there, seeing that it's Saturday, then perhaps I ought to take Barri to the hospital.'

'No, Dr Thomson would be best, as Barri knows him. Be less frightening for him, cariad,' Blodwyn assured her.

'Hurry up, then! You'd better leave the front door open in case I can't put him down to come and open it when you get back.'

Blodwyn arrived back with the doctor within minutes. He took in the situation the moment he came into the house. Deftly, he stemmed the flow of blood from Barri's wrist and applied a dressing.

Holding Barri on his knee and talking to him in a soothing tone to calm him down, Gareth Thomson looked across at Donna, his dark brows drawn together in a puzzled frown. 'How did it happen?' he asked.

'Today is his birthday, it was one of his presents,' Donna explained abjectly, her lower lip trembling.

His eyebrows went up as he looked at the rubber hammer and the broken dish. 'A very silly sort of toy to buy for a child of two!'

'Dammo di! Hold on! It was nothing to do with Donna, I was the one who bought him that toy,' Blodwyn blustered. She was still puffing from having rushed to the Crwys Road surgery, but she didn't intend letting Donna take the blame for the accident.

Gareth Thomson's mouth clamped shut in a tight line, but he said no more. Still cradling Barri in his arm he walked up and down the room, all the time talking to him soothingly.

In next to no time Barri had stopped crying and was laughing up at him.

'His wrist may be sore for a few days, but

it will heal quickly. Provided the wound is kept sterile there shouldn't be any problem. I'll call in and change the dressing, so don't attempt to do it yourself,' he added.

'Thank you!' Donna said gratefully. She hesitated, then asked nervously, 'Since it's Barri's birthday would you join us for a cup of tea and a slice of Barri's birthday cake? It's only a home-made sponge,' she added shyly.

He smiled back at her and nodded. 'I think I've earned such a treat, don't you?'

'I'll make a fresh pot, the kettle is boiling,' Blodwyn volunteered. 'It's the least I can do, seeing it was all my fault that the accident happened,' she added ruefully.

'I think you need to do more than that in order to make amends for what has happened,' Gareth Thomson told her sternly as she poured out his tea.

'You do?' Blodwyn looked startled and put the teapot down with a thump. 'The young boyo is going to be all right once the cut's healed, isn't he?' she asked anxiously.

Gareth Thomson looked at her gravely. 'Barri will be fine in a couple of days. Even so, you've upset Donna very badly.'

'Darw, I know that and I am very sorry,' Blodwyn sighed. 'Thoughtless I was, and I regret it.'

'That's why I'm going to give you a chance to make amends,' he pronounced.

Blodwyn looked puzzled. 'What do you mean?' she asked apprehensively.

'I want you to stay here for a couple of hours, and take care of Barri and keep Mrs Evans company, while I take Donna out. I think it is what she needs to make a full recovery,' he added, with a twinkle in his dark brown eyes.

It took Blodwyn a few seconds to comprehend his meaning and then she smiled widely, her double chins shaking as she nodded her head enthusiastically.

'The perfect medicine,' she agreed heartily. 'Go on, Donna, go and get yourself ready.'

Donna looked from Blodwyn to Gareth Thomson in confusion. 'I don't think I understand what you are both talking about?'

'Of course you do, cariad,' Blodwyn laughed. 'The doctor is going to take you out and I'm going to stay here and look after Barri and your mam. Go on, then, don't keep the doctor waiting.'

Donna felt the colour flooding her face as she tried to convince herself that she wasn't dreaming. It was as if one of her many fantasies was suddenly coming true, and she found it hard to comprehend.

The very fact that Gareth Thomson was there in the house again was disconcerting enough. The thought of being taken out by him, after the way she had inadvertently upset him, was beyond her greatest expectations.

'Off you go, then! I'll clear up here,' Blodwyn repeated. She gave Donna a little push. 'You two go out and enjoy yourselves. Stay out as long as you like, I'll be quite happy sitting here chatting with your mam, Donna.'

'Yes, but what about Barri? It is his birthday, so I should be here with him,' Donna protested half-heartedly. 'I really do think so, especially after the terrible fright he's had.'

'He's quite all right now, you have nothing to worry about,' Gareth Thomson assured her. 'By tomorrow morning he will have forgotten all about it. Children are very resilient, you know.'

'That's right. He's had a lovely little party and enjoyed himself no end, even though he's too young to know what it's all been about,' Blodwyn agreed.

She picked Barri up and cuddled him. 'I'll put him to bed and tuck him in later on when it's time to do so. He'll be safe enough with me, so you run along and have a nice time.'

Donna looked at her mother, but Gwyneth had her eyes closed and was snoring gently.

'Hurry up, then, Donna,' Blodwyn urged. 'Nip and change your dress, cariad, it's got splashes of blood all over it. Go and have a nice time. It's what the doctor ordered, remember,' she chuckled.

Donna looked down at her light green cotton dress, shocked to see the mess it was in. There were brown specks where Barri's blood had splattered onto it and bigger blotches from where she had been nursing him.

'I'll have to put this one to soak in cold water right away,' she said ruefully. 'Even then I'm not sure that these marks will come out.'

'I'll see to your dress,' Blodwyn offered. 'You get changed and I'll put it to soak for you.'

As she went upstairs, Donna's heart was singing. She couldn't believe she was actually going out with Gareth Thomson.

She had no idea where he was taking her, but she decided it called for something smart. At the back of her wardrobe, covered over with a piece of sheeting to keep it in pristine condition, was a pretty blue crêpe-de-Chine dress that her mother had made her for a special occasion. She had never worn it because Dylan had gone off with Tanwen.

She slipped it on and was delighted at the transformation. The softly draping skirt clung to her curves like a second skin, making her look extremely sophisticated.

Even though she knew that his invitation was only a friendly gesture because she had been so upset by the accident, she felt as elated as if she was a young girl on her first date.

Chapter Twenty-Six

Donna's evening out with Dr Gareth Thomson was far different from anything she had imagined in her wildest fantasies.

She had expected him to take her to the Capitol Restaurant in Queen Street, which was why she had put on her blue dress, but she was mistaken. Once he had settled her in his car, which was parked right outside her front door, he drove straight through the centre of Cardiff, past Cardiff General Station, and then headed west.

It was a lovely warm August evening and a heat haze shimmered on the road as they drove towards Penarth. When they reached the headland Gareth drove slowly along the Esplanade. Then he stopped, and they both sat there for several minutes in silence, looking out over the bluff headland to the sparkling waters beyond.

Gareth looked at his wristwatch and frowned. 'I was planning to take you to the

Esplanade Hotel, but it is a little too early. I doubt if they have started serving dinner yet. Shall we go for a walk?'

'Yes, I'd like that,' Donna nodded, and waited for him to open the car door for her.

As they joined the knots of people already strolling along the promenade, Donna wondered if it was all a dream. She almost had to pinch herself to be convinced that she was actually in Penarth and walking side by side with Dr Gareth Thomson as if they were old friends, and not simply imagining it.

She kept glancing sideways, surprised to find he was not as tall as she had thought. He was so broad-shouldered that it gave him a powerful presence, an air of authority that made him appear to be a bigger man than he was.

Donna felt proud to be seen with him. He was so good-looking. His face looked lean and strong, with his thick dark hair brushed back from his broad brow and his perceptive dark eyes. As they strolled beneath the cliffs in Windsor Gardens he appeared so smart in his grey flannels and cream linen jacket that she felt everyone was giving him admiring glances.

She wished she knew more about him. Blodwyn had done her best to find out about his background but to no avail. All she had discovered was that he lived at the surgery in Crwys Road and that he didn't appear to be married.

'He has a housekeeper, mind! She's a crabbed-looking old biddy with grey hair drawn back in a bun and sharp black eyes. She looks at you as if she doesn't believe a word you're saying,' Blodwyn reported after one of her visits.

'You mean she acts as his guardian angel?' Donna smiled.

'She's more like a watchdog than an angel,' Blodwyn laughed. 'She's always dressed in black with a starched white apron covering her dress. She reminds me of a matron in charge of a hospital more than someone's housekeeper.'

'Perhaps that is exactly what she was in an earlier part of her life,' Donna reasoned.

'Yes! The matron from the hospital where he did his training?' Blodwyn had suggested.

Glancing sideways, Donna wondered if she dared to ask him about his housekeeper. If she did then perhaps once the ice was broken he would tell her more about himself.

She hesitated to do so because at the moment she was enjoying his company so much that she didn't want to spoil the magic of the occasion.

They paused further along the Esplanade and leaned on the railings. Seagulls were swooping and skimming over the water and there were yachts sailing in the waters ahead. Donna was taken by surprise when a group consisting of two men and a young lady stopped to speak to them.

Gareth shook hands with the two men and kissed the young woman on the cheek. Donna felt a mixture of curiosity and dismay that was almost akin to jealousy churning inside her as she saw the delight on the girl's face.

As Gareth introduced them to her she felt gauche and out of place. The two men, William and Freddy, were wearing immaculate white trousers, and smartly tailored navy blue blazers which had gold emblems on the breast pockets and shiny gilt buttons. They both had white caps trimmed with navy and gold braid which they wore at a jaunty angle.

Rebecca, who had a pert young face and short-cropped fair hair, was very self-assured. She was dressed in a short white skirt and a navy blazer almost identical to the ones the men were wearing.

Donna was conscious of Rebecca giving her an appraising look, and that her lips were twitching as if she was trying to stop herself smirking.

As their eyes met, Rebecca looked away and concentrated her attention on Gareth. Donna felt uncomfortable. It was almost as if she was being dismissed as of no importance. She was acutely aware that although her dress would look perfect once they were in the Esplanade Hotel she must appear rather overdressed for strolling along the promenade.

She felt so excluded as Gareth exchanged banter and news of mutual friends with them that she was tempted to walk on, even though she knew that it would be very rude of her to do so. Then she remembered that she had to rely on Gareth Thomson to take her home in his car, so she bit down on her lower lip and tried to concentrate on the scenery.

'We've booked a table for dinner at the Esplanade Hotel. How about joining us, Gareth?' William suggested. He grinned self-consciously 'That's, of course, if you don't mind us being in our naval attire. We've been sailing all day, and we've only come ashore to eat.'

'Please do come with us, Garry,' Rebecca begged, clinging to his arm, her blue eyes pleading. 'It would give us a chance to bring you up-to-date on all the gossip. You can tell us whether being in general practice is better than walking the wards.'

Donna held her breath. Gareth had already told her that he was taking her to the Esplanade Hotel for dinner. The thought of making up a party with his friends sent shudders through her. It seemed that not only had they all been at university together, but that they were all in the medical profession. How could she hope to understand half of what they'd be talking about, she thought miserably.

She felt both relieved and very grateful as she heard Gareth say, 'That would have been pleasant, but I'm afraid it's out of the question. We've already made other arrangements.'

Rebecca pouted prettily as she looked up at him, fluttering her lashes provocatively. 'Promise me you'll get in touch very soon, then, so that we can have dinner together,' she insisted.

It reminded Donna very much of Tanwen's behaviour. Briefly, some of the sunshine went out of her day.

'Sorry about that, Donna,' Gareth apologised as they walked away 'As you probably gathered, they are old friends from university days. I'm sure you don't want to spend your evening listening to us reminiscing about past events,' he smiled.

'If you would rather be with them I do understand,' she said stiffly.

'Of course I wouldn't! There is one problem, of course! We can't have dinner at the Esplanade Hotel now, so we will have to look for somewhere else. I'm not sure if we'll find anywhere else in Penarth that comes up to quite the same standard.'

Eventually they found a delightful, small restaurant further along the promenade. They were given a table by the window, and, as they sat looking out over the Bristol Channel, Donna felt it was a corner of heaven. It was far better suited to her taste than the grandeur of the Esplanade Hotel.

Being with Gareth Thomson was what mattered to her. She wanted them to be on their own, not in the company of his university friends.

They talked very little during their meal, too busy concentrating on the delicious food and wine. Afterwards they moved out on the balcony where the air was cooler, and Donna felt completely enchanted by her surroundings.

She had never witnessed such an impressive sunset. It was as if someone had used a giant paintbrush to splash golds and reds in a glorious riot across the deep azure sky. The gulls still swooped and dived, their keening plaintive on the still evening air. Slowly the sun dipped into the sea, leaving a dull orange band on the horizon.

As they lingered there, drinking their coffee in the warm darkness of the late August evening, Gareth started talking about himself.

'Those friends we met were at medical school as well as at university with me,' he explained. 'William and Frederick now specialise in their particular fields. Rebecca works in a hospital in Swansea. All three of them are mad about yachting.'

'You're not keen on sailing?'

He shrugged. 'It's a very expensive pastime. It's not one I've ever been able to afford. My father died before I was born and my mother died while I was still at school.'

'That's very sad,' Donna murmured.

'My Aunt Menna, my mother's sister, paid for my university education,' Gareth went on. 'As soon as I qualified she was keen for me to have my own practice. I was working at Llandough Hospital for just over three years when she heard that Dr Morgan was about to retire and wanted to sell his practice in Crwys Road.'

'So you have no other family at all?' Donna said in surprise.

He frowned. 'No, only my Aunt Menna, who lives with me and acts as my housekeeper.'

It had probably been his Aunt Menna that Blodwyn had described as a dragon, she realised with amusement. She certainly did sound a rather formidable person, but at least he wasn't a married man, Donna thought with relief.

He sipped his coffee. 'I suppose I should have been more adventurous after I qualified. I did once have the idea of becoming a ship's doctor. I thought that way I could travel all over the world before settling down.'

'What made you change your mind?'

He shrugged. 'I felt I owed it to my Aunt Menna to do as she'd asked. She wanted me to take on the practice in Crwys Road so that she could live with me. She'd been so generous paying for me to go to medical school that I felt I owed it to her to keep her company as she grew older.'

'Have there always been doctors in your family, then?'

'Yes, my father, and grandfather both practised medicine in mid-Wales. Aunt Menna was Matron at a hospital in Machynlleth.' He smiled. 'The only break with tradition that I have made is to come to Cardiff instead of staying in the shadow of Cader Idris.'

'Why did you do that?'

'Cader Idris was the mountain that claimed my father's life,' he said in clipped tones. 'He went to help rescue a climber who had been injured. It was midwinter, the mountainside was covered in snow and ice. He slipped and fell to his death.'

The memory seemed to cast a shadow and bring their evening to a sudden end. Pushing back his chair he held out his hand and pulled Donna to her feet.

'We ought to be getting back to the

invalids,' he smiled. 'I'm sure Blodwyn will be ready for her own bed by now.'

'It has been a wonderful evening and I've enjoyed every minute of it,' Donna told him as he pulled up outside her front door.

He leaned towards her and the next moment she felt his breath warm on her face as his lips met hers. Her heart quickened as she felt their firm pressure.

'Good! So have I!' He took her hand, 'We must do it again. Sometime soon if we can persuade Blodwyn to look after your mother and Barri again.'

When she went to bed that night Donna went over every minute of her outing, especially their fleeting goodnight kiss and the words he had said afterwards, about wanting to take her out again. She wondered whether he had meant them or merely said it out of politeness.

She went over every moment of the time they had spent together. His kiss, though brief, had left her in a state bordering pure happiness, and on reflection she felt convinced that he had meant it when he said they must go out together again.

Chapter Twenty-Seven

As he drove away from Rhymney Street, Gareth Thomson was humming happily to himself. He had enjoyed his evening.

He had found Donna such a sympathetic listener that he'd told her far more about himself than he'd ever revealed to anyone.

Mentally he compared her with Rebecca. He could never have confided in her as he had in Donna, he thought with surprise. Even if he had tried to do so she would not have concentrated on what he was saying. Instead she would have interrupted and started chattering on about some concern of her own.

He had meant it when he'd told Donna that he hoped that they could go out together again. He didn't see anything to stop them doing so. Not as long as there was someone available to keep her mother company and look after the baby.

He must try to find out more about Donna's background and how she came to have such a young child. Not that he'd given her much chance to talk about herself, he thought with a rueful smile. He had been too busy divulging his own history.

He wondered what Aunt Menna would think of Donna? She'd probably like her quiet manner and neat appearance. Would his aunt hold it against her that she had a little boy of two and yet she wasn't married?

A dark presentiment of what her opinion would be swept over him. Despite her wide experience of human nature, which she had gleaned from working as a hospital matron, he knew to his cost that Aunt Menna had a strong puritanical streak.

Somehow, before he introduced them to each other, he had to find a way of telling Aunt Menna about Barri. Perhaps arranging for her to meet the little boy might be one solution. For all her apparent starchiness she had a very soft heart when it came to children.

He often wondered why his aunt had never married. She was far too reserved to discuss such matters with him and he'd never had the temerity to ask her. He might be almost thirty but he still held her in awe, and he wouldn't dare to ask her such a personal question.

He was very fond of Aunt Menna and knew that he had a responsibility to incorporate her future welfare in any plans he might make. He would never forget all she had done for him since his parents had died. For that reason alone he felt that it was his duty to look after her and provide her with a home for the rest of her days.

The present arrangement, whereby she acted as his housekeeper, suited them both very well. It made her feel wanted and involved. He found it reassuring to know that he could call on her skill and expertise in an emergency.

Until this moment, though, it had never crossed his mind how things would work out if he ever told her he was planning to get married.

A great deal, of course, would depend on the girl of his choice. She would have to like Aunt Menna, and she would have to be able to get along with her. Equally important, Aunt Menna would have to approve of her. They would need to get on well if living in the same house was to work smoothly.

The alternative, he mused, would be to divide up the house in Crwys Road into separate establishments. His surgery and waiting room already took up most of the ground floor, apart from the large living room at the back of the premises. That, and the kitchen behind it, was where Aunt Menna spent most of her day.

Would there be enough space in the rest of the premises to provide Aunt Menna, as well as himself, with separate living space, he wondered.

He had never even considered such an arrangement before. Now, suddenly, it seemed to be of paramount importance. He couldn't wait to check it out so that he knew whether it was feasible for them to have separate establishments.

The moment he arrived home, despite the lateness of the hour, he found pencil, paper and tape measure. Then he began going around the building and taking measurements.

Disturbed by his activities, Menna Vaughan came to see what he was doing. She had been getting ready for bed and was wearing a long red flannel dressing gown over her white cotton nightdress. Her iron-grey hair, by day constricted in a tight bun, was hanging loose to her shoulders and made her look older and more vulnerable.

'What on earth do you think you are doing, Gareth? I thought the place was being burgled!'

'Sorry, Aunt Menna, I didn't mean to disturb you. I simply wanted to work out how much living space we had here.'

'More than enough for the two of us, as you would know if you were the one who had to keep it clean,' she told him balefully.

'Then you must have more domestic help,' he told her, sitting back on his heels and taking the pencil from between his lips so that he could answer her. 'I told you before that I didn't think a woman coming in three times a week to do the heavy cleaning was

314

anywhere near enough. I'm sure we can make better arrangements than that.'

'I've already told you that I can manage perfectly well!' she said sharply. 'Anyway, I'm sure you're not measuring up the place this late at night in order to discuss our cleaning arrangements,' she challenged pointedly.

He shook his head. 'It was merely an idea I had about the place. I won't trouble you with my thoughts at this time of night.'

'Now that I'm here, perhaps I should make us both a cup of cocoa and then you can tell me where you went tonight.'

As he followed her into their cosy living room, Gareth wondered whether to mention his idea of dividing up the house or not. He didn't want to worry her in any way. It wasn't as though there were likely to be any developments in his personal life that would call for such action for a long time yet.

Instead, as they sat there drinking their cocoa he told her about meeting up with William, Freddy and Rebecca.

He saw her mouth tighten the moment he mentioned Rebecca's name, and too late he remembered how much Aunt Menna disliked her.

'And I suppose Rebecca was simpering and fluttering her eyelashes and fawning all over you,' she murmured contemptuously.

'I'm surprised that you're still seeing her after the way she treated you.'

Gareth felt his colour rising. 'It was an accidental meeting!'

'So what was she doing here in Cardiff? How did she know where you were living if you haven't been keeping in touch with her?' Aunt Menna asked in an irritated voice.

'I didn't meet her here in Cardiff. The three of them had been sailing at Penarth.'

'Penarth! So what were you doing there? Trying to escape from your patients?'

'No,' he smiled. 'Nothing like that. I ... I was taking a friend out for dinner.'

'Not a patient I hope. Surely you know better than to commit an indiscretion of that sort,' she said sharply.

'No, she's not a patient, although I do attend her mother. That is how we met,' he explained.

'Ah!' Her sharp eyes gleamed. 'You mean you've been taking the Evans girl out. Her name is Donna, isn't it? Hmm! You do know she has a child?'

Gareth looked taken aback. 'Yes, of course I do! He's called Barri, he's just turned two years old. How do you know so much about her?'

'I live here in Cathays, too, remember. I use several of the local shops. While I'm waiting to be served I listen to the women gossiping. Patients also talk amongst themselves in the waiting room, you know.'

'I see!' Gareth frowned. 'So you've picked up all this information merely by listening to what other people are saying.'

'How else? I've never met the girl! You've never brought her back here,' she added blandly.

'I've only been out with her once! I'm hardly likely to bring her home to meet you on such a short acquaintance,' he pointed out.

'I did consider going along to her house in Rhymney Street and asking her to make me a dress. That way I thought that perhaps I could find out more about her and even see what sort of home she came from,' she told him. 'I didn't, though! I thought it might prove embarrassing when you eventually brought her here and she found out who I was. She might think that I'd been spying on her,' she added with a twinkle in her sharp eyes.

'When I brought her here?' He felt bewildered. He'd never even mentioned Donna to his aunt and yet she knew more about her than he did himself. What was more to the point she was already assuming that he had serious intentions towards the girl.

Aunt Menna put down her empty cup on the table and looked at him gravely. 'Don't rush things, Gareth.'

'I don't know what you mean, Aunt Menna. You are the one who is rushing ahead and assuming things before they have even entered my head. I took Donna out for a meal tonight, that's all there is to it.'

'She seems to be a very hard-working girl and she's devoted to her mother and to that little boy,' his aunt said cautiously.

'Donna doesn't go out to work!' Gareth responded, running his hand through his thick hair in bewilderment.

'She did! Until quite recently she worked at The Cardiff Drapers, James Howell's emporium on St Mary Street,' she told him.

'Really?'

'Her mother did dressmaking from home before she was taken ill. Now, I understand, the daughter is trying to run the business and look after her mother and the child at the same time.'

'You've certainly done your homework, Aunt Menna,' he conceded dryly.

'Yes, well, you were about to do some yourself, weren't you,' she replied calmly. 'You were trying to work out if there was room for her to come and live here if you did decide to ask her to marry you and she accepted.'

'If you say so,' he grinned. He felt too bowled over to enter into an argument with his aunt. He couldn't fathom how she had managed to glean so much information about Donna when they had never even spoken to each other.

'I'm not sure if she would be the sort of girl I would pick for you,' Aunt Menna told him bluntly. 'Of course, she is certainly a far better choice than Rebecca Hughes.'

'Is that a half seal of approval?' Gareth grinned.

His aunt didn't smile. 'I think you should wait until you know her a lot better before you commit yourself,' she warned.

'Are you trying to tell me that I should find out more about her background?'

'She's had a very different upbringing to you, Gareth. She left school at fourteen and went straight to work as an apprentice dressmaker. You've not only had a university education but you come from a medical background. There's a wide cultural difference.'

'Aunt Menna, I never thought of you as a snob!' Gareth exclaimed in a shocked voice.

'I'm not being snobbish, purely realistic. This Donna is a pretty little thing, but remember that looks fade and by the time she is middle-aged all her physical appeal may have gone. That is why you need a wife who has been educated to the same standard as yourself if you are to be lifetime companions, otherwise you'll outgrow her.'

'What an utter load of nonsense!' Gareth

retorted angrily. 'I'm surprised to find you thinking like that.'

'These things are important, Gareth. What do you know about the rest of her family? There's a lot of gossip about her twin sister. I don't suppose she's ever mentioned that she has a twin. Another thing, has she ever told you anything about the child's father?'

His eyebrows went up. 'You mean you haven't managed to get those details, Aunt Menna?' he asked sardonically.

'Not yet, but I shall do so in time. I only hope I'm not in for too many shocks. Now, I'm off to bed, and I think you should leave your conversion ideas until tomorrow.' She gave him a probing glance. 'There isn't any immediate hurry, is there, my dear?'

Chapter Twenty-Eight

Gareth Thomson found himself rushed off his feet when an influenza epidemic hit Cardiff in mid-September 1932. He was so busy night and day that he frequently slept in his clothes. Often he relied on Aunt Menna to deal with patients who were well enough to call at the surgery about their condition.

He'd had no time at all to make any progress with either his friendship with Donna or developing his ideas about his plans for the house.

He'd not seen Donna on her own since the night in August when they'd gone to Penarth. He'd asked her out twice, but on both occasions she'd had to decline. The first time her mother had not been very well and she hadn't wanted Donna to leave her. On the second occasion Blodwyn had not been feeling well enough to sit with Gwyneth Evans and Barri.

He kept thinking about all the things his Aunt Menna had told him about Donna and was puzzled by some of them. He wanted to hear the facts from Donna and not rely on gossip or information his aunt had over-heard.

As he hurried from one house to the next in Cathays, Gareth Thomson kept wondering when the epidemic was going to peak. Equally important, he wondered if he could manage to keep going until it did.

It raged for another three weeks before the calls began to slow down. By that time he felt utterly exhausted, and also deeply worried about his Aunt Menna who looked worn out.

It seemed incredible that neither of them had caught flu, and he hoped that now the outbreak seemed to be abating they wouldn't do so. In another week things should be back to normal. Once that happened he hoped to pick up the threads of his personal life once again.

When Blodwyn called into the surgery to ask if he could visit Gwyneth Evans because she'd gone down with influenza, he felt concerned yet at the same time pleased at the thought of seeing Donna.

To his dismay he found that because of all her other complications, Gwyneth was in a very bad way.

He sent Blodwyn along to the chemist to collect the medicines he prescribed, and he promised Donna he would return again later in the day to see how her mother was. 'It's highly infectious so try and keep little Barri out of the bedroom, you don't want to have him ill as well,' he warned.

When he returned later that evening, Gwyneth was still running a high temperature and she was having trouble breathing. 'Send for me if you are worried or if she gets any worse, no matter what time it is,' he reminded Donna as he was leaving.

The first light of a damp early-October morning was bringing in a new day when Donna hammered on the surgery door in Crwys Road.

Menna Vaughan, shrouded in her red flannel dressing-gown, her grey hair hidden inside a black hairnet, answered the door.

'Worse, is she, Donna?' she said tersely.

'Doctor will be with you in about ten minutes.'

Donna nodded. As she hurried back to Rhymney Street it crossed her mind that she hadn't said who she was or where she lived.

Flustered, she wondered if she ought to go back. As she hesitated she recalled that his aunt, or housekeeper, whatever she was, had called her Donna.

It surprised her, but she accepted that Gareth had been in practice for several months now so it was probably natural that she knew all that was going on and even recognised his patients.

Blodwyn was standing on her doorstep when she got back home. 'Duw anwyl! What are you doing out, my lovely? Your little boyo's awake and crying his heart out.'

'I've been along to Crwys Road to ask Gareth Thomson to call.'

'Why on earth didn't you bang on my door, cariad? You know I would have nipped to the surgery for you. Your mam's worse, is she?'

'Yes, but I didn't want to disturb you, Blodwyn. You didn't get to bed all that early yourself.'

'I don't need all that much sleep, cariad. You don't as you get older, see. Now what can I do to help? Is the doctor on his way?'

Donna nodded. 'Yes, his housekeeper said she'd call him and he'd be with me in about ten minutes.'

Blodwyn nodded. 'Would you like me to take little Barri back to my place. I can give him a wash, get him dressed and give him some breakfast. That way he'll be out of your way while the doctor's looking at your mam.'

'Oh, Blodwyn, that would be a wonderful help,' Donna told her gratefully.

Blodwyn had just taken Barri to her house when Gareth's car drew up. He examined Gwyneth Evans very thoroughly, talking to her gently and trying to allay her fears. His face was grave, though, as he turned to Donna.

'How bad is she?'

He shook his head. 'I am very concerned about her condition. Her heart is very weak and she is having tremendous difficulty breathing. That is the reason I am going to send her to hospital.'

'No! Not hospital, please, doctor!' Gwyneth pleaded weakly.

'I think Mam would far sooner stay here and have me looking after her,' Donna said uneasily.

'I'm sure she would, but I'm afraid she is far too ill. As well as constant supervision your mother needs help with her breathing,' he said firmly.

Donna blinked away the tears that threatened. She had been afraid he might say something like this. Even though she had mentally prepared herself to expect it, his decision still came as an unwelcome shock.

'May I go to the hospital with her? It might help her to settle in.'

'Yes, of course you can.' He frowned. 'What about Barri, though? You won't be able to take him with you.'

'That's all right,' Donna said quickly. 'He's next door with Blodwyn. She'll look after him. I'll just go round and let her know what is happening.'

'Right.' Gareth Thomson picked up his medical bag. 'Try not to worry.' He smiled encouragingly. 'I'll call into the hospital later and check on your mother's progress,' he promised.

There was so much else he wanted to say. He wanted to take Donna into his arms, to kiss away the threatening tears and comfort her. He refrained from doing so because it might be construed as unprofessional. All he could do at the moment, he reasoned, as he walked towards the door, was to give her all the support and advice possible.

Blodwyn was full of concern when Donna went to see her. 'Of course Barri can stay here with me,' she agreed. 'I'll pop round and get his pram in a minute. Then I'll walk to the shops with him and he won't even know you have gone.'

'You're sure it's not too much trouble?'

Donna said anxiously.

'Of course it isn't! Now don't give it another thought, cariad. You stay as long as you like with your mam. Poor dab, she hates the hospital. It's such a shame she has to go in there again.'

Donna tried to explain to her mother what was happening, but since being told she would have to go into hospital Gwyneth was so delirious and rambling that she wasn't sure her words meant anything. As she packed a bag with things she thought might be needed, Donna wondered if she ought to let Tanwen know how ill their mother was.

Remembering what had happened the last time she'd phoned to say their mam wasn't well, she wondered if there was any point in bothering to do so. There wasn't time now, she reflected. The ambulance would be here any minute so she'd wait and see what they said about her mam's condition once they got her to hospital.

The Sister and nurses were brisk and efficient as they tended Gwyneth Evans. Their voices were muted and their manner concerned. When Donna questioned them they were noncommittal about her mother's condition. They insisted that she must wait until either the hospital doctor or her own doctor came to see her mother, and ask them.

Donna was relieved when Gareth Thomson

called into the hospital after his morning surgery ended. She waited nervously as he consulted with the hospital doctor and the ward Sister.

'Your mother is gravely ill, and there is not very much chance of her pulling through,' he told Donna gently, his hand resting on her shoulder consolingly.

She nodded in silence. He was confirming her worst fears.

'Is there any other member of your family you should inform?' Gareth asked quietly.

Donna chewed her lower lip uneasily. 'Only my twin sister, Tanwen,' she said in a low voice.

He was surprised she'd not mentioned her sister before, but he tried not to show it because he remembered Aunt Menna had said there was a lot of gossip surrounding Tanwen. 'I think you ought to let her know at once. I suggest you tell her to come immediately. Does she live locally?'

Donna shook her head. 'She lives in London.'

'Can you telephone her?'

Donna nodded, but her eyes were deeply troubled as they met his.

'I think you should get in touch with her right away,' he repeated. 'You can telephone from here.'

She shook her head. 'I'll have to go home for the telephone number. While I'm there I can let Blodwyn know what is happening.'

'My car is outside, shall I drive you there?'

She looked at him uncertainly. 'Perhaps I should stay here with my mother in case she needs me?'

He shook his head. 'She's drifting in and out of consciousness all the time, so I don't think she knows whether you are here or not,' he explained kindly.

To Donna's surprise and relief it was Tanwen who answered her telephone call.

'Is it really necessary for me to come to Cardiff right away?' Tanwen asked petulantly.

'Yes, I think it is, and so does the doctor who is attending our mam. She's very, very ill, Tanwen.'

'You told Dylan that once before and it wasn't necessary,' Tanwen reminded her.

'This time she is very much worse than she was then.'

'It's only flu she's got, though, isn't it?'

'It started out as influenza, but now it is affecting her heart and her lungs. She's been in poor health for such a long time that she's too weak to fight it. That is why she is so gravely ill, Tanwen. She can hardly breathe!'

'Well, if you really think it is necessary,' Tanwen said sourly. 'I shall be furious if it is another of your false alarms.'

'So when shall I expect you?'

328

'At the weekend?'

'I ... I think that may be too late, Tanwen.'

'Oh, for heaven's sake! How melodramatic can you be!' Tanwen snapped. 'Very well, I'll come tomorrow. It will have to be late on in the day, though. Dylan's got an important photographic session planned for me in the morning,' she gushed.

'Can't you come today?' Donna pressed. 'Dr Thomson thinks that you should.'

There was a long, uneasy silence.

'Please, Tanwen!'

'Oh, all right, if I must.' Her voice was sharp with irritation. She slammed down the phone at her end before Donna could say anything else.

It was almost seven that night before Tanwen arrived at the hospital.

'You could have told me to come straight here,' she scolded Donna. 'I went all the way to Rhymney Street. It was a good thing I'd told the taxi driver to wait while I made sure there was someone there.'

'You only had to ask Blodwyn, she knew I was at the hospital.'

Tanwen's lip curled. 'Don't worry, she heard the taxi-cab drawing up and was out like a shot. I left my suitcases with her and came straight on here.'

Tanwen looked down at her mother and her face changed. 'What on earth has happened to Mam? She's shrunk to nothing!'

she exclaimed.

'She's been ill for a long time. I did phone and tell you ages ago. I spoke to Dylan. He wouldn't bring you to the phone but he did promise to tell you.'

'You haven't been looking after her properly,' Tanwen said accusingly. 'She wasn't in that state when I left home.'

'Your mother has been extremely ill, Miss Evans. I can assure you that your sister has done a perfectly wonderful job in caring for her.'

Neither Donna nor Tanwen had heard Gareth Thomson approach the bedside. Tanwen's scowl immediately transformed itself into a ravishing smile as her vivid blue eyes raked over him appreciatively.

'You must be Dr Thomson,' she breathed, holding out her hand. 'Donna has mentioned your name so many times that I feel we are old friends.'

'Really?' His heavy dark eyebrows lifted in surprise.

Tanwen nodded and fluttered her thick eyelashes. 'Hasn't she told you all about me? I know I don't visit my old home in Cardiff as often as I should, but I have a very demanding career.'

Gareth Thomson nodded dismissively and turned his attention to Gwyneth. Her breathing was now so shallow that her chest barely moved. She showed no response at all when he took her wrist between his thumb and fingers to check on her pulse.

'Does my mam know I'm here, doctor?' Tanwen asked plaintively, a sob in her voice. 'She hasn't opened her eyes since I arrived.'

He lowered Gwyneth's arm gently and moved to one side. 'It's just possible that she may rally when she hears your voice.'

'Mam! Can you hear me? It's Tanwen. I've come to take care of you,' she murmured, moving close to the bed and bending over her mother.

Gwyneth's eyelids fluttered but her eyes didn't open. A smile flickered over her dry, cracked lips as she muttered Tanwen's name in a hoarse voice. 'I knew you'd come, cariad,' she gasped. Her voice was so faint it was almost inaudible.

The next minute she gave a rasping wheeze, as if the effort of saying those few words had exhausted her. Then a deep sigh shuddered through her body and her face became slack.

Gareth Thomson elbowed Tanwen aside, calling out urgently for the Sister and nurse. They did all they could to revive Gwyneth Evans, but their efforts were in vain.

'I'm sorry, there's nothing more we can do,' Gareth Thomson told them. He placed his hand on Donna's arm consolingly.

'Surely you can do something,' Tanwen sobbed. She grabbed at his arm, her vivid

331

blue eyes swimming in tears. 'I've come all the way from London and hardly had a chance to speak to her.'

'I'm sorry! There is nothing further that any of us can do,' he told her. 'Your mother has been ill for a long time now, and she has been growing weaker all the time. Donna has done a wonderful job looking after her over the past months. The influenza, however, has been more than your mother could contend with since she's become so frail.'

Tanwen brushed a hand across her eyes and faced him angrily. 'I don't agree. I'm not sure that she has had the right treatment or proper care,' she stormed, her vivid blue eyes hostile. 'My mother isn't all that old. She's only in her forties!'

'I am well aware of that fact,' he told her. 'She has had a hard life, though.'

'Really? What trumped-up stories about our family affairs has Donna been telling you?'

'Donna hasn't told me anything about your family matters. I am referring to your mother's medical records,' he informed her in clipped tones. 'You don't seem to be aware of the fact that your mother has been in poor health for quite a long time.'

He didn't wait for an answer, but turned away and spoke directly to Donna. 'The death certificate will be ready tomorrow. In the meantime I think you should take your sister home and try and explain to her how ill your mother has been over the past months.'

Donna nodded, pushing back her froth of hair from her face and biting back her own grief. 'What time shall I call at your surgery to collect the certificate?'

'There's no need for you to do that. I'll drop it off while I am out on my rounds tomorrow morning. I'm sure you will have enough to contend with at home,' he murmured, looking towards Tanwen who was clinging to her mother's hand and sobbing hysterically.

Chapter Twenty-Nine

Tanwen stretched sleepily when Donna took a cup of tea up to her first thing the next morning.

'What time is it?' she yawned. 'I've hardly slept at all. Where on earth did you get this bed from, it's like a bag of rocks!'

'It's the bed you slept in all your life until you left home to go to London,' Donna told her.

Tanwen shuddered. 'No wonder it's so uncomfortable if it's all that old! Why on earth don't you get a new one?'

'I can't afford to,' Donna told her. 'I haven't been able to work because Mam's been so ill. I'm trying to get her dressmaking business going again but it's uphill work.'

Tanwen yawned again. 'We send you money almost every month.'

'I know, and I'm very grateful. I had hoped to save it for Barri when he's older, but I've had to dip into it to keep us going and put food on the table. At the moment it's almost all we have to live on. Barri still only gets bread and jam for his tea at night, just like we did when we were small and Mam was struggling to make ends meet. Cake is a special for Sundays. When Blodwyn gives him an apple or an orange that is a real treat.'

Tanwen pulled herself up in bed, plumped the pillow up behind her slim shoulders and patted her gleaming hair into place. 'What time is it?' she asked as she reached out to take the cup of tea Donna was still holding.

'Almost eight o'clock.'

Tanwen shivered. 'I never get up before ten!'

Donna gave a small tight laugh. 'I'm usually up, and have got Barri washed and dressed and given him his breakfast by this time.'

Tanwen drained her cup and handed it back to Donna, then she slid down into the bed again, pulling the covers up around her shoulders.

'Breakfast is on the table,' Donna told her.

'Forget it! I never eat first thing in the morning.' Tanwen stretched out a hand and began searching amongst the things on the table by the bed.

'If you're looking for your cigarettes, I moved them and the matches out of Barri's reach.'

'Darw! What the hell for? He's not going to smoke them, is he?'

'I don't think you should be smoking in the bedroom,' Donna protested.

'Why ever not?'

'It's not healthy when there's a child sleeping here.'

Tanwen looked at her scornfully. 'He's not here, anyway, he's next door with Blodwyn, isn't he?'

'For the moment, but she will be bringing him back any minute, and since this is now his bedroom he's bound to come in here. Anyway, I don't want the house smelling of smoke when Dr Thomson calls. He doesn't approve of smoking.'

'What on earth has it got to do with him?'

'Look, Tanwen, you may not like him, and you may think he hasn't done the best he could for Mam, but you are quite wrong,' Donna told her hotly.

Tanwen's eyes narrowed. 'You don't have to defend him quite so fiercely! Anyone would think you had a soft spot for him.'

'We are very good friends,' Donna said abruptly. She knew her face had gone red and she felt covered in confusion. 'All I'm saying is that he's been absolutely wonderful, and done all he possibly could for Mam. He's also taken good care of Barri.'

'Perhaps I was a bit hasty,' Tanwen admitted. 'I was so upset. You should have let me know sooner how ill Mam was, then it wouldn't have been such a terrible shock.'

Donna said nothing. What was the point in arguing about it, she thought bitterly. She'd done all she could to contact Tanwen the last time her mother had been unwell, but it had done no good.

Deep down she wondered if it was partly her fault. She had never asked them to come and stay. She knew that everything was over between herself and Dylan, but she still felt uncomfortable in his company. However, she could never forget that he was Barri's father, even though, like Tanwen, he wanted nothing at all to do with his child.

Every time she looked at Barri she could see something of Dylan in him. At times, too, the thought came to her that if he had never met Tanwen then Barri might have been hers.

'I must get on,' she sighed, turning away from Tanwen. 'There's Mam's funeral to be arranged.'

She didn't want to stand there talking. She

still felt resentful that Tanwen had been the one holding their mam's hand when the end came, and the last person their mam had spoken to.

'I would have thought you'd need to have the death certificate before you could do anything about that,' Tanwen commented.

'I know, but Dr Thomson said he would bring it round after his morning surgery ends.'

Tanwen looked thoughtful. 'What time is that?'

Donna shrugged. 'Half past ten or eleven o'clock. It depends on how many people go to see him.'

'Then I'd better get up and get dressed,' Tanwen smiled.

'There's no need. You don't have to sign anything.'

Tanwen smiled complacently. 'I know that, but I thought that perhaps I ought to tell him how sorry I am for the things I said yesterday, seeing that you appear to regard him as someone very special.'

Donna saw the smug look on Tanwen's face and felt uneasy. She wondered if Tanwen suspected the friendship that existed between herself and Gareth Thomson. They had certainly not said anything or acted in any way that could have led her to think that there was any closeness between them.

The way Tanwen had come between her

and Dylan and then stolen his affection filled Donna's thoughts as she cleaned the house.

To her relief, Tanwen was still in her bedroom when Gareth Thomson called with the death certificate. She invited him in and tried to express her gratitude for all he'd done for her mother over the past few weeks.

'I'm so sorry that there wasn't any more I could do,' he told her earnestly, holding both her hands between his own.

'You did everything you could, and I am deeply grateful,' she told him softly.

He touched her brow with his lips. 'You must tell me if there is anything further that I can do to help you, Donna.' His dark gaze held hers. 'Promise me, now.'

'Thank you, Gareth. You've been a tower of strength. I don't know how I would ever have managed without your help and kindness.'

'I'd like to add my thanks as well,' a voice breathed softly close to them.

Donna and Gareth Thomson sprang apart guiltily. They had been so absorbed in each other that they hadn't heard Tanwen come into the room.

'I do hope you will forgive me for all the horrible things I said yesterday,' Tanwen murmured, placing a hand on Gareth's arm and looking up into his face, a challenging look in her vivid blue eyes.

He returned her gaze in mesmerised silence.

Tanwen was wearing a close-fitting black dress, which hugged every curve of her slim figure. The colour enhanced her flawless complexion and her shining gold hair. She looked every inch the film star she claimed to be.

Donna compared her own tired appearance with Tanwen's sleek sophistication and felt disheartened. In Gareth's eyes, when he compared her with Tanwen she must appear dumpy and dowdy. Her hair was untamed and she had no skill at applying make-up, so how could she possibly compete with her slim, glamorous sister.

'Please forgive me!' Tanwen breathed, gazing at him wide-eyed. 'It was shock. I was so upset I didn't know what I was saying.' She dabbed at her eyes delicately with a tiny, lace-edged handkerchief. 'Poor Mam, she was always so wonderful to me,' she sobbed.

With an effort Gareth Thomson pulled himself together. 'Think no more about it. As you say, a shock reaction.'

Tanwen looked contrite. 'I should have been thanking you for the wonderful way you've looked after my mam, not saying such horrid things like I did.'

He patted her shoulder. 'It's all right, really it is. I do understand.'

She dabbed at her eyes again. 'Donna is

about to make some tea. Will you stay and have some?'

Gareth looked at his watch. 'I still have a great many calls to make,' he prevaricated.

'Five minutes to prove you have forgiven me?' She gave him a tremulous smile. 'Donna is still cross with me, and I need to be able to talk about my mam to someone who knew her and cares.'

He hesitated for a moment, checking his watch again, then nodded his assent. 'Very well.'

Tanwen smiled contentedly. 'Will you make the tea, then, Donna, while Dr Thomson and me have our little chat?'

Donna watched, speechless, as Tanwen sat down on the sofa, patting the seat beside her and looking up at Gareth Thomson invitingly.

As she walked through to the kitchen Donna heard their voices mingling, and heard him say, 'Please call me Gareth. Think of me as your friend, not as a doctor.'

As Donna waited for the kettle to boil, tears welled up into her eyes. It was a repetition of what had happened before. Tanwen was exerting her charm like she always did when it suited her. Doubts and fears crowded Donna's mind as she wondered how this was going to affect her own friendship with Gareth Thomson.

By the time she took in the tray of tea,

Tanwen was in the throes of telling him about her career as an actress and about the film she was starring in.

He was listening intently, so utterly absorbed in what she was saying that he barely looked up when Donna placed a cup of tea in front of him.

Donna felt so bitterly hurt that she walked away, leaving her own tea untouched. She felt she couldn't stay in the house a moment longer. Her eyes blurred by unshed tears, she went next door on the pretext of collecting Barri.

As she took Barri in her arms and buried her face in his mop of soft hair, Blodwyn looked at her shrewdly.

'What's your Tanwen been doing to upset you, then, cariad? Up to her old tricks again, is she?' she asked.

Donna hesitated. She wanted to confide in Blodwyn, but pride wouldn't let her. She smiled faintly. 'She's trying to apologise to Dr Thomson for all the unpleasant things she said to him last night.'

'Oh yes!'

'I'd better get back,' Donna said uncomfortably.

Blodwyn didn't try to stop her. She walked to the door and opened it for her and Barri.

'You can bring him back and leave him here with me, mind, whenever you want to, cariad,' she told Donna emphatically.

Gwyneth Evans's funeral was held the following Thursday. Donna intended it to be a very modest affair because there was only her mam's insurance policy to cover the cost. Tanwen was indignant when she heard this and insisted on things being done in grand style.

'Don't worry about the cost, I'll pay,' she said flamboyantly.

Out of respect, the blinds were drawn at every window in Rhymney Street. Many of the women, who had been Gwyneth's neighbours for years, attended the funeral service. The others stood on their doorsteps to watch the cortège depart.

Blodwyn was looking after Barri for the day. He was sitting on her doorstep playing with his train when the hearse arrived. He clapped his hands with glee when he saw the two black horses with their nodding black plumes stopping in the street outside their door. Blodwyn held him up and let him pat their necks before whisking him away out of sight.

The number of people who not only attended the service but also went with them to the cemetery surprised Donna. All of them were women, and most of them had been customers of Gwyneth's when she had been doing dressmaking.

Carina Price came, and Donna was glad of

her support. She looked so grief-stricken that Donna wished she could find the right words to comfort her. She was, after all, her mam's oldest friend, and although she'd stayed in the background she'd been very kind and helpful.

As they left the cemetery, Donna was aware that Carina had stayed behind at the graveside and she agonised about whether she should go back and speak to her, but then decided that it was kindest to leave her to say her farewell in private.

As well as looking after Barri, Blodwyn prepared sandwiches and refreshments for those who returned to the house afterwards.

Tanwen drew all eyes. She was wearing a short black velvet jacket over her black dress, black silk stockings and high-heeled black court shoes. The stylish black hat perched on her sleek golden head had a small veil that almost hid her eyes.

Donna was relieved that Dylan didn't put in an appearance. She had expected him to come for the funeral, even though Tanwen said that it was quite impossible. One of them had to stay in London, she claimed, to let people know where she was if they needed her urgently.

It meant that apart from the priest who conducted the service, the only other man present was Dr Gareth Thomson. He attended the short service but afterwards explained to Donna that he couldn't go to the interment as he had an afternoon surgery. He promised he would call at the house later in the day to check that she was all right.

To Donna's annoyance, Tanwen made sure that she was the centre of attention when people returned to their house for refreshments after the funeral. She told everyone in great detail about her wonderful new career in films. She also sought their sympathy for the fact that she had been forced to stay in London working while Donna was able to be at home and care for their mother.

By the time Gareth Thomson arrived everyone had gone home, and Donna was busy clearing away and washing up all the cups, glasses and plates that had been used. She had persuaded Blodwyn to take Barri for a walk in his pram while she tidied up, and said she would collect him as soon as she was finished.

Tanwen was lying down on the sofa complaining that she was utterly worn out and feeling too devastated about her poor mam to help, when there was a knock on the door.

'Can you answer that, Tanwen,' Donna called out, 'I'm up to my elbows in soapy water.'

'No, I can't, I'm feeling far too exhausted,'

Tanwen called back.

Without stopping to take off the apron that had once been her mother's, and which she'd put on to save getting her black dress splashed as she washed up, Donna went to do it herself.

The moment Tanwen heard a man's voice she came sashaying into the hallway. 'Donna, darling, I told you I would answer the door.' Then she paused, and with a look of surprise on her face exclaimed, 'Oh, it's you, Gareth! I was about to ask Donna what time you held your next surgery.' She raised her hand to her head. 'I have the most terrible headache,' she lamented. 'The pain is absolutely excruciating. Can you recommend something to take it away?'

Donna saw the concern in his dark eyes and didn't know whether to laugh or warn him. Before she could do either she realised he had been taken in by Tanwen's little pantomime.

'Lie down and take some aspirin,' he advised. 'I'll ask Donna to make you some tea. It's been a very exhausting day for you.'

Tanwen smiled bravely. 'Did you hear that, Donna? Could you make some tea and bring it through? I'm going to lie down on the sofa. I need to ask Dr Thomson's advice about another of my little problems.'

To Donna's annoyance Tanwen closed the door between the living room and the kitchen so that she was unable to hear what Tanwen was saying.

As the kettle came to the boil and she made tea for Tanwen, a wave of anger swept over Donna. It really was like a replay of the time when Tanwen had taken Dylan from her, she thought furiously, but this time she wasn't going to sit back and let Tanwen ruin her life again. This time she'd fight back, especially since Gareth was worth ten of Dylan.

Chapter Thirty

To Donna's dismay Tanwen didn't go back to London immediately after their mother's funeral as she had expected her to do.

Instead, she stayed in bed the next morning and complained that her headache was far too bad for her to travel.

'I think you'd better send for Dr Thomson,' she murmured plaintively when Donna took her in a cup of tea.

'You've already told him about it so I shouldn't think there is much more he can do for you,' Donna quibbled.

'It must be more than a headache, I feel shivery as well. Perhaps I've contracted flu, the same as Mam had,' Tanwen moaned weakly.

Although all her instincts told her that Tanwen was shamming, and that to send for Gareth Thomson was asking for trouble, Donna gave her the benefit of the doubt and reluctantly did as Tanwen requested.

When she asked Blodwyn if she would leave a message at the surgery for him to call when he was doing his rounds, Blodwyn's eyebrows went up in surprise.

'Is she really ill, cariad, or is she having you on and playing one of her crafty little games?' she asked dubiously.

'I don't know what to think!' Donna admitted worriedly.

'Well I do!' Blodwyn declared fiercely. 'I reckon she's setting her cap at that doctor.'

'Blodwyn! What are you suggesting?'

'Dammo di! We've both seen her put on a performance like this once before, and who was it that ended up with heartache? Now, think about it, cariad? Do you still want me to ask Dr Thomson to call in?'

Donna hesitated, then she nodded her head. 'Yes,' she said resignedly. 'You'd better do so. She could be telling the truth and it might be influenza.'

Tanwen made a miraculous recovery before Gareth Thomson had arrived. By the time he had knocked on the front door she was downstairs, reclining gracefully on the sofa.

Her face was carefully made up to make

347

her appear pale and fragile. She wasn't fully dressed, but was wearing a black silk-embroidered kimono edged in gold that enhanced the charms of her slim curvy figure and creamy skin.

Donna saw the look of admiration on Gareth Thomson's face as he walked into the room and her own heart sank. What hope did she have of keeping his interest now that he had met Tanwen?

If it came to a choice between herself and Tanwen she knew quite well which of them would win. She was no good at all when it came to putting up a fight. It simply wasn't in her nature, and Tanwen knew this and took advantage of it.

It had always been the same, she thought resentfully. She'd seen that look in people's eyes ever since they were tiny tots. As they'd grown older the difference between the two of them had become even more apparent. Even so, she was fed up of hearing about it.

When Gareth Thomson had arrived, Donna had only just put Barri down for his morning nap. Hearing his voice, Barri began calling out excitedly, 'Doco, doco,' and refusing to stay in his cot because he wanted to come downstairs and see him.

Donna tried to pacify Barri but to no avail, so she decided the best thing was to let Gareth come upstairs and speak to him.

Obligingly, Gareth spent a few minutes

playing with Barri and promised him he would come again soon. Then, with an understanding smile at Donna, he left her to settle him back for his nap.

It was almost five minutes before Barri's eyes finally closed in sleep. At the back of Donna's mind the whole time was the fact that Gareth hadn't had a chance to talk to her.

As she tiptoed from the room and made her way downstairs she was surprised to find Tanwen dressed in her outdoor clothes. She looked round for Gareth but he was nowhere to be seen.

'Gareth thinks that what I need is some fresh air,' Tanwen told her with a smug smile. 'He has offered to take me to Roath Park for a walk. I'm quite looking forward to it, I haven't been there for years!'

'Surely he can't spare the time to do that. He's in the middle of his rounds,' Donna protested.

Tanwen shrugged her slim shoulders. 'He's waiting for me outside in his car. I must go! Doctor's orders!' she added flippantly.

Before Donna could credit what was happening Tanwen was gone, slamming the door behind her with such force that it wakened Barri. Once again he began shouting, 'Doco, doco!' at the top of his voice.

Astounded by the turn of events, Donna

felt bitter resentment burning inside her as she went upstairs to pacify Barri. Knowing that there was no possible hope of him going to sleep again she picked him up out of his cot, burying her face in his hair, comforted by the smell of his baby freshness.

As she came downstairs with him in her arms there was a knock on the front door, and for one hopeful moment she thought it was Gareth Thomson coming back on his own. To her disappointment it was Blodwyn.

'Duw anwyl! Was that your Tanwen I saw driving off with Dr Thomson,' she exclaimed, even before she stepped over the doorstep.

'Probably. They've only just this minute left,' Donna told her.

'So what's going on, then? Not taking her to the hospital, is he?'

'I wish he were!' Donna said with a bitter laugh. Then she pulled herself together and shook her head. 'No, I didn't really mean that. Do you want a cup of tea, Blodwyn?'

'Only if you arc going to tell me all about what's happening, cariad,' Blodwyn chuckled. 'Here my lovely boyo,' she held out her arms to Barri. 'Let me hold him while you get the kettle on, cariad.'

'So is that Tanwen up to her old tricks again?' Blodwyn asked as Donna brought in the tea. She put Barri down on the floor so that he could play with his train, and settled herself at the table. 'I thought you said she seemed to think she had the old flu, and that was why you asked me to go for the doctor?'

'Yes, she said she had a headache and that she felt shivery and not well enough to travel back to London,' Donna admitted as she poured out the tea.

'So what's she doing gallivanting off out with Dr Thomson, then?'

'Apparently he told her that she needed some fresh air.'

'Then why couldn't she have taken little Barri for a walk in his pram? She'd have got plenty of fresh air doing that, wouldn't she?'

Donna laughed. 'I can't see Tanwen pushing a pram, can you?'

Blodwyn took a sip of her tea. 'I was watching her yesterday when everyone came back after your mam's funeral, cariad,' she said thoughtfully. 'She completely ignores little Barri, doesn't she.'

Donna shrugged. 'She has never wanted to have anything to do with him, not since the day he was born, as you very well know.'

'Yes, but what's going to happen now? Without your mam here to help look after him you're not going to be able to manage on your own.'

Donna squared her shoulders. 'Don't worry, I'll deal with it somehow.'

'I'm sure you will, cariad, but it's hardly

fair, now is it. Tanwen's the child's mammy and she ought to be the one looking after him.'

'She's got her career. She can hardly take him to London with her.'

'You have your career to consider as well, Donna,' Blodwyn persisted.

Donna pushed her hair back from her face again. 'If you mean my job at The Cardiff Drapers, then that's all over,' she said resignedly, 'I'll never be able to go back there, not now that I have to look after Barri.'

'You could if you arranged for someone to look after him full time.'

Donna shook her head. 'I don't want to do that. It would be far too upsetting for him, being pushed from pillar to post.'

'So you're going to go on struggling to make a living by doing dressmaking from home, and looking after him at the same time, are you?'

Donna nodded. 'Quite a few of Mam's old customers have proved loyal. With not having Mam to look after I will have more time, so I should be able to make a living,' she said optimistically.

Blodwyn drained her cup. 'You're a fighter, I'll say that for you, cariad,' she said admiringly.

She pushed her cup across the table and waited for Donna to refill it.

'Talking of fighting,' she said, helping herself to sugar, 'I hope you are going to put up a fight and show that Tanwen where she gets off.'

'What do you mean?'

'Dammo di! You're not going to let her steal Dr Gareth Thomson away from you, are you, like she did with your last fella!'

Donna felt hot colour flooding her face. 'I don't know what you're talking about,' she mumbled, avoiding Blodwyn's eyes.

'Oh yes you do, cariad. I'm not blind. I know he's sweet on you. I'm the one who looked after Barri and sat with your mam that time he took you out, so don't try and pull the wool over my eyes!'

Donna let out a long sigh. 'Yes, I do like him, and we do get on well together, I must admit.'

'Not for much longer unless you take a stand. Your Tanwen's the most selfish little bitch I've ever known,' Blodwyn told her fiercely. 'She'll take him off you just for the fun of it.'

'If he's that easily swayed then she's welcome to him,' Donna said tartly.

'That's rubbish and you know it,' Blodwyn admonished. 'He thinks the world of you, it shows on his face every time he calls.'

Donna shrugged but said nothing.

'She's still got Dylan in her clutches don't forget,' Blodwyn went on.

'She's very welcome to him,' Donna snapped.

'You don't want him back, then, my lovely?'

'No! I most certainly don't!'

Donna could see that Blodwyn seemed astonished by the force of her reply, but she meant it. Thinking of him and Tanwen being together left her unmoved.

The same was not true, though, when she thought of Tanwen being out with Gareth Thomson and enjoying his company. Until this moment she'd been so sure that Gareth cared a great deal for her. They'd only been out together once, but it had been very romantic. He had made her feel so special that she remembered every minute.

It was only because her mother had been so ill that she'd turned down his last two invitations. If that hadn't happened then she was sure that their relationship would be at a very different stage than it was at present.

She had been looking forward to getting to know him even better, but now, in the light of his sudden interest in Tanwen, she was wondering if all that had been ruined.

'You ought to make that sister of yours shoulder her own responsibilities over Barri, you know, cariad,' Blodwyn stated pragmatically, cutting into her thoughts abruptly.

Donna looked at her in exasperation. 'You

know quite well that Tanwen wants nothing to do with him. If she'd had her way then he would have gone for adoption the minute he was born. When she found we hadn't done that then she wanted him to be put in an orphanage.' She shook her head sadly. 'I know quite well that Tanwen will never accept responsibility for him, but the way I feel about him I can give him all the love and care he needs.'

'You can't support him unless you have a man of your own to help provide for him,' Blodwyn persisted stubbornly.

'Mam did! She brought us up on her own after Dad died.'

'Yes, and look at the struggle it was for her to make ends meet, poor dab. She never had a penny to spare. She often went hungry to make sure you two girls had a full belly. Never spent a penny on herself. Do you want to live like that? You also want to remember that not many men want to take on someone else's child.'

Donna felt a shiver run through her. Was Blodwyn right, she wondered? Gareth seemed to be so fond of Barri that it had never entered her head that if their relationship ever became really serious then he might object to the child.

As she looked down to where Barri was playing happily on the floor with his little train, she knew that he would always have a special place in her heart as well as in her life.

No matter what price she had to pay, or how it might affect her own life, she would never give him up.

Chapter Thirty-One

Donna felt so upset that the moment Blodwyn went home she decided that she had to get out of the house in order to think clearly. With her mam gone it was as if the walls were closing in on her. She felt trapped. Everywhere she looked there were visible signs of Tanwen's presence. She could even smell her perfume.

Leaving the cups on the table and the house in disarray, she pulled on her coat, dressed Barri in his outdoor things, and popped him in his pram.

It was warm for early October, but she hardly noticed the blue sky and light, scudding clouds as she headed towards Cathays Park. Lulled by the motion of the pram Barri fell asleep almost at once.

Once there she sat on one of the marble slabs that surrounded the edge of the cenotaph and tried to control the feeling of rage that was burning inside her.

Blodwyn was so right. Tanwen hadn't been near all the time their mam was ill. Now she was up to her old tricks. She had already taken Dylan so surely she couldn't want Gareth Thomson as well! Why, then, was she behaving like this? Donna couldn't stop asking herself the same questions over and over again, without finding an answer.

She failed to understand Tanwen's motive. Had she somehow guessed that there was a special relationship between herself and Gareth, and so determined to ruin it, Donna mused. Or was she intent on breaking them up purely out of spite.

She'd always needed to prove that her charms were so great that she could captivate any man. It's as though she's playing some childish game simply to annoy me and to amuse herself, Donna thought angrily.

Whatever her reason, Donna felt that Tanwen was being cruel and vindictive. She had her own life and career in London, surely that was exciting and fulfilling enough for her.

Blodwyn was right, of course. She couldn't let Tanwen steal Gareth Thomson. It would ruin all her dreams for the future. If only she knew how to stop her. She wasn't as clever or as sharp-witted as Tanwen. Nor was she as devious.

She certainly wasn't anywhere near as attractive, either. What you see is what you get, she thought wryly. Plain in looks and in manner, and without any frills or make-believe assets.

She knew it was hopeless putting on an act, pretending to be something she wasn't. She wasn't even any good at flirting. All she could offer Gareth was deep, sincere love.

She really had thought that he felt the same way about her as she did about him. She remembered the evening they had gone out together, when his friend Rebecca had exercised her charms on him. He had been courteous but unresponsive. He had clearly indicated to her that he wasn't interested in Rebecca, and that it was Donna's company that he preferred.

So why was it so different with Tanwen, she asked herself. Rebecca had been attractive, as well as being an old friend. Furthermore, she came from his own sort of background.

She couldn't believe that it was Tanwen's film-star attributes that impressed Gareth. He was far too pragmatic to be taken in by that sort of tag.

Barri was still sleeping soundly so Donna moved away from the cenotaph to a more comfortable seat. The sun was warm and she found herself slowly relaxing. In a semi-daydream she thought about the future.

She'd really meant it when she'd told Blodwyn that she wouldn't be going back to

The Cardiff Drapers to work, and that she intended to take over her mother's dressmaking business. It was the only way she could earn a living and look after Barri at the same time.

For a fleeting moment the thought crossed her mind that maybe Tanwen had been right after all, and she should have let him go for adoption. Perhaps it still wasn't too late. If only she could be certain that whoever took him would be good to him, show him love and understanding as well as providing him with material benefits. Could anyone love him as much as she did, she asked herself. She thought not.

Yet what did the future hold for him, or for her, come to that? If only her dreams could come true, she thought plaintively. If only she could give Barri the home life he deserved.

Barri stirred, his eyes slowly opened and she saw his lower lip tremble as he gazed round, unsure of where he was. Then he saw her and his face became radiant as he beamed a happy smile at her.

As he held out his arms to be picked up, Donna felt a lump in her throat. At this moment she knew beyond any doubt that the decision she had taken to bring him up herself was the right one. They'd manage to get by, one way or another.

Glancing up at the City Hall clock she

realised that the morning was gone.

'I bet you're hungry,' she said as she sat him up in his pram. 'I know I am,' she smiled.

She couldn't face going back to Rhymney Street. Tanwen was bound to be back from her outing in Roath Park and she couldn't bear the thought of seeing the smug, self-satisfied look on her face.

Although she intended to take Blodwyn's advice and fight Tanwen over Gareth Thomson, she wasn't ready to do so yet. She needed to think very carefully about what action to take. It was going to take nerve as well as determination.

Briskly, she set out for the nearest shops. Fish and chips were the answer, she decided. She'd bring them back to the park and they'd eat them out of the paper. She'd buy some milk for Barri and a chocolate bar as well. They'd have a picnic, Barri would love that.

It was late afternoon, the sun going down in a blaze of red, before she went home. As she approached her own front door she braced herself for her encounter with Tanwen. She'll probably be furious at being left to fend for herself all day, Donna thought, as she parked the pram outside and went into the house.

Complete silence greeted her. She called out Tanwen's name, but there was no reply.

She looked in all the rooms, upstairs as well as down, but Tanwen wasn't there.

Surely she wasn't still out gallivanting with Gareth Thomson, Donna thought angrily.

She went back outside to collect Barri and bring him and the pram indoors.

As she undid the pram harness, lifted him out and put him down on the pavement, Blodwyn came rushing out of her house.

'Your Tanwen's gone back to London,' she said gleefully. 'Called a taxi-cab and went off in a right huff, I can tell you.'

'Really? What time was this?'

'About an hour after you went out. Dr Thomson brought her back, but he didn't even turn the engine of his car off. Tanwen had a face like thunder. She slammed his car door so hard that it's a wonder she didn't break it. He drove off without even a glance in her direction. Then half an hour later the taxi-cab pulled up and she piled into it and was gone.'

'So how do you know that she's gone back to London?' Donna asked, perplexed.

'Well, cariad, where else would she be going with her suitcases?'

'Yes, I suppose you're right.' Donna felt uneasy. It wasn't like Tanwen to give up so easily.

'Hasn't she left you a note or anything?' Blodwyn asked in surprise.

'I don't know. I didn't know she'd left so I

haven't looked.'

'Where've you been, anyway, cariad,' Blodwyn probed. 'Getting quite worried about you, I was.'

'I went for a walk in Cathays Park. As it was such a nice day I decided to get some fish and chips and have a picnic. Barri loved it!' she added defiantly.

'I bet he did, and you as well. Anything would be better than coming home and facing that sister of yours, I suppose,' Blodwyn added shrewdly. 'And to think it wasn't necessary, she'd packed her bags and gone long before midday.'

Donna gave her a wide smile. She suddenly felt light-hearted. She didn't know what had gone wrong between Gareth and Tanwen but something told her that he hadn't fallen for her wiles after all. She'd been worrying about nothing. All that thinking and planning about how she was going to tackle Tanwen had been a waste of time.

Life was suddenly good and full of promise. She felt so optimistic that she couldn't stop smiling.

'Fancy a cup of tea, Blodwyn?'

'Well, I wouldn't say no, cariad. You know me, I can drink tea any time of the day or night. I've just made a batch of bakestones so I'll bring a plateful of them with me. That's if you've room for cakes after that picnic the pair of you have just enjoyed.'

'Yes, we can eat one of your bakestones, Blodwyn. It was a couple of hours ago that we had our fish and chips and it's been a long walk home since then.'

They had finished their tea and Blodwyn was on the point of going home, when Gareth arrived.

'I'll take young Barri back home with me for half an hour to play with my Tiggy,' Blodwyn offered, pulling herself out of her chair. 'That cat really loves him!'

Donna nodded gratefully. There was an air of impatience about Gareth and she wondered what it was he had to tell her.

'Tanwen gone?' he asked crisply.

'Apparently. According to Blodwyn she left while I was out. She said it was about half an hour after you brought her back from your trip to Roath Park,' she added.

He shook his head angrily. 'I know she's your twin sister, Donna, but two people less alike would be hard to find.'

'What's that supposed to mean?' she frowned.

'Oh, Donna!' He pulled her into his arms and buried his face in her froth of hair. 'You are so warm, so lovely. Say you will marry me?'

'What!' She pulled away and stared at him in astonishment.

He sighed. 'That wasn't the most romantic proposal, was it? I know I'm rushing you, but we've wasted far too much time already.'

'Do you know what you are saying?'

He pulled her back into his arms. 'You must have had some idea of how I felt about you.'

She hesitated. Her heart was thundering. She knew only too well how she thought about him, but she had hardly dared hope that he felt the same way about her.

'You've been a wonderful friend,' she admitted disarmingly. 'You have been tremendously kind and very supportive.'

'Surely more than that,' he groaned. 'I've been in love with you from the first time I came here to see your mother.'

She looked at him in astonishment. 'You criticised everything I did!'

'I never meant to,' he said contritely. 'From our very first meeting I felt you were special. Since then, Donna, my feelings have grown stronger and stronger.' He smiled ruefully. 'So much so that when Tanwen began sniping about you I lost my temper. I turned the car round and brought her back before we even reached Roath Park. I told her the sooner she got back to her friends in London the better.'

Donna looked at him in disbelief. 'Why did you take her out in the first place?'

He shrugged. 'I did it to please you. I knew there was nothing wrong with her, but I thought I would be pleasing you if I humoured her.'

'Oh dear, and I thought you'd fallen under her spell!' She sighed. 'She is very lovely, you must admit. I really did think you'd succumbed to her charms.'

He shook his head. 'She's a painted doll, nothing more. There's no warmth or compassion in her. I can't even like her.'

Donna tried to stop herself from laughing outright. 'I hope you didn't tell her that,' she chuckled.

'Let's forget about her, shall we? She's gone back to London. I want to talk to you about us, about our future. I really meant it when I asked you to marry me, Donna?'

She wanted so much to say 'yes'. To hold on to his hand and never let him go. She couldn't believe he meant those wonderful words. She found it incomprehensible that he should choose her. All her life, ever since she'd been a small child, she'd always thought of herself as inferior in every way to Tanwen. She had always been the one who was overlooked, so how could he prefer her?

'For weeks I've been thinking and planning our future,' he went on. 'I wanted to share my ideas with you, but I could hardly do so while your mother was so ill and you had so many other things on your mind.'

'What sort of ideas?' she asked curiously.

'Mainly about where we would live. I've

even measured up my place in Crwys Road and drawn up plans of how the living quarters could be divided up to give both us and Aunt Menna separate areas.'

'Aunt Menna!' She drew in a quick breath. She'd only ever met her once when she'd called there early one morning to ask if Gareth could come because her mother was so ill. Blodwyn had heard a lot about her, though, and described her as a right tartar.

'Does your aunt know about me and all your plans for the future?' she asked cautiously.

He frowned. 'In principle, but not the fine details. I wanted you to be the first to hear those.'

'So your Aunt Menna would be living with us?'

'Yes, I'm afraid so. I did explain that I was her only relative and told you about all she had done for me after my parents died.'

'I understand!' She smiled ruefully. 'I have a similar commitment.'

'You mean Barri?'

Donna nodded. 'Does that bother you?'

He hesitated for a moment, then shook his head vigorously. 'No, of course it doesn't,' he said firmly.

'Tanwen has always thought he should go into an orphanage!'

'She would!' he said scornfully. 'Of course

you couldn't let that happen. He's a delightful child and I am very fond of him.'

'Fond?' Donna looked doubtful. 'Is being fond of him enough if you're going to accept him as part of your new family and provide him with a home?'

He nodded. 'I'm quite happy about that. We both have baggage to bring with us.' He smiled. 'You have Barri and I have Aunt Menna.'

Donna looked thoughtful. 'It sounds easy, but how will your Aunt Menna react to Barri?'

'I'm confident she'll love him from the moment she meets him.'

'He's a little charmer, but he can be quite a handful. She might not like the idea of having him living under the same roof.'

'If you are at all worried about what Aunt Menna will think of him, then why don't you bring him round to meet her. Shall we say teatime tomorrow?'

Donna smiled. 'I'd like to do that, I'd like to meet her properly.'

'And then will you put me out of my misery and give me your answer?'

Chapter Thirty-Two

Donna suspected that meeting Aunt Menna was going to be a very important step in her relationship with Gareth. She wanted to make a good impression, but at the same time she was determined to be herself.

After a great deal of consideration she decided to wear a pale pink cotton dress. It was trimmed with dark pink at the neckline and the colour suited her. She brushed her mop of fine hair vigorously and did her best to tame it into a semblance of smoothness.

When she was ready to leave she studied her reflection resignedly. Despite all her efforts she looked much the same as when she was taking Barri to the park or going into the centre of Cardiff to do some shopping...

She made sure that Barri looked his best. Instinct told her that it was important that Aunt Menna took to him from the very first moment they met.

He was too young for her to explain the importance of their visit so she could only silently pray that he would behave himself.

Normally he was a happy little boy and not given to crying or tantrums. Like all very small children, however, he was highly susceptible to atmosphere.

Donna knew in advance that there would be tension. She was aware that it was absurd, but she was already keyed up and jumpy. Gareth was bound to be anxious, too, because he wanted his aunt to get on with both of them.

She couldn't tell what Aunt Menna's attitude would be, but she suspected that she would be highly suspicious of both her and Barri. After all, Donna reasoned, in a sense they would be taking Gareth away from her. If she had brought him up from when he was still a schoolboy, and he was her only family, then it was understandable that she felt apprehensive and perhaps even resentful at any intrusion or disruption to her ordered way of life.

Blodwyn had said she was a tartar. Donna didn't understand how she could know that for sure. She tried to dismiss it, suspecting it was merely based on gossip Blodwyn had overheard.

Gareth had already told her that his Aunt Menna had been a matron so she probably had an authoritative manner, but it didn't mean that she was unapproachable, Donna told herself.

If she'd worked in a hospital then surely she would understand that small children could be unpredictable when they were in strange surroundings, she consoled herself.

Gareth had said to be there at four o'clock. Donna was ready a good half an hour before it was time to leave Rhymney Street. She was so afraid that Barri might get grubby before they arrived that she decided to put him in his pram and take him for a walk.

It was a dull, overcast day, and the weather seemed to make Barri grizzly. In despair she laid him down in the hope that he would go to sleep. At first he struggled to stay awake, then suddenly, five minutes before they were due to be at Gareth's home, he dozed off.

Donna didn't know what to do for the best. She debated with herself whether she should leave him to sleep or wake him up. To rouse him when he had only just dropped off to sleep might mean he was irritable. Yet to turn up with him fast asleep somehow seemed discourteous.

She bounced the pram as she approached Crwys Road, hoping to waken him, but when she arrived at the house he was still dead to the world.

Gareth's face lit up when he opened the door to her. He kissed her warmly and then helped her to bring the pram indoors.

'We'll leave his pram in the waiting room. We'll be able to hear him when he wakes up,' he told her. 'Come on, Aunt Menna is waiting to meet you.'

Donna felt so nervous she could hardly walk. Gareth squeezed her hand and grinned encouragingly at her. 'She doesn't bite, you know,' he whispered. 'She's probably feeling just as apprehensive as you are.'

Donna smiled tremulously. 'I doubt it! My knees feel like jelly!'

Aunt Menna's greeting was restrained, but not unfriendly. Donna was aware that she was eyeing her critically, and she was glad she had taken as much trouble as she had with her appearance. She felt her neat dress and only the minimum amount of make-up had been the right decision. The only thing that she felt self-conscious about was her hair. Going for a walk had not been a good idea. The light wind had lifted it back into its usual halo around her face.

Well, she thought resignedly, that's what I usually look like. If she doesn't like what she sees then there's not a lot I can do about it.

Aunt Menna seemed to relax. 'You sit and talk to Gareth while I bring in the tea. We may as well make the most of the time your little boy is asleep and have our chat and a cup of tea in peace,' she smiled.

Conversation flowed smoothly. They exchanged views about Cardiff and how Aunt Menna had settled in to living in Cathays. Donna told her about the work she'd been doing at The Cardiff Drapers. She went on to explain that she had taken over the dressmaking work her mother had used to do at home so that she could be there to look after Barri.

They had almost finished their tea by the time Barri woke up. At first he was shy, burying his face in Donna's neck and refusing to have anything to do with Aunt Menna.

Donna felt embarrassed, but Aunt Menna seemed unconcerned. She just carried on talking and drinking her tea. She ignored Barri for so long that in the end he was the one who was seeking attention.

The offer of a glass of milk and a biscuit won him over completely. He sat on Aunt Menna's lap quite happily.

Donna was delighted to see that they bonded so quickly. Aunt Menna seemed to be absorbed as Barri chattered away to her.

'Since Barri is so content with you, Aunt Menna, could you keep an eye on him while I show Donna over the rest of the house?' Gareth suggested. 'I want to tell her about the idea I mentioned to you about splitting it up into separate accommodation.'

Aunt Menna stiffened. 'If you wish,' she said curtly. 'I thought Donna was coming to have tea with me and give us a chance to get to know each other.'

'Well, we've done that,' he smiled. 'It's all been so pleasant that I want to take the opportunity of talking to her about my plans for the future.'

Aunt Menna's lips tightened into a hard line but she said no more. She turned her attention back to Barri but the ambience had changed. Donna felt a prickling down her spine and she looked anxiously at Gareth.

Everything had been going so well up to this point that she wished Gareth had held back and not mentioned his plans for the future. It was obvious that it was something that Aunt Menna found disturbing.

'Are you sure she is going to be happy about such a tremendous change,' Donna asked anxiously the moment they were out of earshot.

'In time! It may take a little while for her to get used to it but I'm sure she'll accept it in the end. Anyway, see what you think after I've shown you round and explained what I intend to do.'

The double-fronted, detached Victorian house was immense. It had four bedrooms on the first floor, one of them large enough to put the whole lot of her bedrooms in Rhymney Street inside, Donna reflected in amazement. There were also two more attic bedrooms on the floor above.

'There is certainly plenty of space,' she agreed. 'Why is it necessary to divide it up into two separate households, though?'

He looked at her in astonishment. 'Are

you saying you'd be happy to have Aunt Menna living in with us?'

'Of course I would!' She frowned. 'She mightn't like the idea, mind. Not with all the noise and disruption young Barri can cause.'

Gareth looked bewildered. 'I never thought of even asking if you'd have her living with us,' he murmured. 'I'll sound her out and tell you what she says.'

'Point out that she could always have her own sitting room. She might like somewhere where she can go to get away from us and from Barri when she feels tired or needs a little peace,' Donna told him.

He nodded. 'That sounds like an admirable arrangement.' He put his arm round Donna and pulled her close. 'You really are a wonderful person, you know,' he told her warmly. His lips found hers and for the next ten minutes, Aunt Menna and Barri were forgotten by both of them.

There was still an uneasy atmosphere when they returned to the sitting room. Aunt Menna was obviously enjoying Barri's company as he was still sitting on her lap, but her attitude towards them had changed. Her replies when Gareth and Donna spoke to her were stilted and abrupt.

Donna summed up the situation and thought it might be wise to go home.

When Gareth offered to walk back with

her, his aunt frowned and reminded him sharply that he should be getting ready for evening surgery.

'I hope you know exactly what you are doing, Gareth,' Menna Vaughan said worriedly as the front door closed behind Donna and Barri.

He frowned. 'You mean you don't approve of Donna?' he said in surprise.

'Oh, Donna is admirable. She would make any man a good wife. No, I am referring to the child.'

'Barri?' Gareth Thomson's face softened into a smile. 'He's a delightful little lad, isn't he?'

'So he may be, but have you considered all the implications of taking on another man's child?'

'Well, you did,' he told her with a grin. 'If you hadn't then where would I be today?'

'It's precisely because I know all about what is entailed that I'm warning you to think very carefully before you make such a commitment,' she said.

There was a look of pride on her stern, wrinkled face as she spoke, but the speculation in her dark eyes was clear nevertheless.

'I had hoped that you would approve, Aunt Menna, and give me your blessing,' he persisted.

'If your mind is made up that you are going to marry Donna Evans then you'll not be worrying about a blessing from me, any more than you will heed my warning,' she told him dryly. 'There's been a streak of stubbornness in your make-up since you were a tiny lad.'

'I wonder where I get that from?' he asked with a teasing smile.

She shook her grey head, her thin lips compressed tightly.

'But you do like Donna?' he persisted.

'There is nothing at all wrong with either her or Barri, I'm simply asking you to make quite sure you know what sort of responsibility you are taking on when you undertake to bring up another man's child,' she reiterated.

'I think of him as being Donna's.'

His aunt looked at him speculatively. 'I take that to mean that she has never told you anything at all about the child's father?'

Gareth shook his head. 'I don't think I want to know the details,' he said flatly.

'So what happens if he turns up on the doorstep one day and demands to see his son? He has that right, you know.'

'You are simply looking for trouble, Aunt Menna,' he told her sharply. 'For all we know his father may be dead.'

'Very true! Wouldn't it be wise to ascertain that fact before you ask her to marry you?'

Gareth shook his head. 'If Donna doesn't want to talk about it then that's all right with me,' he said stubbornly.

'Have you thought about the problems that might arise when you have children of your own?' his aunt went on doggedly.

'None of this matters at the moment, Aunt Menna! They're things that we will deal with when the need arises. I love Donna, I want to marry her, and I fully accept that means including Barri in the arrangement.'

'So you have talked about it?'

'Not specifically. When we were talking about the future and I said that whatever happened you would still go on living with me, Donna accepted that fact without hesitation. She reminded me that likewise she was responsible for Barri's welfare.'

'You'll be responsible for Barri for a great deal longer than you will be for me,' Menna Vaughan told him tartly.

Gareth smiled broadly and gathered the tiny figure into his arms. 'He won't be half as much trouble,' he teased as he kissed the top of her grey head. 'Now, don't you want to hear what Donna had to say about dividing up the house?'

When he told her about Donna's idea that they should all live together as one family, he saw some of the tension go out of her taut frame. When he went on to suggest that she should have her own sitting room, a retreat when she found living as a family too much for her, she nodded her head in agreement.

'That sounds like a sensible arrangement. It means you can banish me off to my room when you've had enough of my company, too.'

He looked at her sharply. 'That's not at all what we meant,' he frowned, squaring his shoulders. Then, as he saw the amused gleam in her dark eyes, he relaxed.

'So you are quite happy with such an arrangement?' he pressed.

Aunt Menna shrugged, her face impassive.

'Well, does that mean "yes" or "no"?'

'If you are still determined to go ahead and get married then I suppose I have no option but to agree to whatever arrangements you decide to make.'

He studied her set face, shaking his head in exasperation. 'You're still not completely happy about things, though, are you?'

She looked away and began clearing the tea things from the table, stacking plates and saucers together.

'I still think you need to give more consideration to the importance of bringing up another man's child,' she repeated stubbornly.

'You like Donna, you like Barri – that is the only criterion I need,' he said simply.

She nodded her acceptance. 'You'd better

cut along and start your evening surgery, then, or you won't be able to support them, let alone provide them with a home!'

Chapter Thirty-Three

Time and time again in the days that followed, Donna asked herself whether she was doing the right thing in agreeing to marry Gareth Thomson.

There was no question of whether or not she loved him. Her heart thudded every time she thought about him and she was filled by a momentary dizziness at the wonderment of it all. It was whether they could make things work out with Aunt Menna. She was so severe, and at the moment seemed to be so critical of everything they said or did. She would be with them constantly, day in, day out, an inner voice reminded Donna.

Was it going to be feasible to have a happy home-life for herself, Gareth and Barri at Crwys Road? Menna Vaughan had been in sole charge there ever since she and Gareth had first moved to Cardiff. It was her home. How could she possibly welcome the idea of another woman sharing her home, let alone allow her to take over the housekeeping?

'Yet if I don't play my part as Gareth's

wife, how can I possibly run my life as I should?' Donna asked herself out loud.

The nerve-racking silence brought no answers.

Donna began to dread the time when Barri was asleep because the house was so desolate. Equally, when he was awake his constant chattering confused the thoughts that were filling her head from dawn to dusk.

Even when she went to bed at night her head was full of disturbing contemplation and dreams. One minute she was convinced that everything would turn out all right, the next that she was being submerged up to her neck in an uncharted morass.

Donna wished that there was someone other than Blodwyn to confide in, even Tanwen if they'd remained friends. If only it was possible to turn back the clock to the days when her mother was alive and well.

She tried to imagine how her mother would have dealt with the problem. What sort of answers could she have expected from her to all the many questions that were buzzing round in her head like a swarm of wasps.

Carina Price might know what she should do. Or would she only advise her to find someone to look after Barri and come back to work?

She felt so terribly unsettled that she

wondered if she would feel better if she got on with some dressmaking. Concentrating on sewing might help to take her mind off her problems and she certainly needed to earn some money. There had been none from Dylan since Tanwen's visit and she was beginning to wonder if there would be any more from them.

When she mentioned it to Gareth he frowned. 'Do you really want to do any more dressmaking? Wouldn't it be better for us to get married right away,' he urged. 'Why postpone things. You love me, I love you, so why the delay when it is the logical thing to do?'

When she was cradled in his arms she knew he was right and was eager to accede to everything he suggested. She could even convince herself that Aunt Menna was not really a problem.

A little bit of tact, some careful planning, and everything will be plain sailing, she told herself.

'Why don't we fix the date,' he urged. 'You'll feel much more settled once we do that.'

'So soon after my mam's death?'

'Would she object?' he asked pragmatically. 'Surely it would please her to know that you were happy and settled.'

Donna knew Blodwyn would agree wholeheartedly with his sentiments, which was why she didn't want to talk to her about it.

Finally, in desperation, she went to see Carina Price.

Carina was pleased to see her. It was the first opportunity they'd had to talk since she had left The Cardiff Drapers. Although Carina Price had attended Gwyneth Evans's funeral she had not come back to the house afterwards, so there had been no chance to say anything to each other apart from the conventional exchanges.

'How are you managing?' was the first question Carina levelled at her. 'Are you going to arrange for someone to look after Barri so that you can come back to work? Aileen Roberts would love to have you back in the workroom.'

Donna shook her head, smiling to herself because that was exactly what she'd thought Carina would say. 'I don't think it would be fair on Barri to do that.'

Carina Price raised her eyebrows. 'So how are you going to earn a living, then? Are you going to do dressmaking from home like your mother did?'

Donna took a deep breath. 'I'm thinking of getting married,' she stated.

Carina Price frowned. 'Surely not to that Dylan Wallis? I thought Tanwen had gone off with him?'

'Yes, she did, and she's still with him.

382

They're living in London and they're both working in films.'

Carina Price nodded. 'Yes, I heard Tanwen giving forth at your mother's funeral about being a film star.' She sniffed deprecatingly. 'She looked like one. Cheap and tarty.'

'Oh, Miss Price!'

'I'm sorry, Donna, but she did. No one would ever believe you two were sisters!'

Donna smiled ruefully. 'No, we're not very alike! Pins and needles, Mam always called us. Tanwen as slim and as sharp as a needle. Me, stumpy and solid like a pin.'

'I'm sure she meant no such thing,' Carina Price defended Gwyneth in a shocked voice.

Donna shrugged. 'It's the truth.'

'Well, pins are the more reliable, and they don't stab you unexpectedly,' Carina smiled grimly. 'So who is this man you are thinking of marrying?'

'Gareth Thomson.'

'I've never heard the name. What does he do for a living? Can he support you and Barri?'

'He's the doctor who attended my mother.'

'Really?' Carina Price looked taken aback. 'Was he the thickset, dark-haired man at Gwyneth's funeral? I thought he was with Tanwen?'

'Yes, that was Gareth. He was wonderful with Mam and did all he could for her.' She wiped a tear away from the corner of one eye and forced herself to smile.

'And have you explained to him about Barri?'

Donna looked uncomfortable. 'I haven't gone into details. He accepts that he is my responsibility and that's it.'

'Don't you think you should tell him all the details?'

Donna shook her head. 'I think it's better not to. He doesn't get on too well with Tanwen, see,' she added uncomfortably.

'A sensible man! It would seem you've found a treasure.'

'You really think so?' Donna looked relieved.

'Yes.' She looked shrewdly at Donna. 'So what's the problem?'

'Well,' Donna hesitated, 'do you think it would be disrespectful to Mam's memory if we got married quite soon?'

'I think she'd be pleased to know that your future was so well taken care of,' Carina Price told her briskly. 'Who is going to object? No one I can think of, except perhaps Tanwen, and surely you don't care about her opinion?'

'Thank you, it's such a relief to hear you say that,' Donna smiled. 'If you think that way then I'm happy to go ahead with our plans.'

'You are quite sure you are doing this for the right reasons? You are marrying him because you love him, not simply for security?'

'Oh, I love him,' Donna confirmed, her eyes shining, her face wreathed in smiles.

'Then go ahead, my dear. Don't forget to send me an invitation to the wedding!'

Carina Price's approval set Donna's mind at rest. She felt so light-hearted as she returned home that on impulse she called in to see Menna Vaughan.

Menna was surprised to see her, but her welcome was cordial.

'Is there anything wrong?' she asked, frowning.

'No, nothing at all. I simply thought you might like the opportunity for us to have a chat, and that this was a good time. I've left Barri with Blodwyn for a little while and I knew Gareth would be out on his rounds.'

'I see!'

'I thought there may be some points about Gareth and me getting married that might be worrying you,' Donna said hesitantly.

Menna Vaughan gave her a shrewd look. 'You'd better come in and sit down. I'll make us a cup of tea. There certainly are several things we both need to discuss.'

Donna found that all the petty worries, which had piled up in her mind until they had achieved mountainous proportions, melted like butter in summer as they talked.

She was surprised to find that Aunt Menna also had doubts about them living together that were troubling her. However, once they were out in the open most of them were so trivial that they were of no importance at all.

By the time they'd reached their second cup of tea both of them were much more relaxed. Even more important, they both had a much clearer idea of what would be necessary in the way of cooperation to ensure that living under the same roof worked satisfactorily.

'Now all we have to settle is the date of your wedding,' Aunt Menna smiled, 'but I suppose we must leave Gareth to decide when that is to be. We don't want him thinking we've made all the plans without consulting him.'

'You don't think it is being disrespectful to my mam's memory, then, if we go ahead pretty soon?'

'I think it is the most sensible thing to do, and I'm sure she would agree with me,' Menna Vaughan said firmly.

'It will be a very quiet wedding,' Donna said apologetically.

'Yes,' Menna nodded. 'I'm the only family Gareth has. What about you?'

'I'd like to invite Carina Price. She's in charge of employees at The Cardiff Drapers and has helped me a great deal. She was a lifelong friend of my mam's, see, and is someone I turn to when I have a problem.'

'Of course you must invite her!' Menna agreed.

'Oh, and Blodwyn, my next-door neighbour. She has babysat Barri whenever I've needed her to do so.'

'And that's it?'

Donna nodded. 'Mind, there might be neighbours and old customers of my mam's turning up. The news is bound to get out.'

'What about your sister?'

Donna looked uncomfortable. 'Would it be very terrible of me if I said I would rather she wasn't invited?'

'On the contrary, after what I've heard about her from Gareth I think it's a very sensible decision,' Menna Vaughan agreed.

'That's it, then!' Donna stood up. 'I must be going or Blodwyn will think I've got lost. I don't often leave Barri with her for this long, but I thought it was a good opportunity for us to have a talk.'

'About Barri, Donna...' Menna hesitated, trying to find the most tactful way to ask who was the child's father.

'Oh, yes! Barri will have to be at our wedding as well, of course!' Donna smiled. 'I'm sure that Blodwyn will keep an eye on him, though.'

As she walked home, Donna noticed that the grey clouds had gone from the sky and that the sun was once again shining. She felt happier and more light-hearted than she had for months.

'So what's been happening, cariad?' Blodwyn greeted her. 'You look as though something has made your day. It's the first time I've seen you smiling for weeks.'

'I've made up my mind about accepting Gareth Thomson's proposal,' Donna told her.

'Dammo di! That's the best news I've heard for a long time. When is the wedding to be, then?'

'I'm not sure. I have to talk things over with Gareth. Quite soon, though.' Her face clouded for a moment. 'You don't think I'm rushing things, do you, Blodwyn?' she asked anxiously.

'Not a bit of it, my lovely! I've already told you that a dozen times. Your mam's probably smiling down on you at this very moment knowing that you and little Barri are going to be well taken care of in the future.' Her face sobered. 'He is all right about Barri, then?'

Donna nodded. 'We've never really discussed it in detail, mind, but he accepts that I am responsible for Barri the same as he is for his Aunt Menna. We've included both of them in all our plans for the future.'

When Gareth called round to see Donna later on that evening he was delighted by the news that she had been to see his aunt.

'Talking about me behind my back, were you?' he teased.

'No, but we did manage to iron out most of the small differences between us. Your aunt seemed to think we should go ahead with our wedding plans.'

'She's a very sensible woman is my Aunt Menna,' he grinned.

'I think we ought to start by furnishing one of the bedrooms as a sitting room for her,' Donna told him.

'Oh, I hadn't forgotten about your suggestion,' Gareth agreed. 'I'm still prepared to split the house in two, though, if you want us to live completely separate.'

Donna shook her head. 'No, I don't think that is either necessary or advisable. Menna would feel so lonely and isolated. You are her only family, after all.'

'All right, we can always do it later on if the two of you decide that you don't like living in each other's pockets.'

'We won't be living in each other's pockets if she has her own sitting room,' Donna reminded him.

Gareth pulled her into his arms and kissed her. 'Everything is going to be perfect,' he breathed. Then he kissed her again, more intensely, making her pulse race.

Donna sighed contentedly. 'I keep having to pinch myself to make sure I'm not dreaming!' she told him.

'So all we have to do now is fix a date,' he murmured. 'Tomorrow would suit me fine, but I suppose that would be too soon for you?'

Chapter Thirty-Four

Donna and Gareth found that arrangements for their wedding seemed to meet with obstacles at every stage.

First there was the question of decorating and allocating the rooms at Crwys Road. Donna was adamant that Barri must have a bedroom as near to theirs as was possible. Menna was already occupying the front bedroom immediately next to theirs and she was reluctant to move into one of the other rooms. It took a lot of tactful discussion and careful persuasion to convince her that because the new room would be so much larger than the room she was at present occupying, it would be more suitable to turn into a bed/sitting room.

Even when this was resolved, redecorating it took far longer than they had anticipated. Christmas came and went and they were suddenly well into 1933. Even worse, when they came to fix the date of their wedding they discovered there was nothing available until Easter Saturday, which wasn't until the middle of April.

'I've already told the landlord I'm moving out of Rhymney Street by the twenty-fifth of March, which is quarter day,' Donna said worriedly.

'Can't you stay on there if you pay another three months' rent?' Menna suggested.

Donna shook her head. 'I've already asked the landlord, but he said the place is let from that date to someone else.'

'Then you'll have to move in here with us before the wedding,' Gareth stated.

Although Donna knew it was the sensible solution she still didn't like the idea. Even if the decorating was complete, where were she and Barri going to sleep? Surely Gareth didn't intend for her to share the bedroom that they had decided would be theirs after they were married.

Blodwyn suggested that the alternative was to move her furniture to Crwys Road and then for her and Barri to stay at her house until the wedding.

Donna thought that was the end of her problems until Gareth broke the news that it was impossible for them to be married on Easter Saturday as they had planned because of some error that had led to a double booking.

'We can, however, be married two weeks

later, on the twenty-ninth of April,' he told her.

Donna looked at him, bemused. 'Do you think so many things going wrong is some kind of warning?' she asked shakily.

'Of course not!' He pulled her into his arms and kissed her soundly. 'It's just a few hiccups, we'll soon sort them out,' he assured her.

To recompense for all their disappointments, Gareth suggested that they should spend Easter weekend away on their own. He was astonished when Donna turned down the idea.

'Why ever not?'

'We're not married!'

'We will be getting married a couple of weeks later. Since we've already booked the hotel in Swansea and arranged for Barri to be looked after, it's an ideal opportunity for us to enjoy some time together on our own,' Gareth persisted.

Donna reluctantly agreed, but she had very mixed feelings. She'd never been away on any sort of holiday in her life and she'd been looking forward to going on honeymoon in Swansea. As the time drew nearer, however, she was filled with apprehension.

Part of her concern was the forthcoming ordeal of spending her first night with Gareth.

Much as she loved him and was conscious

of the ever-mounting passion between them, she had refused to agree to consummate their love until they were married because she was completely inexperienced when it came to bedroom activities. He was a doctor so he knew all there was to know about the physical aspects, but for her their first night was going to be a tremendous ordeal.

Sometimes he'd seemed annoyed, sometimes bemused by her refusal, but he hadn't pressed the matter.

She felt she owed Gareth an explanation about why she was so reticent, especially after they'd set the date for their wedding, but she was too embarrassed, too tongue-tied, to talk to him or anyone else about why she felt as she did.

To Donna's surprise both Blodwyn and Aunt Menna agreed that she and Gareth should take advantage of the arrangements already made.

'You'll only be away for a couple of nights, and Blodwyn will take good care of Barri and bring him to see me every day,' Menna Vaughan assured her.

'Why ever shouldn't the two of you go away together?' Blodwyn asked. 'You'll be getting married two weeks later so it's not really a sin. Think of it as a trial run, my lovely. It's a wonderful opportunity! You've never stayed in one of them hotels before, cariad, so it will give you a chance to find out what's what. It will also set your mind at rest about Barri being left with me, so that when you go away on your honeymoon you'll have no worries at all about him,' she added.

Their room at the hotel in Swansea was so well appointed that Donna felt over-whelmed by the luxury of it all. Gareth hung a 'Do not disturb' sign outside, closed the door and took Donna in his arms.

'Happy you decided to come away?' he asked.

Donna nodded nervously.

'And we've got the whole weekend with no one to worry about, no interruptions, just the two of us.' He tipped her head back and his lips covered hers in a long, deep kiss that set her pulse racing.

She made no protest when he started to undo the fastenings on her dress and she felt it slither to the ground around her feet. She stepped clear of it as Gareth kissed her even more passionately.

Her fingers sought the buttons on his shirt, feverishly undoing them, running both her hands up inside, eager to feel the warmth of his body and his bare skin against her palms.

As Gareth's lips trailed down her neck and over her breasts her breathing became ragged. She was filled with so many strange sensations that she lost all sense of time or place.

Automatically they moved towards the bed. As they collapsed onto it, Donna gave herself up to Gareth's ministrations.

He was a skilled lover. Building up the tension, layer upon layer, until her entire body felt on fire. She found herself wanting to cry out with pleasurable anticipation as well as a longing for release.

She offered no resistance when his hand moved down over her flat stomach, stroking her thighs and spreading them wide.

The physical reactions she was creating in him filled her with wonder. His erection was like a solid rod between them. Timidly she held it in her hand and shuddered with anticipation of what she knew would follow.

He raised his body above hers and held her firmly as he prepared to enter her. Her breasts rose sharply as she drew in a deep breath. She felt a searing pain and then she cried out in agony.

He stopped immediately, a look of bewilderment and shock on his sweat-soaked face.

'I'm sorry ... I had no idea,' he gasped hoarsely.

Donna fought back her tears. 'Don't stop,' she whispered. 'It's got to happen sometime, hasn't it,' she breathed. 'And I want you so much.'

Seconds later the agony had passed and they lay locked in each other's arms, utterly exhausted.

'You should have told me, my darling, that it was going to be your first time,' he murmured gently. 'I had no idea...'

'Would it have made all that much difference if you had known?' she smiled.

He hugged her close, breathing sweet words of love, but refrained from asking the hundred and one questions that were buzzing inside his head.

Gareth was awake before Donna the next morning. He raised himself on one elbow and looked down at her in wonder. With her halo of light brown hair frothing around her face she looked so young and innocent. Even so, he was deeply puzzled by what he had discovered the night before.

How on earth can she still be a virgin when she has a two-and-a-half-year-old son, he asked himself.

He'd assumed that her reluctance to make love before they were married was because she had already been made pregnant and was scared of it happening again.

He remembered his Aunt Menna's concern that he should find out about Barri's father, and how he had refused to do so because he felt it was invading Donna's privacy.

Now he wished he had taken his aunt's advice. After last night he knew Barri couldn't be Donna's child, so who was his mother? Could it be that he was her little brother?

Gwyneth Evans had told him that she'd been widowed and left to bring up her twin girls on her own ever since they were six years old. She had only been in her forties when she died, though, so she could have had a man-friend and have had Barri as a result, Gareth reasoned.

This would account for Donna's determination to bring Barri up, and why she had told him that Barri was her family when they'd been discussing their responsibilities.

He went over the various possibilities, searching in vain for an answer. He tentatively rehearsed what he would say when he asked Donna to explain the relationship. It wasn't going to be easy. She might be upset, outraged, even, if he said he'd thought all along that Barri was hers.

They made love when she woke up. Slow, languorous passion that was a release of abundant happiness between them. It was so different from the painful coupling of the previous night that they were both overwhelmed by their love for each other.

Gareth waited until they'd enjoyed a leisurely breakfast and had set out for a walk along the seafront before he broached the subject. It was an idyllic morning; the sun was warm and sparkled on the sea, with gulls noisily swooping and diving overhead.

Donna gave him an easy opening when she murmured, 'I wonder if Barri is all right with Blodwyn and your Aunt Menna.'

'Of course he'll be fine,' he told her, squeezing her hand reassuringly.

'It's the first time we've ever been parted,' she sighed.

'How about when you were at work? He was left with someone then!'

'Yes,' she smiled, 'with my mam, but that was different.' She sighed. 'He loved his nana so much!'

'His nana?' He felt mystified. His theory that Gwyneth Evans might have been his mother was blown, he thought ruefully.

'Obviously Barri is not your child, though, Donna,' he said quietly.

When she made no reply he looked sideways at her. She avoided his gaze. 'No,' she admitted, 'he's not really, and ... and yet he is,' she said adamantly.

'What's the full story?' he persisted.

Donna took a deep breath. 'It's not easy,' she said hesitantly. 'You mightn't like what you hear. It was wrong of me not to have told you earlier. You seemed to accept him as belonging to me and I love you so much that I didn't want to complicate things.'

Gareth felt uneasy. It looked as if Aunt

Menna had been right after all, and he should have questioned Donna earlier.

'Come on, let's hear all about it.' He put his arm around her shoulder and hugged her close. 'You've got to tell me sometime, you know.'

'Can we sit down somewhere?'

They found a wooden bench and sat in silence for several minutes. He waited patiently. Suddenly she began to speak and the whole story came pouring out in sharp, stilted bursts, like oil erupting from a well.

'Dylan Wallis was my boyfriend until Tanwen stole him from me. When she became pregnant she tried to get rid of the baby, but it didn't work. When Barri was born she refused to have anything to do with him. She wanted to have him adopted or put into an orphanage. Mam and I couldn't let that happen. We kept the baby at home and looked after him. You know the rest.'

It took Gareth a few minutes to digest what she had told him. It was outrageous that Donna was saddled with Tanwen's child. Unbelievable that Tanwen refused to have anything whatsoever to do with him.

He found himself seething with indignation. He felt so angry that he knew he must be careful what he said. He'd been ready to accept Barri as their responsibility when he'd thought he was Donna's, but if

Tanwen was his mother that was a very different situation.

He turned the problem over and over in his mind. It was a difficult decision. He knew how much Donna loved Barri, but the fact that he was Tanwen's, and she was so heartless, and conniving, could mean trouble for all of them in the future.

Chapter Thirty-Five

'So how do we deal with this situation?' Gareth's face was strained as he faced Donna. 'You really should have told me the whole story from the outset.'

She shook her head. 'I wasn't holding out on you. I simply took it for granted that since you accepted Barri it didn't matter that Tanwen was really his mother. Dylan feels the same way as she does, neither of them want anything to do with him.'

'That's what they tell you now, but what happens if they change their minds?'

'They won't!' Donna twisted her hands together. 'I know they won't. I keep telling you, Tanwen wanted to have him adopted.'

'So what if, later on, Barri's father changes his mind and decides he wants him back?'

'He won't. He's been sending money for

his keep, but he's insistent that he doesn't want anything to do with him other than that. He only started sending the money when Mam became too ill to work.'

'Unless Barri is formally adopted, either of them can claim him back at any time they want to do so,' Gareth persisted.

Disbelief mingled with alarm registered on Donna's face. Then her mouth tightened. 'In that case I'll adopt him.'

'Hold on, it's not quite that easy!'

Donna's face tightened. 'I love Barri as if he was my own child. I've been a mother to him ever since the day he was born. No matter what happens I'll never give him up.'

She turned away so that he wouldn't see the tears in her eyes. 'I mean it, Gareth. Much as I love you and want to marry you I can never give Barri up,' she repeated shakily.

'What are you saying, Donna? Are you saying that you would choose Barri over me?'

Her voice was a ragged whisper. 'If I have to!'

'Donna!' The shocked agony in Gareth's voice ripped through her. She clenched her hands into fists. She wanted to throw herself into his arms, to beg for his understanding, but she was afraid he might make conditions.

When she felt his hands on her shoulders

she stiffened.

'In that case we'll have to adopt him, won't we.'

Relief flooded through her. 'Do you really mean it? That would be wonderful! Thank you, Gareth.'

As she turned to him one of his hands went under her chin, lifting her face and tilting it so that he could look deep into her eyes. His lips covered hers and she felt such an enormous surge of happiness that her legs went weak. She was sure she would have fallen if he hadn't been holding her so tightly.

'I want both of you,' he told her gently. 'It has to be done legally, though,' he added firmly.

She frowned. 'So how do we do that?'

'We'll ask Tanwen and Dylan to meet us and discuss the matter coolly and calmly. When we all agree about the legal details then we'll arrange for a solicitor to draw up adoption papers.'

She began to breathe more easily. 'That shouldn't be too great a problem.'

'Provided they agree to our terms, for everything to be done legally. Don't build your hopes up too much,' he cautioned. 'Tanwen might decide to agree, but this chap Dylan mightn't want to give up his son.'

Donna felt so confident that her only

worry was how soon she could persuade Tanwen and Dylan to come and talk to them.

When she phoned the number they'd given her, Tanwen became rather off-hand as soon as Donna told her that she was going to marry Gareth Thomson.

'If you are asking me to come to the wedding I am far too busy to spare the time,' she said abruptly.

'Very well, but Gareth says he wants to talk to you and Dylan before he'll take on the responsibility for Barri.'

'Who the hell does he think he is, dictating his terms.'

'He's the man I'm about to marry, Tanwen, and it's very important that we sort things out!'

'He can't think much of you, then, if he's making all this fuss to break things off over someone else's brat.'

Donna bit back the retort burning on her lips. She needed their cooperation. She didn't want to lose either Barri or Gareth, or to have to choose between them.

'Please come, so that the four of us can talk things through,' she begged.

'Very well, if we have to,' Tanwen said churlishly.

Gareth looked doubtful when Donna told him that Tanwen and Dylan would meet with them.

'Are you quite sure they'll come? We'll need to have a solicitor and a witness present, you know. I don't want to go to that much trouble and then find they don't turn up or they refuse to sign.'

'Don't worry, Gareth, they'll come and they'll sign.'

As the weekend drew nearer, some of Donna's confidence began to wane. Supposing Tanwen did change her mind about coming. Supposing she wouldn't sign. Even worse, what if she made stipulations that weren't acceptable to Gareth?

She couldn't sleep. Not only her waking hours but even her nights were filled with disturbing doubts and speculation.

She said nothing to Gareth and left him to make all the legal arrangements. The document was drawn up, the solicitor arranged, and Blodwyn agreed to act as witness.

'I bet your Tanwen can't wait to sign those papers, cariad,' Blodwyn cackled.

'I hope you're right,' Donna said nervously.

'Of course I am! Dammo di! She wanted to be rid of him the moment he was born. She's never bothered with him from that day to this. No problem there at all, my lovely.'

As she and Gareth arrived at the Capitol Restaurant in Queen Street, where they had arranged to meet Tanwen and Dylan for lunch, Donna felt panic surging through her. She hoped that a good meal with plenty of wine would put Tanwen and Dylan in a relaxed, friendly mood.

Blodwyn had agreed to look after Barri and to take him round to Menna Vaughan's for lunch. Afterwards she was leaving him with Menna while she came to the solicitor's office to sign her name as a witness.

Because of Barri, and the planning for the forthcoming wedding, the two older women were spending more and more time in each other's company, and seemed to get on very well.

Tanwen and Dylan were so fashionably dressed that they caused raised eyebrows as they entered the restaurant. They seemed to be delighted by this, and by the general atmosphere. They made a tremendous fuss of greeting Donna and Gareth before acknowledging the waiter hovering by the table and deciding what they wanted to eat and drink.

The food tasted like sawdust to Donna she felt so anxious. She sipped nervously at her glass of wine, hoping it would give her the courage to stand up to her sister.

No mention was made of the real reason for their visit to Cardiff as they ate their meal. Tanwen and Dylan dominated the conversation, talking about themselves and their latest successful film.

When the coffee was served it was Tanwen who broached the reason for their visit. 'Before we discuss Barri I think we should tell you that we are leaving London quite soon. We've signed a very lucrative contract with an American film company and we've decided that's where our future lies. We are planning to make our home there permanently.'

Donna had a queasy feeling in the pit of her stomach. Was Gareth right? Was Tanwen going to take Barri away from her after all?

'Then it's a good thing we've met today,' Gareth said coolly. 'We want to discuss the future, too.'

'Donna said you were getting married.'

'That's correct, which is why we have to discuss your little boy's future.'

Tanwen's face darkened. 'What's Donna been saying,' she snapped. 'Tired of looking after him, is she? Or is it you who doesn't want to be bothered with him? Dylan's always sent money for his upkeep,' she added belligerently.

'That hardly makes him a good father,' Gareth said mildly.

'Well, it's all he's going to get from us, isn't it, Dylan.'

'You mean you don't intend to take him to

America with you, Dylan?' Gareth pressed, ignoring Tanwen.

'No! Never!' Tanwen interposed before Dylan had a chance to answer. 'I warned Donna the day he was born that she should let him be adopted, but she refused to listen. If she's fed up of looking after him then she'd better put him into an orphanage.'

Gareth nodded. 'What about you, Dylan? How do you feel about Barri? Is this the sort of future you want for him? You are his father after all.'

Dylan looked uncomfortable. 'Tanwen's spoken for both of us. I'm willing to help support him but I'm not having him living with us. We couldn't cope with him, he'd hamper our careers.'

'So you'd like Donna to go on looking after him and bringing him up?'

'That's up to her,' he said aggressively. 'As Tanwen said, she can always put him in an orphanage if she finds he's too much trouble, especially now she's getting married.'

'You don't intend to come back in a few years' time and claim him then?' Gareth asked mildly.

'What the hell are you on about?' Dylan snapped.

'You're not going to want Donna to give him up so that you can have him back to live with you sometime in the future?'

'Duw anwyl! What do you take us for,'

Dylan blustered. 'We've no feelings at all for the boy. That's why we wanted him adopted. It's probably too late for that now so he'll have to end up in an orphanage.'

'Not if Donna and I adopt him legally,' Gareth said quietly. 'We'll do that if you sign the necessary documents.'

Donna waited for their replies with bated breath. She saw Tanwen hesitate and her heart sank. She could hardly believe her ears when Tanwen said, 'We'll sign the necessary papers provided we don't have to support him financially, and you agree never to tell him who his real parents are.'

Donna gasped at her audacity. She was on the point of telling Tanwen how selfish and heartless she was, but stopped herself in time. This was what she wanted, she reminded herself. She'd probably never see Tanwen or Dylan again if they went to America. It would sever all contact between them and Barri need never know anything about them.

Chapter Thirty-Six

Donna Evans and Gareth Thomson were finally married two weeks after Easter, at midday on Saturday, 29 April 1933. It was a glorious spring day, with the sun shining down from a cloudless blue sky.

Donna and Barri had spent the previous night at Blodwyn's house. When it was time for them to leave for the church all the neighbours in Rhymney Street came out onto their doorsteps to wave Donna on her way.

Donna was transformed from a young woman weighed down by running a home, looking after a small child and trying to earn enough money to make ends meet, into a fairytale vision.

She was wearing a simply styled white satin dress that she had made herself. The edge of the long skirt, as well as the high round neckline and the deep cuffs on the long sleeves, were all trimmed with heavy lace. There were even tiny lace bows on her white satin shoes.

On her head, restraining her froth of light brown hair, a short veil was held in place by a half hoop of artificial orange blossom. She was carrying a fragrant bouquet of spring flowers.

She came out of the house hand in hand with Barri, who was dressed in a white satin sailor suit, white socks, and white patent leather shoes.

They were accompanied to church by Carina Price, who had not only accepted the invitation to attend the wedding, but since Donna had no other family member present had agreed to give Donna away.

Tanwen and Dylan had said that they couldn't spare the time to come to Cardiff for the wedding. It was too near the date of their departure for America.

Blodwyn was Matron-of-Honour. She followed them looking very smart in a new blue dress and loose matching coat that Donna had made for her specially for the occasion.

When they arrived at church Donna held Barri's hand as she walked down the aisle to where Gareth was waiting. Before she reached Gareth's side she let go of Barri's hand, and Blodwyn, who was walking behind her, gently guided him towards the front pew where Menna Vaughan was waiting to take charge of him. She was looking very smart in a flower-trimmed silver-grey hat, and a dark grey dress worn under a silver-grey coat, and for a moment Barri stared at the small elegant lady as if he didn't recognise her. Then a wide smile lit up his face and he clutched at her hand and scrambled into the pew alongside her.

The ceremony had a dreamlike quality for Donna. She and Gareth had eyes only for each other as they exchanged their vows.

Afterwards, as they gathered outside for photographs to be taken, it seemed to be a comparatively small group. Even so, as she posed with one hand resting on the arm of her new husband and the other on the shoulder of the little boy she loved so dearly, Donna knew she was surrounded by the people she loved most in the world.

Knowing that Barri now really belonged to her and Gareth, and that Tanwen could never take him away, had been the best wedding present Gareth could ever have bestowed on her, she thought contentedly. She had never felt so happy in the whole of her life as she did at that moment.

The quiet ceremony over, they went back to Crwys Road and Blodwyn and Menna supervised the meal that they had already laid out for them.

An hour later, with Carina's help, Donna changed from her wedding dress into a simple cream dress and matching jacket in readiness for their honeymoon journey.

'I'm so happy that things have turned out so well for you, Donna,' Carina murmured as she kissed her goodbye. 'Your mother would have been so pleased that you have such a wonderful husband, and relieved to know that Barri is in such good hands.'

Gareth had wanted to take her to Italy, but since they could only be away a week because of his surgery duties it had been impossible. Instead, Aunt Menna had suggested that they should go to Portmeirion.

'You'll love it,' Gareth told her. 'It's the next best thing to being in Italy. It's a village built right on the tip of a promontory in North Wales looking out over the sea. The entire complex is fashioned on an Italian-style village. We'll be staying in the Portmeirion Hotel, which is very luxurious, so I'm told. James Wylie, who is the manager of the hotel, is an old friend of Aunt Menna's. He's also a painter and there's one of his pictures hanging in her bedroom.'

It sounded enchanting. Donna's only concern was over leaving Barri. When it was time for her and Gareth to be on their way, Donna hugged Barri close and kissed his chubby cheeks.

'Dammo di! He'll be as right as rain with me and Gareth's Aunt Menna, so set your mind at rest and enjoy yourselves,' Blodwyn told her.

'It's been a long day for him and I know he'll sleep like a log tonight,' Donna agreed. 'It's when he wakes up in the morning and I'm not here that I'm worried about,' she added uneasily.

'He knows this is his home now,' Menna reminded her. 'I'll be here with him and so too will Blodwyn. The days will pass in a flash, he'll hardly have time to miss you.'

Donna knew they were right. She didn't want to spoil things by letting Gareth know how worried she was after he had gone to so much trouble to plan everything so well for her. The fact that Blodwyn would be staying at Crwys Road all the time they were away would help to reassure Barri.

Gareth had hinted that since Blodwyn and his Aunt Menna had become such good friends then if they got along together being in the same house it might be a good idea to suggest to Blodwyn that she should move in permanently.

'I thought it would help take some of the load of looking after the house and organising the surgery off Aunt Menna's shoulders,' he explained.

'Blodwyn might like that!' Donna agreed thoughtfully. 'She'll be pretty lonely without Barri being around all day.'

'It will, of course, mean that we'll have to do some more reorganising, but I think it would be worth it,' Gareth enthused.

'Perhaps we could turn the two rooms at the top of the house into a bedroom each for Aunt Menna and Blodwyn and then convert Aunt Menna's big bedroom into a sitting room that they can share.'

'That sounds like a perfect arrangement,' Gareth agreed. 'Even more important,' he grinned roguishly, 'it means that not only will Blodwyn and Aunt Menna have each other for company, but they will be on hand to look after Barri so we will be able to spend more time on our own.'

The publishers hope that this book has given you enjoyable reading. Large Print Books are especially designed to be as easy to see and hold as possible. If you wish a complete list of our books please ask at your local library or write directly to:

Magna Large Print Books
Magna House, Long Preston,
Skipton, North Yorkshire.
BD23 4ND

This Large Print Book, for people
who cannot read normal print,
is published under the auspices of

THE ULVERSCROFT FOUNDATION